Bonbon with the Wind

A SOUTHERN CHOCOLATE SHOP MYSTERY

Dorothy St. James

Barking Dog Press

Visit Dorothy St. James at:

http://www.dorothystjames.com

http://www.facebook.com/dorothy.stjames

Published by Barking Dog Press, LLC

"Bonbon With the Wind"
All rights reserved
Copyright © December 2019 by Dorothy McFalls

This is a work of fiction. Names, characters, places, brands, media, and incidents are either the product of the author's imagination or are used fictitiously. The author acknowledges the trademarked status and trademark owners of various products referenced in this work of fiction, which have been used without permission. The publication/use of these trademarks is not authorized, associated with, or sponsored by the trademark owners.

Publisher's Note: The recipes contained in this book are to be followed exactly as written. The publisher is not responsible for your specific health or food allergy needs that may require medical supervision. The publisher is not responsible for any adverse reaction to the recipes contained in this book.

Hardcover ISBN: 978-1-0878-5580-6

Cover art: Nicole Seitz
Cover design: John Chitwood, Renaissart Design
Editor: Nicki Richards

Dedication:

For My Readers.

Like Penn, I don't always take praise or kindness well. But if not for you and your support over the years, this book would have never been written. Thank you.

Chapter 1

Everything looked gray in the dim predawn light. The damp sand. The cresting waves as they reached up in an attempt to touch the endless stretch of sky. The blurred shapes of people walking along the shore. It was all colorless. And silent. The air stirred only a little. It felt as if the entire world was holding its breath.

Here on Camellia Beach, we were all holding our breath—and worrying. The South Carolina island town, a thirty-minute drive from the historic city of Charleston, had become my adopted home less than a year ago when I'd inherited the local chocolate shop from my maternal grandmother, a grandmother I'd never known existed.

My best friend's murder had brought me to this little island town. I'd come chasing after answers. When I'd first saw the beach's shabby downtown, I'd thought to myself that only a bulldozer could improve it. That was before I'd learned what a true paradise looked like.

Now, I couldn't imagine living anywhere else. On my way to the beach, I had made an effort to etch into my memory each of the humble clapboard, concrete block, and brick shop fronts. I trembled at the thought that my beloved town might be gone in the next twenty-four hours and there was nothing I could do to stop it.

Standing on the sandy shore where the land slipped into the ocean, I watched the beach in all that grayness. The tall sea grass rose up from the gently sloping dunes. Further inland silhouettes of the palm trees and scrubby oaks with their twisting branches and trunks waved in the building wind. This quiet, spit of sand at the edge of the Atlantic Ocean had become my personal paradise and my refuge. And yet, already, nothing appeared quite the same.

Nearly every house and shop on the island had been boarded up tightly. Porch swings fashioned from bed frames, rocking chairs used for lazy days, and family picnic tables were missing from the cottages' welcoming, wide porches. The twinkling holiday lights (displayed year-round) were gone. Sandbags had been piled up against doorways. The town reminded me of one of the many forgotten and neglected neighborhoods in the Midwest abandoned when all the jobs had moved to other areas. Nearly the entire town's population had vacated Camellia Beach.

A few islanders lingered, though. The surfers, who talked excitedly about the challenge of the storm-churned waves, had completely ignored the governor's mandatory evacuation order demanding residents flee inland. They bobbed like seals in a line just beyond the breakers as they waited to drop in on the next big swell. There were also shop owners, like me, who had agreed to stick around and serve the community until the very last minute and a handful of stubborn residents who believed that by staying they could singlehandedly hold back a hurricane and keep it from ravaging their homes.

Rough sand grated against the bottom of my bare feet. I continued down the beach with Stella, my five-pound papillon dog, at my side. The black silky fur on her wing-shaped ears—ears that were bigger than her head—shuddered. She gazed out over the water. I stopped and squinted to see what she saw. On the far horizon, dark clouds had lined up like soldiers of an advancing army.

I tightened my grip around the leash until my fingers cramped.

This was really going to happen.

I stood frozen in place when what I really wanted to do was fall to my knees and sob at the unfairness of it all. It'd taken me thirty-eight years to find it, the first place that had ever felt like home. How could I lose it now?

Stella quickly lost interest in the storm rolling toward us. She tugged at her end of the leash, urging me to get moving again. With her nose half-buried in the sand, she moved her head from side-to-side like a tiny metal detector in search of treasure.

Treasure to Stella meant ghost crabs. She loved rousting them from their holes and chasing them down the beach. I let my pup lead me just a bit farther past the pier and in the direction of the old, abandoned lighthouse. Although I didn't want to leave the water's edge—or turn my back on those portentous storm clouds—I desperately needed to return to the shop. My to-do list had grown as long as my arm overnight. And time was definitely running out.

"I thought I'd find you here, Penn," Althea Bays called from one of the wooden walkovers that provided access points from the interior of the island to the beach. I turned to watch as she moved with enviable grace down the steps and toward me.

Althea, short and slightly waifish, had an otherworldly glow this morning. She'd wrapped a colorful yellow scarf around her hair. Her skin appeared even darker than usual against the backdrop of the bleak landscape and the bright yellow of her scarf. She wore a matching yellow sundress. Its flared skirt flowed like the rising tide around her legs with each step. I don't know how she did it. Even at the edge of disaster, she looked stunning.

Stella barked wildly while tugging even harder at the leash. "Let me at her," her actions were saying. "I'll protect you. I'll bite her toes until she cries. Come on. Let me get her."

While Stella had never taken a liking to Althea—nothing against Althea since I suspect my dog only barely tolerated me—Althea and I had grown to be the best of friends. When I'd first arrived in Camellia Beach determined to single-handedly solve a murder, Althea had offered advice and help. She owned the local crystal shop and believed in magic and witchcraft and things that go bump in the night. I had just left a career in advertising and needed all the help I could get in figuring why my friend had died in a giant vat of chocolate.

We'd had a shaky start. At the time, I had been unwilling to trust anyone on this strange island. But Althea had been tenacious.

She'd eased her way into my life. Even though I thought she was a weirdo for believing in magic and crazy woo-woo crystals, I'd started to feel comfortable around her. We made a good team. With her help, I managed to solve several other murder mysteries.

But then, two months ago, a lie had come between us, a lie that had nearly caused me to lose the chocolate shop. As much as I wanted to forgive and forget, I couldn't seem to manage it. Not that my reluctance to let her back into my life seemed to matter to Althea. She kept coming around and acting like nothing had changed. While I bristled at the sight of her, she offered a wide, guileless smile.

Stella continued to bark with a crazed frenzy.

"Quiet," I commanded. When my little dog paused in her hysterics to take a breath, I tossed her a small bit of bacon from the stash I kept in my pocket. She gobbled it and looked up at me expectantly for another. "Good girl," I said, then tossed her a second piece. "Sit."

The hours and hours *and hours* I'd spent working with Stella were finally starting to pay off. She sat beside me, her entire body shivering with excitement while she waited for yet another treat. I praised her and told her how wonderful she was before saying to Althea, "Please don't tell me there's a new crisis. Don't tell me the chocolate has been stolen. Don't tell me someone set off a bomb in the shop. And certainly don't tell me someone found a dead body. Even if it happened, just-just don't tell me. I don't think I can take it."

Althea shook her head. "No crisis. No dead bodies." Her brows furrowed as she thought for a moment. "At least, none that I know of. Just coffee. Mama's in the Chocolate Box already. She brewed a big urn to offer those who haven't evacuated yet."

When Althea got close enough, she handed me a cup that smelled like caffeinated heaven.

"Bertie added a shot of the Amar chocolate?" I asked as sweet and bitter scents swirled around me. I took a long sip and sighed.

"Just to yours. Mama suspected you'd need an extra boost this morning," Althea said. Her mother and I shared the apartment above my chocolate shop. Although I owned the shop, Bertie Bays was the real talent behind the chocolates we crafted at the Chocolate Box.

I was, without doubt, the apprentice while Bertie was the master chocolatier. I'd inherited the Chocolate Box after taking a couple of chocolate making classes from my maternal grandmother, Mabel Maybank. Occasionally, Bertie threatened to retire and move to Florida. So far I'd been enough of a disaster in the kitchen to keep her from considering leaving town too seriously.

"Mama sent me out to deliver that cup of coffee to you. She said you'd need it like a fish needs water."

While I sipped, Althea stared out over the ocean. "This isn't the first time." Her voice sounded oddly subdued as she gave a nod toward the ominous clouds gathering on the horizon. "I think Mama asked me to find you because she wanted me to make sure you weren't freaking out."

"Me? Freaking out?" I laughed. The rusty cackle sounded rather hysterical. "I'm totally freaking out," I admitted.

Althea put her hand on my arm. "No matter what happens, you're not going to lose anything important." She sounded sure of herself.

Too sure of herself.

"What did you do?" I demanded. The muscles in my back tightened. I jerked away from her to put some distance between us. "You didn't use some *mystical* divination to peer into the future, did you?" I asked, not that I believed in that kind of claptrap.

I was the rational one. The sane one. I knew better. Magic didn't exist.

"Don't go and get all snippy," Althea said. She softened her words with a good-natured smile. "What I mean is that no matter what happens tomorrow, you won't lose me or Mama or Harley or anyone

5

else who's important to you. We'll all come back. We'll rebuild if we must. Camellia Beach is our home. Nothing can change that."

I hoped she was right.

But I feared she wasn't.

One little lie had already wedged its way between Althea and me, and I wasn't sure if I could ever allow myself to trust her again. If one lie could do that kind of damage to our relationship, I hated to imagine the kind of strain the destruction of a town would put on the relationships I had with everyone else who mattered in my life.

"They're saying Avery is the hurricane of the century," I reminded her. "They're calling it a superstorm."

The weather forecasters were now on air twenty-four hours a day reporting on Hurricane Avery's slow churn toward our coast. The storm was supposed to be even more powerful than Hurricane Hugo, which had devastated the South Carolina coast back in 1989.

"They're saying there's going to be nothing left of any of the islands." I was starting to sound as shrill as the excited weather forecasters. I even flapped my arms a bit. "They're saying there might not even be enough of an island left to even be able to rebuild."

"They always say that." How could Althea sound so calm? "It's rarely as bad as any of the forecasters predict. Still, we take precautions." She gestured toward the plywood covering the doors and windows on the houses facing the beach. "We leave before the storm hits. And when it's all over, we return to see what needs to be done. It doesn't do anyone any good to fret so over what might or might not happen."

Stella, bored with our conversation, started pawing at a nearby ghost crab hole. The morning breeze was starting to build. The wind smelled moist and salty and portentous.

Despite Althea's upbeat wait-until-tomorrow attitude, I saw plenty of reason to fret right now. But instead of telling her that, I buried my nose in my rich coffee with its dark chocolate undertones and took several deep breaths.

"Isn't that Joe Davies?" Althea asked.

I followed her gaze. Several hundred yards down the beach I spotted the hazy figure of a hunched man pulling a beach cart toward us from the eastern end of the island.

"It looks like him," I said.

Old Joe Davies, with a crooked back and perpetually sunburned bulbous nose, spent nearly all his time walking up and down the beach or through the marshes, dragging that old beach cart made from stained PVC pipes with him. It was loaded down with shovels, sieves, and all sorts of equipment that he said was essential to his search for pirate treasure. Joe liked to tell anyone willing (or not so willing) all about his theory that there was gold hidden just under our noses on Camellia Beach.

I'd heard his fantastic story more than once. He would launch into the lecture about how he was destined to find this fortune in treasure every time he came into the Chocolate Box. And he came in nearly every day to purchase a piece of Bertie's dark chocolate sea salt caramel. According to Joe, the infamous pirate, Blackbeard, had buried his treasure on Camellia Beach shortly before his ship, the Queen Anne's Revenge sank in 1857.

I was surprised to see Joe out searching for treasure this morning since the island was under a mandatory evacuation order. I was planning on leaving as soon as Bertie and I had finished up all the preparations to the shop. And Joe struck me as a careful guy who followed the rules and liked to make sure everyone else around him was following the rules as well.

"Who's he talking to?" I asked as a woman appeared at Joe's side from out of nowhere. Like everything else in the dim pre-dawn light, her shape was gray and somewhat blurry. Even though I couldn't get a good look at her, something about her felt familiar.

I leaned forward, trying to make out her features.

Was that Florence, my on-again-off-again mother? No, it couldn't be. What would she be doing out here? On the beach? She never went out to the beach. The sand would ruin the fancy shoes she liked to wear. And why would she be talking to Joe Davies?

Whatever the woman was saying to him, seemed to cause him a great deal of upset. Joe shook his head violently, then with a jerky movement, he pulled his cart away from her as fast as his short legs could carry him.

By the time he reached us, he had his head down, and he was muttering to himself, turning his head side-to-side with an agitated jerky motion.

"Are you okay?" I rushed to his side, concerned for the poor man. If he had indeed encountered Florence, I understood his upset. She often reduced me to a nervous, dithering idiot whenever I encountered her.

"Am I—?" He looked up at me with surprise. "Oh, um, hello Althea, Charity."

"It's just Penn," I corrected. He *must have* been talking with Florence. She was one of the few people on the island who still insisted on calling me by my cringeworthy first name, *Charity*.

"Who was that woman?" Althea asked.

"Did she say something to upset you?" I asked at the same time.

"Just-just seeing her was upsetting enough, don't you think?" His pale brown eyes grew wide. "But, yes, she warned me. And…oh!" he exclaimed as if he'd just realized something. "Do-do you know what that means?"

"She threatened you?" I'd experienced the wrong end of her anger a time or two myself. Florence loved to issue her tight-lipped threats.

"Ain't that what she does?" he asked.

"That's my experience," I said.

At the same time Althea cried, "Who? Who were you talking to?"

"The Gray Lady," he growled. His thinning hair, dyed an unnatural shade of orange, lifted from his head in the stiff pre-storm breeze rushing in from the ocean and waved around like tentacles.

"*No*," Althea gasped. She pressed a hand to her mouth.

I frowned.

"Who else would it be?" he shouted. He then shook his head seemingly startled by his own outburst. "Of course it was her. She told me—" He swallowed hard. "She told me the storm would be bad." Moving quickly, he slammed his metal detector into its slot on his beach cart. "I've got to get out of here. I shouldn't have stayed so long."

Althea grabbed his arm to keep him from escaping. "That was her? Really her?"

I turned back searching for the woman who had been talking with him. But the beach was empty.

That was impossible. People didn't simply vanish.

"As ghostly as they come," Joe was saying to Althea. "Could look straight through her and see the dunes and houses beyond her as clear as if she weren't there at all."

"Ghost," I hesitated to even say the word. "As in...?" I couldn't even complete the thought because it was nonsense.

Both Joe and Althea nodded in unison.

"She's as fearsome a sight as they've said she would be," Joe said and then shivered.

"The Gray Lady," Althea whispered with what sounded like a great deal of awe.

"Sounds like a bunch of nonsense to me." I snapped. Talk of the supernatural always made me prickly and rude.

"Not nonsense. Not at all. She's an apparition that appears to people on Camellia Beach before storms," Althea said. "She's not nearly as popular as the Gray Man who shows up to warn residents on nearby Pawley's Island. He'll tell them that a hurricane is on its way. He's achieved international fame. I think he even has a Twitter account." Althea paused for dramatic effect. "The Gray Lady doesn't simply warn residents of hurricanes. To see her is a warning of impending doom. How she does it seems rather cruel. According to the lore, nothing you do can change your fate. You're doomed. The storm is going to wreck your life. And now you know it."

Even in the early morning light, I could see that Joe's complexion had paled.

"Althea! You're scaring poor the man for no good reason. There's no such thing as ghosts. And even if there were, they wouldn't go around scaring random beachgoers."

"Sorry, Joe," Althea said. She really did sound sorry too. "I-I didn't mean...I mean, the tales might not be one hundred percent correct. There might be a way to—"

"I don't think that's helping," I said. "Joe? Are you okay?"

He wasn't okay. The words had barely escaped my mouth when he pitched forward and landed hard on the ground right next to where Stella had been digging. His unexpected fall frightened my little pup so much she darted behind my legs and started barking again.

Good gracious. Had the poor man dropped dead from fear?

Alarmed, I knelt beside him. "Are-are you okay?"

I didn't know what I'd do if we suddenly found ourselves dealing with a suspicious death. Hours before a hurricane made landfall certainly wasn't a good time...as if there could ever be a good time for someone to die.

He didn't move.

"Joe?" I whispered.

His body remained as still as death.

Oh, no...

Without warning, Joe rolled over onto his back.

I screamed.

He thrust a sandy lump of rock toward me.

I lurched back and screamed again.

"What's wrong with your friend?" he asked Althea.

"I thought you were dead," I answered for her.

"Dead? Hardly." He shook the sandy lump at me again. "Do you know what this is?"

Both Althea and I shook our heads.

He scrambled to his feet. I followed.

With his wide, flat thumbnail, he chipped away the dried sand to reveal a round disc that glimmered kind of like gold. "It's a Spanish gold coin, possibly from the eighteen hundreds."

"Cool," I said peering at the coin closely. "So you didn't suffer from some kind of attack or faint?"

"Me? Faint?" He snorted. "I'm as healthy as a twenty-year-old. I saw your dog playing with this. And I had to get it."

The sun was starting to rise. A red glow formed right under the dark clouds on the horizon, making them look as if the storm clouds were bleeding. I shook that crazy thought away. Worry over the hurricane was making my thoughts as fanciful as Joe and Althea's. "I need to get back to the shop. Stay safe, Joe. And don't worry about silly ghost stories. Make good decisions, and you'll be fine."

"You don't understand what this means." He grabbed my arm and shook the coin frantically. His entire hunched body started to tremble. "I didn't think anyone would ever find it. Not a bit of it. But we now have evidence that it exists. Heck, I didn't really think it existed. I just…"

"You mean?" Althea sounded almost as excited about his little gold coin as she had about the Gray Lady.

Joe nodded. "Yes. I do mean it. This coin proves that Blackbeard's treasure was actually buried here. And dagnabbit, I can't do a thing about it because of that storm and-and—" He threw a worried look over his shoulder to the place on the beach where he'd spoken to the Gray Lady. "I have to go. I can't stay. It isn't safe. I have to leave the island. It's not safe out here for me. It's not safe for anyone."

Chapter 2

"We expect the first of the outer bands from Hurricane Avery to reach our coastline by five P.M. This is going to be a devastating storm, y'all. If you haven't already evacuated, do so now," the announcer on the shop's radio implored shortly after I'd returned from the beach.

The two-story white clapboard building was home to my chocolate shop and the Drop-In surf shop next door. Upstairs were two apartments. I shared the apartment directly above my shop with Althea's mom, Bertie Bays. Harley Dalton, the island's surfing lawyer, rented the other apartment. The entire building leaned to one side as if the prevailing winds were slowly pushing it over. It'd survived more than a hundred years of storms.

Even though the Chocolate Box wasn't officially open for business, it was already buzzing with activity. Althea, her face flush with excitement, rushed through the front door of the Chocolate Box shortly after me.

Wanting to keep Stella close to me (but out of trouble), I took her to the shop's back office where I kept an overstuffed dog bed and two ceramic bowls. I filled one with cool water and the other with a carefully measured serving of her food. Before closing her inside the office, I told her to behave herself. She nudged my hand with her coal-black nose as to say, "Have you just met me?" She then barked several times to make sure I understood who was actually in charge.

I chuckled and shook my head. That dog of mine always had to have the last word.

When I returned to the front of the shop, I found Bertie tending the coffee station, filling to-go cups and handing them out. I recognized among the crowd several town council members, half the fire department, a few young police officers, several fellow business owners, and contractors who'd been working day and night to board up the island's houses and businesses.

Bonbon with the Wind

Nothing was for sale today. We were providing coffee and tea and what was left of our chocolate stock as a thank you to those who had to stay and work to keep the island safe.

The Chocolate Box had been in operation in this same building in Camellia Beach, making chocolate from the cacao bean, for generations, being passed down from family member to family member. It had been my grandmother's dying wish that I did everything in my power to continue the work my ancestors had begun. While I knew I'd never match Mabel's ability to run this shop while also protecting the island's tight-knit community, I took the heavy mantle of responsibility seriously. Even if the only thing I could do was to hand out coffee and good cheer before the storm arrived, that was what I planned to do.

"I double-checked all of the equipment in the kitchen before unlocking the front door. You did a good job sealing everything in plastic," Bertie said to me. She then handed a cup of coffee to Camellia Beach's police chief, Hank Byrd.

Bertie was dressed in another one of her touristy Camellia Beach T-shirts. This one had a cartoon picture of a muscle man flexing his arms while dressed in nothing but a tiny red swimsuit. The caption said, "I don't need a permit for these guns."

Her black hair was meticulously curled. Her neatly trimmed nails had been painted the same shade of red as her cartoon man's swimsuit. I puzzled over that. She never painted her nails. Why would she start now when we had so much else to do to get ready for the hurricane?

But then Bubba Crowley, the president of the local business association who resembled a gentle giant, wandered over and bussed a kiss on her cheek. Bertie blushed and batted him away. Her reaction answered my question about her painted nails. Bubba must have finally started to succeed in his quest to win her over.

Before I could tease her, Bertie blurted out, "Althea told me about what Joe Davies saw."

13

"About the gold coin? I hardly think one old coin proves there's pirate treasure on the island," I said.

"I agree." Bertie handed a cup of coffee to Bubba and winked at him. "I meant about the Gray Lady."

It was as if someone had flipped a switch and turned off the sound in the shop. The cacophony of excited chatter and nervous laughter came to an abrupt stop. The only sound for nearly a minute was the hiss of the growing wind outside.

"He clearly didn't want to tell us who he was really talking to." I turned and frowned at Althea. "I think she looked like Florence."

"The Gray Lady?" Bubba drawled in that deep and slow good-ole-boy tone of his. "Joe actually spoke to her?"

"Poor devil," the police chief grumbled.

Before anyone else could offer their opinion, the copper bell above the door rang. An older man dressed in wrinkled dress pants and a stained white button-up shirt staggered in. He swept off his tweed hat to reveal a bald head and said somewhat breathlessly, "I need to find Joe Davies."

"Why do you need to find him?" I asked.

"If he has any kind of brains in his head, he'll be long gone by now," Bubba told the man before he'd had a chance to answer me. "You should wait until after the storm to look for anyone. The residents will be scattered to all corners of the Southeast by now."

"He might have decided to stay," the stranger said. "Don't some people stay and ride out storms despite the mandatory evacuation order?"

Bubba exchanged a glance with the police chief.

"Only fools with rocks for brains choose to ignore evacuation orders. We can't rightly force them out of their homes. But as soon as we finish here," Byrd said as if he were doing something more important than drinking free coffee and eating fistfuls of Bertie's sea salt caramels, "we're going to go door-to-door and write down their names so we can notify next of kin after the storm."

14

"Have you tried his cottage?" I asked the stranger.

"No one answered when I knocked," the stranger admitted. "But I thought...I mean...I hoped that perhaps he wasn't home and that's why he hadn't opened the door."

That was a curious way to say that. If sounded like he thought that Joe might be hiding inside his own house. But that didn't make sense. Joe would have no reason to hide inside his house just because a stranger came knocking on his door.

"Why do you want to talk to him?" I asked again.

"I...um...it's a private matter," he mumbled.

"We were talking to him on the beach a little while ago. But he rushed off, saying he needed to evacuate," I said. The back of my neck prickled. "Sounds like you just missed him."

"Like Penn said, he's gone inland. Try back after the storm," Bertie suggested as she handed the stranger a cup of coffee. "We'll all be back assessing the damage and putting our lives back in order after the evacuation decree is lifted. I'm sure Joe would appreciate any extra help you could offer cleaning up debris from his yard or getting the boards off his windows."

The man held the cup at arm's length. His brows flattened. His gaze shifted from person to person in the room. With a huff, he jammed his tweed hat back on his head. "I'll be back," he grumbled and then hurried out of the shop.

No one spoke for a few moments.

"And you saw her too?" Bubba leaned in close to my face to ask. "You *and* Althea?"

"What?" I was still watching the stranger through the shop's plate glass window. He'd stopped under the large oak tree in front of the shop. His mouth twisted into a scowl that made the prickles on my neck turn into a full-scale shiver. The Spanish moss dangling from the oak's massive branches waved as if trying to shoo the odd stranger away.

"The Gray Lady? You actually saw her?" Bubba persisted.

"I saw a woman from a distance," I admitted. "She wasn't a ghost. She was a person. Kind of looked like Florence. By the skittish way he was acting I'd guess she was Florence. She tends to scare the heck out of anyone she encounters."

Althea shook her head in disagreement. "The Gray Lady looked all wispy."

Several people in the crowded shop gasped.

"The sun hadn't come up yet. *Everything* looked wispy." I tried to explain.

"Joe said he could see straight through her," Althea argued.

"Joe needs glasses. And it was still dark out," I pointed out. But it was hopeless. Everyone was set on believing some ridiculous ghost story.

"That's bad news for the town," the police chief said as he sipped his coffee. "But there ain't really anything we can do about it."

"We can get out of town," Bubba reminded us.

"Already planned to," someone else said.

"Y'all should be gone already," Hank seemed to direct that comment to me.

I held up my hands. "Once we're done serving the coffee this morning, we're leaving. The car is already packed."

"That's right," a welcome voice rumbled directly behind me. "I caught Troubadour and stuffed him—spitting mad, mind you—in that cat carrier Bertie gave me. I think that's the last of the preparations for upstairs."

A blush must have traveled up my face, because hearing his voice made me feel suddenly all hot and…well…happy.

I spun around and somehow found myself wrapped in Harley Dalton's strong arms. "I'm anxious to get as far away from here as possible and yet I'm also terrified to leave. Does that even make sense?" I asked as I pressed my face to the shoulder of his black cotton T-shirt.

He kissed me on the top of my head. "It makes perfect sense."

Blushing even harder, since I knew everyone was watching and would be talking about how close Harley and I had been getting lately, I peeled out of his embrace.

I'd sort of inherited Harley with the shop. He had been my grandmother's lawyer and he was mine. The sight of him made my heart thump like crazy in my chest.

He was slightly taller than me, which was saying something, since I towered over most men. I liked being able to see him eye to eye. His brown hair was in need of a trim. It curled at the ends in the humid air that had blanketed the island. His soulful green eyes watched me with a look of concern that made butterflies flutter in my belly.

"Let me count your fingers. Any mortal scratches?" I said, reaching for his hands. Troubadour was a hairless cat that had belonged to my grandmother. When Mabel had died, Bertie had adopted him. For the most part, Troubadour was a friendly cat, and he was absolutely in love with Harley, shamelessly rubbing against his legs whenever he stopped by to visit.

However, this utterly docile cat turned downright feral when it came to dealing with Stella or whenever he had to ride somewhere in his cat carrier. He'd also once attacked my mother, Florence. Not that I held that against him. I considered the attack a sign that Troubadour possessed a fine sense of judgment.

Harley wiggled his fingers. "All attached and accounted for."

"And Gavin? Is he coming with us or did he leave with Jody?" I asked referring to his eleven-year-old son. He shared custody with his unpleasant ex, Jody Dalton.

"Jody took Gavin to visit the theme parks in Florida."

I suspected Harley was paying for the trip. Jody rarely paid for anything.

"Of course I'll miss him like crazy," he continued. He put his arm over my shoulder and pulled me close to his side. "But he's excited instead of scared, so I'm glad that's what they're doing. His friend Tom went with them too."

The bell above the door chimed again. And again, the shop fell silent as everyone turned as if expecting the Gray Lady to march in and order the last of the chocolate cherry bonbons. A tall man dressed in a black full-body wetsuit. He had a full head of curly silver hair. His narrow face was covered in a tapering beard that made him look like a pirate.

He raised his hand and called out to Harley, "Bro!"

"Big Dog." Harley answered. Being a competitive surfer himself, Harley knew most of the surfers who came to Camellia Beach. Harley and the new guy did one of those handshakes that involved their entire arms. "I didn't know you were in the area."

"What? You thought I could stay away and miss a chance to ride on waves kicked up by what could be the hurricane of the century? Never. Besides, I had some business to attend to." His playful gaze glided over me. "You must be Penn. Harley"—he nudged Harley's side—"no wonder you've been hiding her from the circuit. Half the surfers would be trying to steal her from you."

I winced. Years ago Harley's ex-wife, a fellow competitive surfer, had slept around with one of Harley's biggest rivals on the surfing circuit.

"Penn's far too smart to be taken in by sweet talk and lies," Harley said.

Big Dog nudged his arm again and laughed. "Glad to hear it. You were never one to repeat past mistakes."

"That's because I've got brains in my head instead of seaweed," Harley agreed, which only made Big Dog laugh harder.

"Wicked good waves," the older surfer mused. "You should be out there."

"Yeah." Harley ran a hand through his hair, making it delightfully disheveled. "I've been busy packing up to evacuate. You know, doing responsible adult stuff."

"He had to catch my mom's cat," Althea said. She wrapped her arms around Big Dog and kissed his cheek. "Good to see you," she said. "It's been a while."

"Seems like y'all were just kids last time I saw you," he said, looking Althea over with an appreciative eye.

"It hasn't been that long," she said with a laugh. "A few years at the most."

"I heard about Mabel," he said, referring to my maternal grandmother. "She'll be missed."

Bertie, who clearly knew him as well, poured him a cup of coffee. He took a few sips before putting the to-go cup down on a nearby table. "Well, I have a few more waves to catch," he said on his way out.

"And then you'll get off my island," Byrd shouted after him. "Idiots, all of them, acting like this is some kind of playground."

"He'll be safe," Harley said, I think for my benefit. He gave my hand a squeeze. "He knows when to leave town."

"It's high time we get out of town too," Bertie announced. "The chocolates are gone. The coffee urn is nearly empty. And weather conditions are only going to get worse."

I looked at the shop. The glass counter was indeed empty. The chairs had been turned upside down and set up on the tables. The cash register had been tightly wrapped in plastic to keep it from getting ruined if the shop flooded or the ceiling leaked. I hated that this might be the last sight I might have of this place. I loved my shop. Leaving it was going to tear my heart right out of my chest.

A quiet voice in my head wouldn't leave me alone. It kept repeating the Gray Lady's warning. I prayed the voice was wrong.

The wind whipped around the motel in the inland town of Summerville where we'd taken refuge. It roared and battered the walls, shaking the entire building. The lights flickered on and off several times before leaving us all in the dark. After that happened, Stella backed herself as far under the bed as she could get herself and refused to come out. Not even her favorite bacon treat could tempt her to leave her hiding place. In the darkness outside, we could hear trees cracking and snapping. Harley tightened his arms around me as we huddled together on the double bed.

Texts pinged on my phone every few minutes, most coming from my favorite half-sister Tina. She was terrified the storm was going to wash me out to sea. Although I texted back, promising her I was safe, she kept asking for updates. And I kept renewing my assurances. That is, until we lost cell service.

The last message I received before the cell phone went dead was a long text from Peach—my mother's younger sister. Earlier in the evening, she had asked where I was staying and insisted I stayed safe. In this text she wrote that the Maybank family, including my uncle Richard and my mother, had taken refuge in the small town of Cypress, in the middle of the state, at a lake house that my maternal grandparents had built. The text had included a picture of the house.

I stared at the picture of the sprawling two-story lake house for half the night, wondering if my mother—who I suspected was too proud for her own good—had asked Peach to check up on me. It was possible, since they were staying in the same house.

I didn't know how I felt about the unexpected communication with the Maybank side of my family. Part of me wanted to be happy that they were making an effort to reach out to me. But that other part of me, the part that was so adamant about protecting myself from ever letting anyone close enough to hurt me, tried to find an ulterior—and sinister—motive for the texts. Perhaps they'd wanted to rub it in that they were together in the family lake house, a place I was neither invited nor welcomed. Perhaps they'd wanted to find more evidence that I was too inept to run their family's chocolate shop. Perhaps—

Oh, the possibilities were endless, and wondering about it was only making me feel incredibly sad. So I tried not to think about it.

On the other bed in the motel room, Bertie and Althea sat together with Beauregard sleeping soundly at their feet. Althea shouted at the hurricane using sorts of colorful language whenever there was a crash outside.

"She's never been afraid of storms before," Harley, who'd once dated Althea, whispered after her last outburst.

"She'd told me not to worry," I said. "But that was before she thought Joe had seen the Gray Lady. Gray Lady, indeed." I snorted. "Like ghosts would waste their time walking around, telling us a storm would destroy us."

He patted my leg. "Well, that explains why she's so scared. You and Althea saw the Gray Lady too." He held up a hand when I started to protest. "From a distance. And you may have not seen anything supernatural. But lots of people around these parts put a great deal of stock in those stories. The folklore surrounding Gray Lady's existence dates back over a hundred years. Just the mention of her can make a brave man tremble."

I thought of how Joe Davies had reacted. He'd been trembling with fear...and with another emotion I couldn't describe. Anger? Astonishment? Surprise? What? I didn't know.

Something smashed against the roof of the building.

I prayed the residents of Camellia Beach had all evacuated the island and had made it to a safe shelter. It sounded as if the world was coming apart at the seams outside our motel room's steel door, and we'd traveled more than an hour inland of the shore. I hated to imagine the beating my favorite little town of Camellia Beach was taking on that horrible night.

Chapter 3

By midmorning, Hurricane Avery had moved to the north of us leaving the town of Summerville eerily quiet. I stood a few steps past the motel door with my hands on my hips. The air outside felt crisp, almost cool. The storm seemed to have sucked the humidity out of the area. Every cell in my body hummed with a need to get back to Camellia Beach and back to the Chocolate Box. Mixed in with that need was an equal measure of dread. Part of me (a big part) expected to find an empty spot where my beloved shop had once stood.

The good news, according to Althea and Bertie, was that the hurricane had weakened before making landfall. It'd also blasted through the area rather quickly. They regaled me with stories of previous storms that had lingered and caused tremendous wind and flood damage. There was one that had bounced up and down the coast, leaving the area only to return a few days later to cause more damage. This hadn't been that kind of hurricane.

But even though the storm was gone, we were stranded for several more days with no electricity or cell service. We ate food out of our cooler that was gradually losing its cool. By the end of the first day, we'd met nearly all the motel guests and employees. By the end of the second day, everyone at the motel had bonded over our shared hardships and were acting like family.

By the time the fourth day came, we were finally given the green light to return to Camellia Beach. Despite the Governor's lifting of the mandatory evacuation order, local officials urged us to wait. We were cautioned that the power hadn't been restored—we still didn't have power at the motel either—and that many of the roads would be impassable. We didn't care. Everyone was anxious to get back to assess the damage to our shops and to our town. After a series of hugs (which I awkwardly endured) and exchanges of email addresses and cell phone numbers, the residents at the motel began to check out and leave en mass.

Harley drove my Fiat that was packed with our essentials. We left the rest of our cars in the motel parking lot. It was as if by mutual agreement we decided to confront what was left of our beach as a united front. Bertie sat in the front seat. Today she was wearing a green T-shirt that simply read "Camellia Beach" in pink curlicue letters. Like her, we were all dressed for comfort in T-shirts and shorts and sturdy athletic shoes. Althea and I had stuffed ourselves in the backseat with Troubadour hissing in his carrying case and Stella barking at him. What should have been an easy one-hour drive back to Camellia Beach took more than three hours as we plodded in heavy traffic through the Lowcountry, weaving around fallen trees and pieces of homes.

At the bridge that crossed onto Camellia Beach, the National Guard stopped us and checked our identification before allowing us to go further.

"How's it out there?" Harley asked a young guardsman wearing a camo uniform.

"Sand everywhere," the guardsman said. "You won't get far in that car of yours. Should have brought an off-road vehicle."

The guardsman wasn't kidding. A mixture of sand, marsh grass, and tree branches covered everything—the road, yards, sidewalks. We had to abandon the Fiat in a parking lot that had been cleared for that purpose. We found one of the last parking places and started unpacking. Stella sniffed the salty air and barked happily as she tugged on the leash.

"I suppose we walk," Althea said as she pulled her rolling luggage toward what used to be Main Street.

I stepped into the sand. My foot sank several inches. Water oozed and soaked my shoe. I lifted my foot and gave it a shake. "It's going to be a long walk."

"Got nothing else on our schedule," Bertie said as she struggled to pull her rolling luggage over a branch as thick as my leg.

"That's the truth." Harley took Bertie's bag from her, which was silly of him. He was already carrying Troubadour's carrier and his own luggage. He didn't have enough arms to carry everything. I hurried over and tried to take Bertie's bag from him.

He resisted. "Penn, stop it. I'm Southern and my mama raised me right. She'd have a fit if she found out that I let you lift this burden from me."

Undeterred, I gave the luggage a tug. "And I'm from the Midwest. Where I was raised, women don't go around letting men parade around pretending they are superior."

"Sweetheart, I already know you have the strength of an ox." He refused to let go of the bag. He flashed me a rakish smile. "I learned that well enough when you socked me in the nose."

"Are you going to keep bringing that up?"

"Until the day I die."

"I hit you because I had thought you were trying to kill me."

"And I had thought you were harmless. We were both wrong. Let me carry Bertie's bag."

"No. That's stupid," I said, which convinced Stella that she needed to start barking even louder.

Luckily, a National Guard truck with huge tires that rolled over the mushy sand as easily as it would over pavement stopped beside us. A cheerful guardsman leaned out the driver side window and shouted, "Need a lift?"

"Dear Heavens, yes!" Althea said faster than anyone else. She glanced at me with a look of exasperation. "You two will be here arguing about who gets to carry the bags until nightfall if we don't accept."

My heart raced as the truck bounced us closer and closer to the shop. I kept wiping my sweaty palms on my pants. We turned a corner onto East Europe Street, the street where the Chocolate Box was located. The air suddenly felt like it was too thick for my throat.

Bonbon with the Wind

Sand covered the road and landscaping. Branches stuck out of the ground like wooden tombstones. The cute cottage that housed a real estate office next to the Chocolate Box had a gaping hole in its roof.

"Can you see it?" I croaked, after tightly closing my eyes. "Is it—?"

"Honey," Bertie said gently, "don't fret so. That building of yours has survived a hundred years of hurricanes."

That wasn't assurance enough for me. "Tell me it's still there."

"It's there," Harley said gently. "Look."

I popped a square of the shop's special Amar chocolate in my mouth and savored its rich, tropical flavors before opening my eyes.

The ancient oak tree that stood sentry outside the shop had lost a few massive branches but was otherwise healthy. The building itself still listed to one side. But like an old friend, it was there waiting for me. Tears welled in my eyes. I breathed a deep sigh of relief.

We all climbed down from the back of the truck and waved goodbye to the guardsmen who were off to help other residents. I stood with my hands on my hips and stared at my shop, still quite unable to believe what I was seeing.

The white clapboard siding was stained where the sea had lapped at the building like a thirsty hound. Dirt and stain, I could handle. The building was there.

"We still have a roof." Harley nodded to the second floor.

"Instead of standing around gaping, let's see what it looks like on the inside," Bertie suggested with a huff.

We had to work our way through a heavy thatch of marsh grass to get to the front door. The plywood boards covering the plate glass display windows were still attached. The sandbags we'd piled in front of the door were still in place, thought coated in the thatch of marsh grass. We began to remove the bags and found starfish, an assortment of exotic shells, and smelly, rotting fish.

"Look at that," Bertie said pointing to something poking out of a mound of marsh grass that had gathered next to the door.

It was a tweed hat. It took me a moment to remember why it seemed familiar. "Wasn't the man searching for Joe Davies wearing a hat like that?"

"I believe so. I hadn't seen as fine a hat in a while. My daddy used to wear one, but Daddy's had a little pheasant feather tucked in its brown silk band," Bertie said.

I picked up it up, plucked off the seaweed before turning it over in my hand. I then read the inside label. Just as I'd thought. It was made by a prominent men's designer. The back of my neck prickled. "I have a bad feeling about this."

"Are you having a premonition?" Althea was quick to ask.

"No." I frowned at her. Why would she think that? "But I do have enough common sense to know a man doesn't simply drop an expensive hat like this one and forget about it. See the stitching? You don't see that kind of tight, even quality every day. It's actually quite difficult to find." I sounded like my half-sister. She was a popular Chicago fashion designer. Apparently I hadn't completely ignored her when she had gone on and on about the troubles she often encountered when working with the garment industry. "Something happened here."

"I hope he wasn't foolish enough to try and ride out the storm on the beach," Harley said.

"I hope—" I started to say. But I didn't want to say it.

Harley's brows rose, but he didn't say anything.

"What?" Althea asked. "You don't think—?"

I shook my head. I didn't want to think about it. For the next ten minutes we continued to move the sandbags away from the front door. It was slow going.

"Not as bad as we'd feared," Bubba drawled as he joined us. He reached down and tossed aside a sandbag as if it weighed nothing.

"Your house and business are okay?" Bertie asked before I could. Her cheeks turned a pretty shade of pink as she watched him heave aside another sandbag.

"The house took a little beating, and there's a bit of water got into the shop. It's the loss of operating days that's going to hurt worse than the cleanup." He wiped his hands on his jeans. "Penn, you do know there are small business loans available to help businesses like ours stay afloat while we recover from natural disasters."

"Hello?" Althea said with a little note of exasperation. "I'm also a small business owner."

"So am I." Harley smiled as he said it.

"And the two of you already know about the loans because we've weathered hurricanes before," Bubba pointed out.

I'd been struggling to drag a sandbag—they were wicked heavy when wet—but stopped to turn to my friends. Dang, I was dense. Althea and Harley both had businesses that could have suffered losses. Instead of visiting their properties, my friends were here helping me. They were here helping because they knew recovery from a hurricane would be a new and frightening experience for me. And Bubba had come too, although I suspected he was here for a different reason. Bertie smiled whenever she glanced in his direction.

My grandmother, who was considered a saint in the town, would have been more worried about the other residents than about the state of this shop. She would have been spending her energies trying to figure out what she could do for them instead of worrying over the damage the storm had done to her building.

I could almost hear Mabel's voice whisper in the light breeze that was tickling my ears saying, *"The older residents won't be able to do this on their own. They're going to look to you, Penn."*

I glanced up to see Althea watching me with a I-know-what-you're-thinking smile. She was acting as if she'd heard the voice too.

"It's my conscience, not the voice of a ghost," I wanted to snap. But to say that wouldn't convince her. And besides, even if she was standing right next to me, it she couldn't hear the thoughts in my head. So instead of saying something crazy, I said what I thought would make Grandmother Mabel proud, "As soon as we get the doors open, we need to make a plan for helping the residents get back on their feet. We need to start a volunteer list and a needs list. I'll keep them posted in the window."

Just as Bubba moved the last sandbag out of the way, Althea leaned toward me and said in a knowing way, "Mabel used to post lists just like those on the shop window after a hurricane. She wouldn't happen to be whispering advice in your ear, would she?"

"Any reports of major damage?" I asked Bubba as I nudged Althea out of my face.

He hesitated before answering. "You saw the roads and our yards. Sand is everywhere. There are damaged roofs. A few buildings are pretty badly beat up. Flooding occurred nearly everywhere. And there was one bad house fire. Because it happened during the height of the storm, the place burned completely to the ground before the fire department could get out to it with their equipment."

"Not Althea's house," I cried.

"See, you do worry about me. We'll be friends again before you know it." Althea patted my shoulder.

I hoped she was right.

"Why would you think it was Althea's house that burned?" Bubba asked.

"Because you seem reluctant to tell us about it, and I'm standing right here where Bertie, Harley, and I live."

"Stop acting like you're on the stage and blurt it out already, Bubba," Bertie said with a huff.

"Very well." He eyed me cautiously again. "But you need to know, Penn, that I'm not saying anything. I'm just telling you what you asked me."

"Why does everyone around here think I have a volcanic temper?" I complained.

"Because you do!" Bertie, Althea, and Bubba all howled at once.

Harley, smart man, had kept his lips clamped tightly shut and his expression fairly neutral.

"It was Joe Davies' house," Bubba said it like he was ripping off a band-aid and then winced.

"That poor man," I said quite calmly. Why would they think I'd react in any other way? "He once told me that he had reams and reams of research stored in his house."

"The Gray Lady had warned him." Althea took a step away from me before making that pronouncement. Her eyes opened as big as an owl's. "She warned him. And now he's lost everything."

I chose to ignore her.

"At least he was smart enough to get off the island. Just think what would have happened if he'd been foolish enough to try and ride out the storm," Harley said.

"Well, I know who'll go on my needs list," I said. A piece of me felt proud—and quite frankly surprised—that I could manage to sound so calm. I hadn't snapped at Althea or lectured that only fools believed in ghosts. Instead, I'd focused on moving forward after the storm.

My aversion to ghosts and magic went back to my childhood. I'd been told (wrongly) that my mother—the woman who'd abandoned me on my father's doorstep—was a fortune teller and a con-woman who took advantage of gullible people eager to believe in the unbelievable. She was the villain in my life's story. If not for her, my father's family wouldn't have suffered the humiliation of my existence. It was people like her, people who claimed to have magical powers who caused the most damage, or so I'd believed.

And then I'd met Althea.

She believed in every kind of magical woo-woo nonsense out there, yet she'd managed to charm her way past my defenses. She was funny and easy-going. She was like a butterfly flitting from flower to flower. One couldn't help but be drawn to her.

29

The last of the sandbags had finally been moved out of the way. I used my shoulder to push open the shop door. The wood must have swollen from the flood waters. The copper bell above the door made a joyful sound like a puppy happy its owners had finally returned home.

There were puddles here and there on the wood flooring, and there was a brown stain low on the walls that reminded me of a ring in a bathtub.

"So the flood waters did get inside," Bertie said pragmatically. "It's nothing a little cleaning can't handle."

Not willing to breathe easily yet, I headed straight to the heart of the shop...the kitchen.

"She'll have to have someone come in to dry out the place and make sure mold doesn't grow," I heard Harley saying behind me as I hurried down a hallway to the back kitchen with Stella following along.

"I know someone who'll give her a good price," Bubba's low voice rumbled.

I stepped into the kitchen and flipped on the overhead lights. Nothing happened. Of course nothing happened. The power still hadn't been restored on the island. While I knew that, it was hard to break old habits. The kitchen was usually a bright, sunny area. But with plywood boards covering every window, including the windows that opened up to the marsh behind the shop, it made the space dark and gloomy.

As I peered into the darkness, suddenly a bright, almost ghostly, light flitted around the room. Startled, I spun around to find Harley standing there with a flashlight in his hand.

"Bertie found this in the office. The carpeting in there is ruined. And you might want to replace that old desk. But other than that, I think it'll be okay."

I nodded somewhat absently while my gaze followed his beam of the flashlight.

Like out front, there were puddles of water on the floor and a watermark stained the walls, but none of the ovens or chocolate making equipment—all of which we'd tightly wrapped in plastic—seemed damaged. Even the burlap sacks of Amar cacao beans were exactly how I'd left them, untouched by the flooding waters. I breathed out a sigh of relief.

It was okay.

I wanted to pinch myself.

My shop had survived.

An hour later, Troubadour was happily munching his food upstairs in our apartment. I had the volunteer and needs lists posted to the newly uncovered storefront window. My name was at the top of the volunteer list. I was ready to help the town get back on its feet.

We followed Bubba as he led the way back to Main Street and the shops there. Harley wanted to take a look at his office, which was on the second floor above Althea's crystal shop and Althea wanted to see how her place had fared as well.

We were halfway down Main Street, which was currently being cleared of sand with a large bulldozer, when Stella slipped out of her collar and took off running.

Thankfully, she steered away from the heavy equipment being used on the road. She zigged and zagged while running as quick as a world-class sprinter toward the beachfront.

"Stella! Come back here!" I chased after her, stumbling several times in the rolling sand dunes where there should have been roads. If anything happened to my little dog, I didn't know what I'd do.

"Go on without me!" I called to my friends and ran even faster after Stella.

The ocean waves were visible as they crashed against the battered shoreline. I half-slid, half-fell down one of the damaged dunes where the storm had sharply eroded the beach just as Stella disappeared over another sand dune far to my right.

"Come back!" I yelled like a crazy person. "Please."

That's when I heard it. A yelp and then a whine.

Oh, gracious no. Stella sounded hurt. I crested the dune she'd disappeared over and found my little dog.

She pawed the sand and continued that odd, deep throated whine. I'd never heard her make a sound like that before.

"Stella?" I whispered as I approached her cautiously. Had she cut her foot? Was that why she was pawing the sand?

I stepped even closer.

What I saw stopped me cold.

Her paw scraped at what looked like a white cotton buttoned-up shirt. But the shirt wasn't wadded into a pile as if it'd been washed out of a house. The material was buried less than an inch under the sand and lying flat and slightly rounded. And the smell...

I scooped Stella up in my arms and hugged her to my chest.

She hadn't found a crab to chase or a piece of detritus from someone's life that had been washed away. She'd found some*one*. Although I wasn't an expert in these things, I guessed by the horrific odor that the body had to have been there for several days.

Chapter 4

I needed to report this. I pulled my cell phone from my back pocket to call my friend, Detective Frank Gibbons who worked with the Charleston County Sheriff's Department. When I hit the call button, my phone beeped twice. A message popped up on the screen that read, *No Service.*

Right. I'd forgotten that cell service in the area hadn't been restored. Losing my phone and access to the outside world felt like someone had cut off my arm. It took me a panicked moment to figure out how to report the body.

I hated to leave whoever was buried in the sand alone. It felt disrespectful. But there was no helping it. I had to hike back to the downtown and hope I'd be able to find someone at the police station who would know what to do.

"Why didn't you listen to the news media and stay away from my town?" Police Chief Hank Byrd complained when he saw me rush into the police department's front office. He tugged at his ill-fitting pants. "We won't have power for days. Go find a safe place to stay and leave me alone."

"I-I—" I stammered, feeling suddenly out of breath from the burst of adrenaline that was coursing through my veins. "Body."

He rolled his eyes to the water-stained ceiling tiles above his head. "Do not tell me you're saying what you're saying. Tell me, instead, that you're getting in your car and going as far away from here as possible."

"I-I—" I dragged in a deep breath as Stella wiggled out of my arms. She sniffed his sandy boots and then growled. "I think I found a body washed up on the beach."

Still gazing at the ceiling—was it drooping?—Byrd heaved a heavy sigh. "Of course you did," he said.

When he didn't say anything else, or even look at me, I asked somewhat hesitantly, "Would you like me to show you where?"

A muscle in his cheek twitched. Sure, in the past year there had been a few incidences involving dead bodies. But no one had died because I'd moved to Camellia Beach. And I had assisted in solving the mysteries surrounding those deaths.

He finally tore his gaze from the water-damaged ceiling. "I had such a quiet life as Police Chief before you moved to town. Never had to deal with a murder or a—"

"I know. I know. The worst crime that you had to handle was speeding cars and rowdy kids on weekends," I said before he could.

"Exactly. Glad you're starting to understand." He hitched up his pants again.

"I'm sure it's an accidental death," he said more to himself than to me. "Let me go see if I can get someone with the EMS to join us out there." He exited through a door on the far side of the police department and left me alone.

The air in the city building felt damp and muggy. I hoped the town would be able to restore power soon. Even though it was the middle of October, there wasn't even a hint of fall this deep in the South. Air conditioning was desperately needed not only to cool things off, but also to keep mold from growing all over...well, all over everything.

While I was standing there with sweat making a path down the center of my back and Stella sniffing a stain on the carpeting, a man burst through the front door. He was older, perhaps in his mid to late seventies. His thinning gray hair stood up here and there. He was wearing a long-sleeved dress shirt and dark blue wool suit pants. Startled by his entrance, Stella jumped in the air and began barking with a high-pitched sound I now recognized as a sign that she was terrified.

"I need to report—" He grabbed his knees in an effort to catch his breath.

"What's with all this infernal racket out here?" Byrd growled as he lumbered back through the same door he'd gone through not a few minutes ago.

At the same time the man dressed far too warmly for the weather blurted, "I need to report a murder!"

"Not this again," Byrd said. He turned to glare at me. "There's no reason to jump to conclusions. Accidents can—"

"No!" he rushed past me and grabbed Byrd's arm. "No! He was murdered. My brother was murdered."

Hank shot me another hard glare before focusing on the man who was gripping his arm. "Who are you, and what in blazes are you talking about?"

He released Byrd's arm. "I'm Silas Piper."

"Really?" Byrd raised his eyebrow with disbelief.

I shared the police chief's reaction. Silas Piper was a multibillionaire with business holdings all over the globe. Why would an important man like him come to Camellia Beach? Wouldn't he hire someone to come and ask questions for him? I knew my father would.

"My brother has been murdered, and I expect a full investigation," Silas said importantly.

"Did he often wear a tweed hat?" I asked.

The man eyed me cautiously before answering. "I don't know much about what he might or might not wear. I haven't set eyes on him in over ten years."

"You'll have to excuse me for sounding callous," Byrd said. "But if you've not been in contact with your brother, why would you even start to think he was killed out here on Camellia Beach? This town is a paradise. Our residents are peaceful and—"

"Because of this." Silas had pulled a crumbled letter from his pants pocket. "I received it yesterday. Taylor wrote the letter. He said it was insurance, the fool. It's a letter that he supposedly left with a friend only to be mailed if that friend failed to hear from him."

He handed the letter to Byrd. The police chief read it through quickly and snorted out a frustrated breath. "This doesn't prove anything. As you might have noticed, a hurricane has hit our area. The power is out. The phones are down. The cell service is down. The only thing that's working for communication around here is our radio system. Give it a few days and I'm sure your brother will call you." He pushed the letter back into the older man's hand. "Now, if you'll excuse me, I'm horribly busy. Penn, you had something to show me?"

"I—um—of course," I muttered while Silas, his shoulders slumped, shuffled toward the door. "Give me a minute. And you might want make sure the EMT has a good shovel."

I heard Byrd groan behind me as I followed Silas out to the street.

"Mr. Piper?" I crossed the distance between us and, after setting Stella down, held out my hand. "I'm Charity Penn. I didn't recognize you at first. You used to visit my father when your business headquarters were in Chicago."

He'd visited my father's house several times when I was growing up, but I'd only ever seen the top of his head. I remember watching from my perch on the stairs as the family butler led the way through the vaulted foyer and down the wide hallway. Silas' purposeful stride had made his shoes clack on the marble floor as he headed toward my father's domain—a study that smelled of leather and books.

"Charity Penn?" His brow furrowed with confusion as he tentatively shook my hand. "And you claim you're George's child?"

My father, like his father before him, was the head of Penn Industries, a multinational conglomerate that bought companies, restructured them, and sold shares of the rejuvenated businesses at large profits. My father's family, especially my paternal grandmother, liked to deny my existence. My mother, who I'd only recently learned was Mabel's daughter, hadn't been a debutant handpicked from a well-heeled blue-blood Chicago family. Worse, my father couldn't even remember my mother's name.

"I'm his oldest child." I drew a deep breath before adding, "I'm not surprised he's never mentioned me. I'm—you know—a bit of a family secret. A black sheep of the Penn clan."

"I see." He wiped the hand that had touched mine on his pants.

"I live here on Camellia Beach. Perhaps there's something I can do to help you?"

He sighed. "I suppose you want a fee for this *help*?"

"A fee?" I hadn't even thought of that. All I wanted was a peek at that letter in his hand. But I couldn't pass up an opportunity to get Silas to release his grip on some of his riches. "I don't need anything personally. My business escaped relatively unscathed. However, you could donate some money to help with the hurricane relief around here."

He shook his head, so I quickly added, "The police chief means well, but with the hurricane and having to protect the shops and homes from being looted, he doesn't have time to search for a missing person on an island where nearly everyone is missing right now. We were only given the go-ahead to return this morning. I, on the other hand, am a business owner and resident. I have time to ask around as a favor to a family friend."

His eyes narrowed. I had a feeling he was trying to figure out what kind of con game I was playing. I locked my fingers behind my back and tried to appear as unthreatening as possible.

"You say you're the black sheep of the Penn family, huh?" he said. "Why didn't you try and hide that from me?"

I smiled awkwardly and shrugged. "I have no reason to deny it. You could find that out with one phone call to my father. It's the circumstance of my existence that makes my family think I'm an embarrassment, not anything shameful that I did as an adult, if that's makes any difference."

"You're a bastard, then?"

"It seems like an old-fashioned term in this day and age, but yes. You could say that."

He nodded sharply.

Undeterred, I asked, "May I look at that letter your brother sent?"

His hard gaze shifted from where he'd been studying my face to my outstretched hand. "It's a copy. The original is at my office."

He slapped the crumpled paper onto my open palm. I unfolded and quickly read the letter before he had a chance to change his mind.

It was exactly as he'd described it. The letter was short, which meant it was also short on details.

It must be a shock hearing from me after all this time. I decided to follow up on that business that caused our family so much pain.

"What business?" I asked.

"It's a private matter," Silas growled.

He reached for the letter, so I started to read faster.

As you might imagine, there are several people who won't welcome my interest. I have followed one of them to Camellia Beach in South Carolina. As a precaution, I have directed my friend to send this letter to you, brother, if he hasn't heard from me for three days. If you have received this letter, know that my efforts have failed and that I am dead. The guilty have murdered me in order to keep their guilt and my innocence hidden.

At the bottom it was signed, *Taylor Graham*, which was interesting.

"Graham? Why a different last name?" I asked him.

"It's a long story."

I waited to hear it.

He kept his thin lips pressed together.

"All right." I handed him the letter. "I don't know a Taylor Graham, but I can ask around. Can you text me his picture? I'd like to show it to some of my friends."

"It wouldn't be a recent picture," he warned.

"It would be better than nothing. Can you get it for me right away?" I dug a scrap of chocolate wrapper from my pocket and jotted my cell phone number on it.

"I'll see what my secretary can do," he said. He then lifted the wrapper to his nose and smelled it. A ghost of a smile flickered across his tight mouth.

"I own the local chocolate shop," I told him. "It's been run by my mother's side of the family for generations. The chocolate we make there is unmatched anywhere in the world. Once the town gets back on its feet, come by and I'll let you have some samples."

He grunted. I wasn't sure if that was a happy grunt or if he thought I was presuming too much.

"If you find out anything, you can contact me through my secretary," he said with a haughty sniff. "If she cannot find a photo, I'll have her send you a text to inform you of that."

His cold manner was probably his way of trying to hide his deep concern for his brother's life. I often acted in the same standoffish manner whenever I felt scared or overwhelmed. Besides which, he didn't know me. I could be a kook who wanted to sell a story to a tabloid newspaper.

"Cell service is down on the island right now. So don't have her send it until you hear it's been restored, okay?" I didn't wait for him to answer. I'd gotten what I'd needed. I had hoped he had a photo of his brother tucked away in his pocket. But he didn't.

I also knew that the police chief wouldn't wait for me for much longer, even if I was talking to one of the most powerful men either of us would ever meet in our lives. There was a body on the beach to be dealt with. He'd come marching back out here, grab my arm, and pull me away if I didn't join him soon.

I ran back up the steps and into the town hall where the police station was located. Byrd, as I'd expected, was heading in my direction. A dark-haired woman about my age dressed in a blue EMT's jumpsuit was at his side. She introduced herself as Marion Olrich. She had a shovel slung over one shoulder and the strap to a large medical bag over the other.

"It's this way." I drew a fortifying breath. Stella yipped softly. The three of us exited the building through a side door. We then headed toward the beach and the dead body buried underneath the sand.

The wind blew the ocean's salty air into my face. I shivered. I feared we were on the cusp of uncovering Silas Piper's long-lost black sheep of a brother.

Chapter 5

"Wait up!" Harley jogged to catch up to us as we made our way toward the beach. Not that we were walking that fast. Marion was weighed down with her equipment and had refused my offers to help carry something. And Byrd rarely moved quickly. He once told me that a hasty police chief stirred an air of panic in the residents of the town. Above all things, he strove for calm and easy in his life.

"What's going on?" Harley asked. His clothes were streaked with mud and wet sand. The cuff of his shorts had ripped since I'd last seen him.

"Are you OK?" I blurted, suddenly more concerned about what had happened to him than some dead body on the beach that wasn't going anywhere. "Are you hurt? How's the office?"

"Um…I'm fine. There was…some damage to the office. It's going to have to be completely redecorated. Luckily all the files had been digitized and uploaded to an offsite server. So I suppose I didn't lose anything important."

I eyed him closely, trying to decide if he was more shaken up about his office than he was letting on. He'd taken over his father's law practice after his father had passed away. The only change Harley had made to his father's office, with its old wood paneled walls and furniture the color of faded avocados from the early nineteen sixties, was to purchase a computer. While money constraints might have kept him from updating and making the office his own, I suspected he'd treated the office like it was one of downtown Charleston's famous historic sites—not changing a blasted thing—as a way of keeping his father's memory alive.

I wanted to say something comforting. I wanted to let him know that he could count on me for any emotional support he might need. But when I opened my mouth none of that came out. Instead, I said, "The carpeting in there was older than the both of us combined." And then I wanted to kick myself for sounding so uncaring.

Harley only chuckled. "It was a classic pattern. Don't know I'll be able to find anything quite that shade of brown with brown highlights to replace it." His entire face brightened as he shook his head. So perhaps I'd said the right thing after all. "But enough about my office, what's going on?"

"Dead body on the beach," Byrd answered for me. "Your girlfriend found it."

Harley tripped over his own feet. "Penn, really?"

I nodded.

"We haven't been back in town for more than"—he checked his watch—"two hours, and you're already stumbling across dead bodies?"

"It wasn't on purpose. Besides, it wasn't me. Stella found it."

"You're blaming the dog?" He scrubbed his hand over his face. "Whatever you do, don't let Fletcher hear about it. He'll declare it was a murder."

"He won't hear about it from me, but this is Camellia Beach. If he's returned, there's a good chance someone has already told him," I said.

Fletcher was my newest employee. He had this unnatural interest in playing amateur detective. It was an interest that had nearly gotten him killed a few months ago.

Harley groaned. "That boy is looking for murders. He was wearing a Sherlock Holmes deerstalker hat the last time we saw him, for goodness sake."

"It might be a murder," I mumbled. Not quietly enough, apparently.

Harley paled.

I felt for him. He was likely remembering the last murder on the island. He'd helped me track down the killer. Things had turned downright dangerous at the end. Matters between Harley and me had

42

also turned steamy right before we'd confronted someone who had no moral qualms against killing anyone who had gotten in their way.

Like Fletcher, we'd also been lucky to escape with our lives.

"Don't misunderstand me," I said. "I hope it's nothing. I hope I'm seeing dead bodies where none exist. But Silas Piper was at the police station just now."

Harley mouthed the name and whistled.

"He was the one who brought up the idea of murder, not me." I told him about Silas' black sheep brother and the letter Silas had received.

Harley's tan returned. "The hurricane has knocked out all communications in the area. I'm sure it's a case of bad timing and nothing else."

"That's what I'm thinking," Byrd said. "If there's a body on the beach, I'd bet good money that it belongs to some brainless lack-wit who thought riding out a hurricane on a barrier island would be a hoot."

"I asked him to get me a picture of his brother, you know, just in case," I said, not able to shake the nagging feeling that something dreadful had happened on Camellia Beach after we'd evacuated, something that had nothing to do with Hurricane Avery.

We arrived where I'd found the suspicious-looking shirt. Perhaps I was wrong. Perhaps that stinky lump in the sand wasn't a dead body. I grabbed Harley's hand and held it tightly as both Byrd and Marion donned plastic gloves.

Marion produced a little whisk brush from her medical bag— not something I was expecting she'd have in there and then squatted next to the suspicious lump. With fast, efficient swipes she removed the top layer of sand from a small area. A moment later, Byrd cursed.

I leaned forward to see what had upset him.

A mistake.

What I saw wasn't something I'd wanted to see. I quickly pressed my face to Harley's chest, sandwiching Stella between me and her arch nemesis. She wiggled and growled low in her throat.

"I didn't want to be right," I choked as I tried to soothe my angry little dog. "Truly, I didn't."

"I know, Penn." Harley rubbed his hand up and down my back.

Marion had uncovered from the sandy grave what was clearly a man's hand. The action of her brush had dislodged something disc-shaped from his fingers.

"Is that a gold coin?" Harley asked.

"Looks like it," Marion answered as she continued to clear away the sand.

"It's evidence and not to be discussed," Byrd snapped. He jumped up from his crouch with surprising speed. "Back up, now. Let the experts work. Ah, here are your colleagues now, Ms. Olrich."

One of the National Guard trucks with its giant tires rolled onto the beach. Two men and a woman dressed in the same blue jumpsuits that Marion was wearing jumped down from the cab. The men went around to the rear of the truck and retrieved a stretcher.

"Go on, get out of here," Byrd made shooing motions toward Harley and me with his hands.

"You'll let us know who it is?" I asked, not moving.

He tilted his head and grimaced. "What do you think? I'm not the news service. This is a police investigation. And last time I looked, you weren't a member of the police force. Now get going."

"But—" I protested. Stella started barking.

"Come on." Harley moved away to give Marion's team room to do their work. Because I still had my arms wrapped around him, it was easy for him to lead me along with him. "Even though communications are down, this is still a small island," he reminded me. "We'll know who it is before nightfall."

He was right. And I really didn't want to stand and watch as they uncovered a body that had been buried in the sand for close to a week. Still, my feet felt like lead weights. Something told me I needed to be there, I needed to see the clues they were uncovering.

"It's an accidental death," Harley whispered in my ear. "Someone stayed during the storm who shouldn't have stayed. It's tragic, but far more common than you might think."

"I hope you're right." It didn't feel like he was right.

The gold coin that had fallen from the dead man's hand nagged at me.

"I'm right," Harley said, but he sounded worried.

The letter Silas' brother had sent, claiming he'd been murdered bothered me.

"We have enough on our plates with the storm damage. We can't go borrowing trouble," he said with an emphatic nod.

"The stranger with the tweed hat," I said. "The one who was looking for Joe Davies. I wonder if he was Silas Piper's brother."

"Even if he was," Harley said, "there's no reason to believe his showing up in Camellia Beach hours before the hurricane has anything to do with an accidental drowning. No reason at all."

"I'm sure you're right. I just have a really bad—"

"Hank, do you recognize this man?" I heard Marion ask. She must have uncovered the poor dead man's face.

"It's kind of hard to tell," Byrd said. "He looks kind of familiar."

I was glad we weren't standing close enough to see for ourselves.

One of the men on Marion's team swore an oath. "Look at the shock of red hair. That there is Joe Davies."

"Joe Davies?" the other man cried. "The Gray Lady did him in!"

The police chief swore viciously.

I felt like swearing too.

Chapter 6

One week later.

"Joe Davies brought this on himself, you know." Ethel Crump, Camellia Beach's head gossip, leaned over her mug of coffee. She let her gaze shift from person to person before whispering, "Hank said it was an accidental death. But we all know this was no accident. When Joe set out to find Blackbeard's treasure he might well have been looking to dig up a grave, for all the ill that it caused him. The unsettled ghosts around here don't cotton to anyone poking into their secrets. If Blackbeard buried his treasure on our island, it's his and anyone who dares to touch it risks otherworldly retribution, as Joe found out."

The residents crowded around her table all nodded in agreement.

I rolled my eyes.

It was Sunday morning, which was the time when the island's nosiest residents gathered at the Chocolate Box to catch up on gossip. Ethel Crump, rumored to be as old as the town's ancient oak trees, twined her crooked fingers together and leaned back in her chair. The woman was in her glory as she spoke of ghosts and death.

Things on Camellia Beach were slowly returning to normal. The shop had only opened for business two days ago. We'd all had to wait several days for the power and cell phone service to be restored to the island and the National Guard to clear the sand from the roads.

But even though there was a feeling of normalcy inside the shop, there were many reminders that the hurricane was still disrupting life outside. Bright blue tarps covered roofs that the wind had torn apart. The sharp rat-a-tat-tat of nail guns and the hum of electric saws could be heard throughout the daylight hours as homes and businesses were repaired. And much of the island's brightly colored wildflowers had been lost under the thick swaths of sand that covered everything.

Bonbon with the Wind

The needs list and volunteer sheet I'd posted on the shop's front window had quickly filled up. Many of the elderly residents who used the Pink Pelican Inn as a low-cost retirement home had returned only to find they were now homeless. The inn's first floor had been flooded by the hurricane's storm surge. The ocean had literally washed across much of the small island. And the inn's second story rooms had sustained rain damage when sections of the metal roof had lifted off. The Pink Pelican was getting a complete makeover, which it had desperately needed anyhow. But in the meantime, we'd needed to find places for sixteen of our most vulnerable members of our community while the place was closed.

It warmed my heart to see how everyone was stepping up to help. Bertie and I had opened our small apartment to two elderly sisters, Trixie and Barbie Baker. I'd given them my bed and had taken to sleeping on the sofa.

I stretched my aching back, before clearing coffee mugs and plates off a table.

Fletcher Grimbal returned from the shop's kitchen. He carried a large tray of peanut butter bonbons that he slid into the glass display case. He was wearing his Sherlock Holmes deer hunter hat. His entire face came alive when he heard Ethel mention Joe's name. His cheeks bloomed red.

"It-it's as if s-s-someone was t-trying to wipe him off the f-f-face of the earth," Fletcher stammered. He had a speech impediment that worsened whenever he was nervous or excited. He drew a long breath and then sang, "It's quite the mystery."

"No mystery," Ethel countered, her voice sounded like the scraping of a tree limb against a window. "The Gray Lady took him. He's trapped in her domain now. Before long, we'll see signs that he's joined with the other unsettled spirits haunting our beach."

Fletcher glanced at me and raised his eyebrows.

The corner of my mouth twitched. I didn't want to say anything, but I agreed with Fletcher's look of disbelief. The Gray Lady was a myth, a story. Myths didn't kill people. The islanders had clearly lost their collective minds if they believed some pretend ghost had anything to do with Joe's passing.

Just yesterday Chief Byrd had told the local newspaper, *The Camellia Current*, that Joe's death had been declared accidental. According to the official report, Joe had bumped his head and then drowned in the hurricane's storm surge. Perhaps he'd been running from his house after it'd caught fire. Perhaps he'd died before the fire. The coroner couldn't tell.

What I didn't understand was why Joe had ignored all the warnings to leave the island. He'd told us that he was leaving right away. Had he stayed in order to search for more of Blackbeard's gold? He'd died with that gold coin in his hand. Not that his holding the coin made any sense. Why was it in his hand and not in his pocket?

I glanced in Fletcher's direction again. His nose was twitching like a rabbit's. That could only mean one thing—he suspected foul play, which would also explain why he'd taken to wearing that silly Sherlock Holmes cap all the time.

The bell above the shop door tinkled sweetly. I looked up, expecting Harley.

It wasn't.

A woman in a crisply pressed baby-blue suit with matching stiletto heels entered. Her short hair curled around her face like a golden frame. She stopped just a foot inside the door and stroked her pearls as she scanned the room.

Everyone in the shop stopped their conversations to turn and stare. I set down my tray of dirty mugs on the closest empty table before hurrying across the room to greet the newcomer.

"Welcome to the Chocolate Box," I said with a smile.

Her perfectly plucked eyebrows flattened. She glanced over my shoulder as if searching for someone, anyone, who wasn't me. Her reaction was not at all what I was expecting.

"We sell chocolates," I said slowly. "We—you know—make them from the bean." I cleared my throat, hoping that would chase away my sudden hesitation to talk with her.

I couldn't put my finger on it, but something about her unnerved me. I wanted her out of my shop. And I had no idea why. There were very few people who caused me to act that way. And none of them were strangers to me.

"You're not here to buy chocolate," Fletcher came up from behind. He put his hand on my shoulder.

I tried not to flinch. I'd always been a flinch-whenever-someone-touches-me kind of person.

"You're here because you're frustrated that the police chief didn't give you the answers you were looking for," he added.

"Why would you say that?" I scolded the younger man. I then quickly said to our customer, "I'm sorry. My assistant loves playing detective. Please, come in. We have coffee, tea, pastries, and a wide assortment of chocolates."

Her silvery-blue eyes flicked from Fletcher to me and back to Fletcher again. "He's right," she said with a long sigh. "Chief Byrd told me the case was closed. Actually, he said there was no case to be opened or even investigated in the first place."

"I don't understand." I really didn't. What case was she talking about? And how had Fletcher guessed that she'd talked with the police chief?

She looked at me as if I should already know everything there was to know about her story and huffed. "Joe was my husband." Again, she said it as if I should have already known.

"Joe was married?" I asked. He'd told everyone that he was a retired fisherman. "He'd once told me he'd been married to the sea."

"Well, as you can plainly tell, I'm not a large body of water. For better or worse, I was married to him." She closed her eyes and gave her head a sad shake. "Only, 'Joe' wasn't the name I knew him by. I was married to John Fenton. He disappeared about eight years ago. I didn't know if he was alive or dead. But when they ran that article in yesterday's newspaper, a friend of mine saw it and emailed it to me. The man in the picture, the man they called Joe Davies, is—I mean— was definitely my John Fenton. I want to know who killed him. And I want to know why."

Fletcher hissed under his breath before saying, "*I-I knew it!*" while beating a fist against his thigh.

I swallowed hard. "I see," I said. I would have said more, but before the words could form, a television crew stormed through the door.

"I'm Stevie McWilson," a tall man with large, gleaming white teeth and a full head of hair slicked back with some kind of thick styling product, announced to the room.

"I've seen you on Channel Six." Ethel Crump rose from her chair with the speed of a much, much younger woman. I don't think I could have moved as fast as she had, and I was at least fifty years younger than her ninety-plus years. "Young man, you make listening to the news tolerable."

Stevie's bright, bleached smile widened. "I'm always pleased to meet a fan. But I must warn you, dear lady"—he showed off a diamond-studded wedding band—"I'm taken."

Ethel hooted with laughter. She loved it when people didn't treat her like a doddering invalid. She wasn't. Although she suffered from stiff joints and some hearing loss, she was as spry and sharp as anyone I knew.

"As you might imagine," Stevie continued, his voice booming with authority. "We're pursuing a story about the Gray Lady and her latest victim. I was told that this was the best place to come on a Sunday morning in search of residents who would know about the ghost and her history."

He shot an inquiring glance at me and then at the woman standing beside me.

"We can go talk over there," I told Joe's estranged wife. She didn't need to be harassed by the press. I was confident that no one in the shop would tell Stevie (an outsider) who she was or why she was in town. While Camellia Beach was a typical small town where there were no secrets, the town was also protective of its own.

The woman pulled away from me. "Mr. McWilson. I'd like to talk with you," she said boldly. She pushed herself in front of Ethel who was giving Stevie a lecture about the Gray Lady. "I'm Delilah Fenton, the dead guy's wife."

Did she actually call her late husband *the dead guy*? Yikes!

"If you'll give me a few moments to fix my hair and freshen my face, I'd be happy to talk with you on camera. My husband, it seems, was hiding many secrets."

"Really?" Stevie flashed a wide smile. "Let me buy you a coffee and some pastries." He hooked his arm through Delilah's and guided her to a private table at the back of the shop.

Everyone watched. Ethel's mouth had dropped open. She quickly snapped it closed.

"I wouldn't have figured she'd want to air her dirty laundry like that," she said.

"I s-suspect she thinks it's th-th-the only way to g-get a police investigation," Fletcher offered. "She's on a qu-quest for justice."

Ethel looked to me, expecting me to comment. I bit my lower lip and kept silent. Not because I agreed with Fletcher—I didn't agree with him. He was young and naive. He didn't understand the heart of a woman scorned. I did.

A woman in her position might be looking for answers. She might be looking for revenge. She might even be looking for a hidden stash of inheritance she thought she was owed. I doubted, however, she'd come to Camellia Beach looking for justice.

I started to wonder aloud why Joe would want to keep his marriage a secret, when I suddenly got an odd feeling that I was being watched. I whirled around, fully expecting to have a quick laugh at my wildly out-of-control imagination. My gaze crashed into Delilah's. While Stevie was sitting with his back to the room, Delilah had positioned herself—going as far as to maneuver her chair so it was at an odd angle to her table—so she could stare at me. Or perhaps she was staring at Ethel or Fletcher and I'd merely gotten in her path. Either way, the look she was directing our way got stuck like a choking lump in my throat. Her silvery blue eyes had frosted over. The gentleness of her features hardened until her pale skin looked like stone. The corners of her mouth turned down in an extremely disapproving manner. Even her hair seemed to bristle. Any one of those things, when taken by itself, hinted at a vague sort of dislike. But when they were added all together, her face became the portrait of pure hatred.

I didn't understand it. And seeing it chilled me to the bone.

Chapter 7

"Did you see who's here?" Bertie grabbed my arm, interrupting my attempt to escape through the door that led to the back kitchen. In the hubbub following the camera crew's entrance, I hadn't noticed that she'd returned from church. Bubba, dressed in his coat-and-tie Sunday finery, followed along beside her like a puppy. A ridiculously oversized puppy.

"I'm kind of shocked about it," I said. "Joe talked and talked and talked, but he never mentioned anything about having a wife."

"That? Oh, yes, there is that." Bertie fluffed her hair a bit. Unlike every other day of the week, Bertie looked like one of the older fashion models that my sister would hire to display her clothing line. Her navy-blue dress was tailored to compliment her pear-shaped contours. Instead of encased in cheap, white sneakers, her feet looked elegant in the dark-blue heels. "But did you see who's with her? That's Stevie McWilson. From Channel Six News. He's such a hottie."

"Hey!" Bubba protested. "A man doesn't like his woman talking about how good another man looks."

Bertie swatted his broad chest. "Don't fuss. For one thing, just because I let you accompany me to church doesn't mean I'm *your woman*. You haven't earned me yet. And for another thing, my eyes won't drop out of my head the moment I decide to let you call me *your woman*. I'm always going to be my *own* woman."

Bubba's shoulders dropped with defeat. "At least do your fawning over other men out of my hearing. It's hard on a man's ego."

Instead of agreeing, Bertie chuckled. I suspected she would go on doing exactly as she pleased when it came to Bubba. I envied her for it.

"We need to get you in front of the camera," Bertie announced.

At first I thought she was talking to Bubba. After all, he was the president of the business association. I realized my mistake when she gave me a gentle nudge.

"Me? Um…no," I said. "I'm not—" I didn't bother to finish what I'd started to say. She wasn't listening.

Instead she was frowning at my jeans with a rip in the knee and short-sleeved white blouse with a coffee stain in the middle where a customer had accidentally spilled their double shot of espresso on me that morning. "Perhaps you should put on one of those stodgy work dresses you used to wear when you first arrived."

"None of them fit anymore." Owning a chocolate shop, while wonderful for my mental health, had been a disaster for my waistline. I'd been shopping local thrift stores to build a wardrobe that wasn't nearly as form-fitting.

"Then one of your sundresses." She herded me toward the back door. "Make sure it's a bright color."

"I can't go on TV." I might have worked in advertising before inheriting the Chocolate Box, but that didn't mean I liked to be in front of the camera.

"Sure, you can," she said, giving me a push.

"No, I can't." My family had once tried to disown me after I'd agreed to be interviewed for a national magazine. I'd been told the interview was for an article about how I was graduating at the top of my class from college. The reporter had lied. The article had ended up being a hit piece against me and my family.

Never again.

"How about that new purple and blue sundress you wore the other night? Bright colors pop on camera. And you'll want to pop."

"You do know that reporter is here to do a piece about the Gray Lady?" I asked.

She still wasn't listening. "Be sure to mention the Chocolate Box in a way that it cannot be cut from the footage."

"He's here about the Gray Lady," I repeated.

Bertie nodded. "Yes. That's why he'll want to get you on camera. You saw her."

"I saw a woman. I didn't see a ghost," I protested. But it was too late. Bertie had already pushed me all the way out the back door and onto the small courtyard that opened up to the marsh.

"I'll stall McWilson for you," she called as she returned to the front of the shop. "And don't forget to put on some makeup while you're up there."

"You heard her," Bubba said, sounding surprisingly serious. "You'll be representing the store and the town. The businesses have suffered in the aftermath of the hurricane. We need you to get people to return to Camellia Beach and start spending money again."

No. No. And no. They could find someone else to field questions about some nonexistent ghost while talking up the town. I wasn't going to do it.

End.

Of.

Story.

Period.

I did go upstairs and change out of my coffee stained blouse. It would have been silly not to. Now that Bertie had returned from church, she could help with the morning crowd.

I usually spent this time working in the kitchen or tackling the business' bookkeeping. But today, I felt restless. My legs itched to get as far away as possible from the reporter and the talk of a haunted island. After slipping into comfortable running shorts and a white Chocolate Box T-shirt—it might have been October, but the high temperature for the afternoon was going to be close to ninety degrees—I snapped the leash to Stella's collar and then headed toward the beach.

Halloween was a week away, which explained why the reporter was hungry for a good ghost story. The real estate office next door had hung ghosts from the eaves of their porch and witches' legs with striped stockings stuck out from the part of the roof that was covered with a blue tarp. Pumpkins with grim expressions lined the front of the Dog Eared Café. Stella barked happily at them, prompting one of the servers to give her a doggie bone.

While I had meant to go straight to the beach, I took a detour onto a side street. I told myself that I'd turned that way because I was enjoying the spooky decorations and because I'd wanted to check on the progress of recovery for some of the houses that had been damaged. It wasn't the truth. My feet knew exactly where they were headed.

I stopped in front of the lot where Joe Davies used to live. The house had been one of the cottages that had been built atop tall towers of cinder blocks to elevate it above flood level. The cinder blocks were still there. Charred wooden beams still connected them to form the bottom part of where a house used to stand. Nothing else remained. What the fire hadn't destroyed, the hurricane had washed away.

Had it simply been a run of bad luck that Joe had died in the storm and his house had burned so completely? It felt as if someone were trying to erase…something. But what? And if that was the case, was foul play involved?

A small Honda with a dented hood and a faded blue paint job pulled up to the lot near where I was standing. A petite woman with flaming red hair stepped out of the car. She looked up at where the house once stood and burst out into ugly, noisy sobs. Her slender shoulders shook violently as she buried her face in her hands.

Who was this woman? Another wife no one had ever met? Or one of Joe's friends no one on the island had known about? Whoever she was, she was obviously distraught by his death.

I debated whether I should leave and let her have this private moment of grief alone or if I should try and comfort her. I'd started to back away from the broken remains of his house when the woman cried out in a raspy voice that tore at my chest, "*Daddy.*"

Goodness, no.

It was bad enough that he'd abandoned his wife. How could he—or anyone—abandon a child? It was a question I'd asked myself over and over from the time I'd learned my own mother had left me outside my father's dorm room door. And I still had no answer.

I took a couple of steps closer to the woman and then cleared my throat.

"Excuse me," I said. I must have whispered it since she didn't look up. I cleared my throat again. "Can I help you?" I drew a breath. "I knew the man who lived here."

She turned toward me with a look of horror.

"I mean…I knew the man he'd presented himself to be," I amended. "I suppose some of it was a lie. He'd told us that he was a retired fisherman."

She sniffled. "He was a car salesman. He didn't retire. He—" She gasped. "I'd assumed he'd-he'd died."

I nodded. "I'm sorry. I know what it's like to have a parent leave. My mother…" I cleared the lump that had formed in my throat. "She left me. If you'd like to talk, I could tell you what I knew about Joe."

"He was John Fenton," she said with a sob. "He lived in Virginia and worked at the Cedar's Hill Imports car lot."

"Did he like to fish?" I asked.

She sniffled again before answering. "Not even a little. Did he fish here?"

"Not that I ever saw. He was more interested in searching for pirate treasure than putting a line in the water."

That bit of news seemed to confuse her. She jerked her head back. "Pirate treasure?"

"Blackbeard's treasure, actually. He was obsessed. He'd tell anyone who he met how he was certain that Blackbeard had buried his treasure somewhere on this beach. He was determined to find it."

"Are you sure? My father actually told people he was looking for pirate treasure? That's not..." Her large gray-blue eyes widened. She shivered. I wondered if she was going into shock.

"Can I buy you a coffee or tea or something?" I asked. "I'm Penn. I run the local chocolate shop."

"Chocolate?" That news seemed to cheer her up a little. "I think I could use some coffee and chocolate right now. I drove all night from Virginia to get here. I'm Mary. And thank you for your kindness. Not everyone would stop to help a stranger."

"You'll find the people in this town are different. In a good way. Come on. If you don't mind walking, my shop is a few blocks down this road. Your mother is there. She came in looking for answers as well."

Her head snapped in my direction. "My mother died twenty years ago." Her words were brittle.

"I'm sorry. A woman who claims to be Joe's—I mean, John's—wife is at my shop. I assumed—"

"She's nothing to me. A gold digger." She had to stop to catch her breath. She held up her hand. "I'm sorry. This-this is just so hard. A friend who lives in Charleston contacted me. After seeing my father's picture in the local newspaper, he called and read me the article. That's how I found out my father been killed in the hurricane. I had to come see for myself. If you see *that woman* again, don't tell her I'm here. She'll only try and kick up trouble for me like she did for my dad."

"Do you have any idea why he might have run away and changed his name?" I asked as gently as I knew how.

Her upper lip trembled as she thought about the answer. "You'd have to ask that woman he married. I wouldn't be surprised if she'd chased him away. She married him for the money that came to him through my mother's estate. And once she ran through it, I heard from family friends that she'd pressured him to get more. She didn't love him. She only loved what he could buy for her."

Mary began to sob again. I wasn't sure what to do. Did I hug her—a stranger? That seemed awkward. But just standing by with my arms helplessly at my side while watching her struggle with her grief felt a hundred times more awkward.

Steeling my spine—hugs never came easily for me—I crossed the distance between us and wrapped my arms around her. "I'm so sorry," I said and immediately thought how inadequate that sounded. And because hugging a stranger was making my skin feel all jumpy, I kept talking. In fact, I couldn't seem to stop talking. "I can't imagine what you must be going through. If there's anything I can do, anything at all, just let me know. Please, I want to help."

She looked up at me with her large tear-stained eyes. "R-really?"

"Um…really. I-I'll do anything I can." I'd jump through fire if it got her to stop crying.

Much to my horror, my offer only caused her to cry harder. She pressed herself tightly against me, wrapped her arms around my neck, and squeezed. "Really? I don't know how to thank you," she managed to get out between heavy sobs.

"Um…" I said. "You could start by not crying." I had no clue what else I could say. I had no idea what she was thanking me for. But whatever it was, I had a bad feeling about it.

After a moment, her sobs quieted. Tears still streamed down her red and blotchy cheeks. She drew a ragged breath.

"I need you to—" she hesitated.

I held my breath kind of needlessly. She had lost her father and had come to Camellia Beach for answers. I'd done the same thing when my best friend had died less than a year ago.

"I need you to help me find who killed my father. And more importantly, find out *why*. Why would anyone do this to a kind old man? Could you help me find out what's going on?"

There was also no stopping me from nodding. If she needed help getting those answers, who was I—a daughter who also knew the bitter sting of abandonment—to deny her?

59

Dorothy St. James

Chapter 8

"I thought I'd find you in here." His voice startled me a few hours later as I worked in the Chocolate Box's commercial kitchen.

I looked up to find Harley leaning against the doorjamb. Goodness, he looked tempting. He was wearing khaki shorts and a white cotton short-sleeved shirt. The top couple of buttons were undone, giving me a nice view of his broad tanned chest. His soulful green eyes sparkled with pleasure as he eyed the double boiler I'd placed on the stovetop. His adorably kissable lips spread into a smile.

"What are you making?" he asked. The man had a sweet tooth nearly as big as mine. "I'd be happy to taste it for you." He was always volunteering to be my taste tester, which was saying something. He was either that brave or that desperate for chocolate. Although I was improving, the chocolate creations I made often turned out horribly wrong.

"Our regular deliveries have been delayed due to the hurricane." I gestured to the nearly empty shelving behind me. Bubba brought by several pumpkins that had survived the storm. He'd bought them as decorations for his shop, but Bertie told him that he'd purchased cooking pumpkins, not gourds." Ten small pumpkins were lined up on the stainless-steel counter.

"And?" He waggled his eyebrows suggestively.

"And I was thinking since it's October, it would be fun to play with pumpkins, spice, and pumpkins seeds. Everyone loves pumpkin spice, right? I'm picturing a bonbon with a double filling. A sweet and salty pumpkin seed butter, surrounded by a spicy pumpkin paste, and dipped in a slightly bitter dark chocolate. Or perhaps the other way around. I haven't quite worked it all out yet."

He pressed his hand to his chest and pretended to swoon. "I'll take two dozen."

"It's still just an idea. I don't yet know if it'll even turn out. It probably won't. Bonbons are my personal Achilles' heel." I often ended up with oozy messes.

"Now be honest with me," he said. He suddenly sounded serious. "You're in here dreaming up new ways to make a bonbon because of the zoo out there. Bertie and Bubba both have their noses out of joint, grumbling that you ran like a scared rat or something."

"Not a scared rat. A rational human. And I'm starting to think Stevie McWilson is planning to move into my shop."

"If he does, it'll be good for business. The line at the chocolate counter nearly reached the door when I came in."

"Everyone wants a chance to experience a moment of celebrity," I said with a sigh. But that wasn't exactly true. When Joe's daughter, Mary Fenton saw the crowded shop and the news crew van parked at the front door, she'd bolted too, yelling as she charged down the street that she'd come back another time.

"I'm not interested in fame or celebrity moments," Harley pointed out. "You're not either."

"I know how the limelight can burn," I admitted. "Besides, I never know how to act when people are watching. It always turns out wrong." Like my bonbons.

"I'm sure that's not true. If you were out there being interviewed about seeing the Gray Lady, you'd have full command of the room. You, Penn, whether you like it or not, are a natural leader."

While I didn't agree with him, his words made me feel all warm and tingly inside. That's why I liked him so much. He made me feel as if I might one day be able to become the woman he believed I already was.

"If I were to talk to McWilson, I'd tell him in no uncertain terms that there is no Gray Lady. Please tell me I'm not the only sane person around here who knows the Gray Lady didn't kill anyone? She didn't because she isn't real," I said and then amended, "Well, there is Fletcher. He's convinced Joe was murdered."

"Do *you* think Joe was murdered?" Harley asked.

"You mean, like by the Gray Lady?" I snorted. "Of course I don't believe in ghosts."

"You saw her."

"No, I saw Joe talking with a woman."

"The Gray Lady," he supplied.

I growled. And he chuckled.

"You know I'm pulling your chain," he said.

"Why do guys do that?"

"I don't know, probably the same reason boys like to play with fire." He shrugged. "Touching danger is exhilarating."

I tossed a dish towel at him.

He caught it like a sport's pro. He then crossed the room to stand toe-to-toe with me. We were on the same eye level, which I liked. "Pulling your chain makes my heart beat faster," he said. The rumble in his voice and heat in his gaze made *my* heart beat faster.

"We can't play this game right now." I gave his chest a friendly shove. "Not if you want me to ever finish making my pumpkin spice bonbons. The pumpkin seed butter needs to come out of the melanger."

I went over to the large metal grinder where two stone wheels had been spinning away, blending the seeds with honey and salt into what I hoped would be a delicious paste for my fall-flavored bonbon. I peeked through the clear cover and saw that the seeds were now smooth and creamy. Good. They were ready. I flipped the switch, turning it off.

"Actually, I came looking for you because something else is nagging me," he said in the sudden silence. "Gavin goes back to Jody's house tonight. And I know that over in your apartment you're sleeping on a sofa. That's all kinds of wrong when you could be using my bed."

"Wow, you'd sleep on the sofa for me?" I said without looking in his direction. I'd removed the melanger's lid and started to scrape the sides with a spatula.

Instead of answering, he chuckled.

"My sleeping on a sofa is bothering you. That's sweet," I said.

"Not sweet," he said.

I lifted the spatula from the melanger and turned toward him. "No, it is sweet. But…" I searched his face and noticed an added layer of tension that wasn't there yesterday. "Something is wrong. What is it?"

He hesitated before saying, "It's what you said about Fletcher."

Well, wasn't that a splash of cold water?

"You're not jealous of him, are you? He's the best worker I've ever hired. He knows the food service business inside and out. But that's all there is. For one thing, he's way too young for me."

"Wow. Why in world would that be the first place your mind goes?" He waved his hands, signaling he didn't want me to answer that. "No, I'm not jealous. That's not what I'm implying. In case you haven't noticed, he's gone full-Sherlock-Holmes about Joe Davies' death. He's convinced that, because Joe had thought he'd found pirate gold, that he was murdered even before Hurricane Avery arrived. And he thinks the fact Joe's house also burned to the ground proves it."

"I may have heard him put voice to that theory once or twice this morning," I said slowly. "But I don't see why his theories bother you. He has to do something to justify the cost of his hat. He paid a couple of hundred dollars for it, you know."

"It's not him I'm worried about. Not really." He took the spatula from my hand and turned me fully toward him. My heart did a little fluttery double-beat. "It's you. It's always been you that I worry about. I asked you if you also believed if Joe had been murdered, and instead of answering you told me you didn't believe in the Gray Lady."

"You noticed that?" Perhaps we were getting too close.

He moved a smidge closer. The heat of his body made me want to melt into him. "Yeah, Penn. I noticed."

"Hank released the coroner's report to the *Camellia Current* yesterday, which concluded his death was accidental," I said.

"And?" he pressed. Our lips were almost touching.

"And I didn't think anything about it." Gracious, I sounded a mite breathless.

"Until...?" he asked.

Oh, he knew me too well. I pulled away from him. "A ghost didn't kill Joe."

"But you did see a lady with him on the beach, a lady you claim made him mighty upset."

I nodded.

"He told you that she was the Gray Lady, but you know that wasn't true. So, now you're wondering who she was and what she said to upset him." Harley had a calm manner about him as he chipped away at my defenses. I felt sorry for anyone who had to face him in a courtroom. He tapped his chin, an innocent gesture, and yet I could tell he was about to make his move. "And then there was that stranger who showed up not a few hours later searching for Joe. But you're okay with Hank's decision not to investigate any of that."

"It's none of my business," I said.

He nodded. The corner of his mouth lifted just a bit. "Your friends and neighbors and now the local news media are in your shop discussing how Joe was killed by a ghost. And you're okay with that too, I suppose?"

My right eye twitched.

"Uh-huh," he said. "Did Silas Piper ever send you a picture of his missing brother?"

"He did," I admitted. I'd gotten a text from Silas' secretary two days after the cell service returned. His brother, Taylor Graham, was still missing.

"Oh?" That seemed to surprise him. He pulled back. "Did he look familiar?"

Instead of answering, I said, "Let's stop playing twenty questions and get down to the question you want to ask me."

"Sure." His lips flattened out. "It's not really a question though, is it? It's more like a realization. You think Joe Davies was murdered. And you think Silas' brother is somehow involved. And you're hiding back here in the kitchen while trying to figure out how to quietly conduct an investigation without me (or anyone else) finding out."

"And why would I do something stupid like that?" I asked. It irked me to no end that he knew me that well. Well, if he knew me so well, he should already know why I was trying to keep him from getting involved in something that could turn dangerous.

"Why would you investigate? Is that what you're asking? That's easy." He nodded toward the door. "Because of what's going on out there. You want to prove to the town that ghosts do not and have never existed."

He was right. There was that. And there was also Mary and her quest to find out what had really happened to her father.

I pressed my fingers to my eyes.

"Penn?" He hesitated. When I didn't open my eyes, he plowed on with a sharp tone I didn't know how to describe. It wasn't quite anger. But it was close. "I thought we had...something. A spark. Tender feelings. Friendship. No, more than friendship. I thought we had...something special. And now I'm finding out that you didn't even think enough about me to tell me that Silas Piper had sent you a picture of his brother. And if I hadn't barged in here and guessed what was going on in that clever head of yours, I wouldn't have heard a word about any of this from you. And I still haven't heard much more than a word or two about any of this from you. I've been doing all the talking. And to be honest, my feelings are hurt."

I didn't know what to say to that. He was right. I had kept the information about Silas' brother to myself. I'd also kept my thoughts about Joe's death to myself. After nearly getting Harley killed not even two months ago, I didn't want to involve him in this. He had his son to think about. He had his own life to protect. It wouldn't be fair to involve him in something that might turn dangerous. I cared for him too much to put his life at risk.

It scared *me* too much.

That's what I should have said to him. I should have said as plain as day, "I care for you too much." But admitting something like that was a step I wasn't ready to take in our relationship. It felt safer if we kept things between us flirty and playful. Safer for him. Safer for my heart.

So instead of saying what needed to be said, with my fingers still pressed to my eyes I blurted, "I don't care what Hank says. Joe was murdered, and I'm going to prove it. I'm sorry, but this is something I need to do. And I need to do it alone."

Silence answered me.

I lowered my hands and opened my eyes to find that Harley had left. But I wasn't alone. Bertie stood at the kitchen door with an empty tray in her hand.

"Child, I never thought you were a fool." She dropped the large tray. It landed on wooden floor with a loud clatter. "If that's the attitude you're going to take with Harley and the rest of us, I don't know what I'm doing here. If you don't need us, then I'm going to Florida where I can play Canasta any time I want." She spun on her heel and hurried back down the narrow hallway while muttering, "Oh, yes, that's what I'm going to do. Don't need to be working my fingers to the bone like this. No, ma'am, I don't. Not for a stubborn goat who can't see what's what and what's important."

"Wait! I do need you. I need—" But it was too late. Bertie had already returned to the front of the shop.

I silently cursed Joe Davies and his obsession with pirate gold. It had gotten the fool man murdered, and now—from the grave—that obsession of his was ruining nearly every healthy relationship I had in my life. If he weren't already dead, I'd have been awfully tempted to kill him myself.

Chapter 9

WE NEED TO TALK, I texted Harley.

He didn't reply.

I'M SORRY, I texted Bertie. I NEED YOU. THE SHOP NEEDS YOU.

She didn't reply.

I stared at the phone, willing it to do something. As if by magic, it pinged as a text showed up on the screen. HOW DID THE CHOCOLATE BOX HOLD UP?

It was from Aunt Peach. Was she asking for herself or as a proxy for my mother? Either way—after they'd worked so hard a few months ago to try and steal the shop from me so they could tear it down—their concern felt empty. After a few minutes, she texted again to tell me that the Maybank family had returned from their lake house. Their three historic downtown Charleston homes had survived.

I didn't reply.

Instead, I went to the front of the shop in search of Bertie.

"I'm sorry, P-Penn. Sh-she blasted through the front of the shop and m-marched with her arms p-pumping like p-p-pistons about t-ten m-minutes ago," Fletcher said as he adjusted his deer hunter hat. "Wh-wh-why? Wh-what did you d-d-do?"

"I've chased Bertie and Harley away," I was ashamed to admit. I dropped a store apron over my head. With Bertie gone, Fletcher would need me as backup to handle the crowd. Though, to be honest, the crowd had dwindled considerably since the last time I'd peeked out to see what was going on. Stevie McWilson, his camera crew, and Joe's estranged wife had all left.

The shop's regular Sunday crowd had gotten their fair share of gossip and then some. The residents would be talking for weeks about the Gray Lady and how her pre-storm appearance was going to make our small town famous. I was sure many of my loyal customers had left to tell their family and neighbors all the excitement that had happened in the Chocolate Box this morning.

"Y-you chased—?" Fletcher demanded.

"She said she's going to retire to Florida because I'm a stubborn goat. Or something like that."

"Retire?" His eyes grew wide. His voice boomed, "N-no!" Fletcher pulled the apron off me before I could tie it. "G-get out of h-here and m-make things r-right."

"I can't leave you here by yourself. You need help handling everything."

"Y-you m-might n-need h-help," he said, arrogant as ever. He pushed me toward the door. "I-I d-don't."

And that's how I found myself wandering around the island searching for Bertie. She wasn't with Bubba at his T-shirt shop. Nor had she gone back to our apartment. The two elderly sisters bunking with us had returned from church and were sitting on the sofa, eating pre-sliced American cheese straight from the plastic wrapping while watching reruns of Golden Girls. Neither of them knew where Bertie had gone. Stella, who usually shied away from everyone, was sitting beside the sofa with her tongue hanging out the side of her mouth and sniffing the air. Clearly, she approved of their choice of snack.

Bertie's car—a rusty Pontiac the size of a boat—was still in its parking place, which meant she couldn't have gone far. Part of me had been terrified that she'd already packed her bags and had left me. I'd checked her closet, just in case. All of her Sunday dresses were still there as well as her deceased husband's favorite leather jacket. She wouldn't leave without that jacket. When we'd evacuated, bringing only the essentials, that leather jacket had come with us.

I suspected I knew where she'd gone. But ever since we'd returned after the storm, I'd avoided going there—Althea's shop.

A knot tightened in my stomach when I thought about seeing Althea. Trust was a funny thing—when broken, emotions tended to spill out like blood from an open wound.

69

Just wondering how I would act around Althea and what I would say awakened an ache that had worked itself deep into my bones. Yes, she'd lied to me. But I'd done something worse. I'd abandoned her when she'd needed me. I should have gone to see what kind of help she needed with her shop right after we'd returned from the storm. But I hadn't. And now things felt awkward. How could I face her?

I couldn't.

I wouldn't.

I'd sit in the apartment with the elderly sisters and eat cheese while watching old sitcoms.

No. Hiding from responsibility never fixed anything. It only added pounds to my hips.

I closed my eyes and huffed angrily at myself.

"Could you move? I can't see what Blanche is wearing," Trixie said. She poked me in the side with her cane.

I opened my eyes to see that I was standing in front of the TV. "Sorry," I muttered and then gave myself a hard mental shake. Yes, that was better. "I have to go down to the crystal shop. Do you need anything?"

"It ain't open," Barbie said.

"Could use a love potion," Trixie said.

"It ain't open," Barbie repeated louder. "And what do you need a love potion for at your age?"

"What do you mean at my age? I'm two years younger than you."

Barbie blew a sharp breath through her lips. "Next thing you know, you'll be running around town in bright pink spandex hot pants."

"Have you been poking around in my shopping bags again?"

"I was with you when you bought them," Barbie screeched.

Stella wagged her tail and barked. Both sisters rewarded her with pieces of cheese, which she gobbled with greedy delight.

"Don't feed her too much," I warned. "She's small and can't afford to put on too much weight."

"She's such a sweet dog," Trixie said. "Don't know why everyone calls her such horrible names."

"People call Stella names?" Learning that made me even more upset than I was a moment ago.

Both sisters nodded.

"Heard her called Demon Dog," Trixie said.

"Snappy Mutt," Barbie added.

"Barky Breath."

"An irritating dust ball."

"Big-Eared Brat."

I threw my hands in the air. "Enough. I get it. Stella is sweet. People are mean. And I need to get going. Stella? Do you want to come with me?"

My dog looked at me and then she looked over at the sisters with their bright yellow cheese and didn't move.

"If she needs to go out, her leash is by the door," I said.

"We know that," Trixie said.

"You tell us that every time you leave without her," Barbie said and poked me in the side with her sister's cane. "Go on. Get out of here."

I dodged the cane when it came at me again and ran out the door. They were right. I had to go fix things.

"And don't forget my love potion," Trixie called after me.

Half a block away, I could still hear the two sisters arguing about whether Trixie should have a love life. I shook my head and laughed. Although they argued all the time, they clearly loved and trusted each other. If one of them did (or said) something stupid, I'd bet my shop the other one wouldn't threaten to run off to Florida. But then again, they were sisters. Not friends. Not business partners.

While I was searching for Bertie, I was also constantly checking my phone for texts. It must have stopped working, because Harley should have answered me by now. He was right. He was more than my friend. Over the past several months, we'd grown close.

He was my…

My…

Um…

Oh fudge cakes.

I'd made it to the middle of Camellia Beach's downtown and still didn't know what to call Harley. He wasn't my boyfriend—and what a stupid term for two fully grown adults. I refused to use it. He wasn't my lover. We'd flirted. Shared a few kisses. Been on a few dates. Evacuated together. Society should invent a word for what we meant to each other. An adult word—one that suggested intimacy and trust.

Perhaps there was already a word for that kind of relationship, and I simply didn't know it. It wasn't as if I were an expert when it came to relationships. Clearly, I was much more comfortable thinking about what had happened to dead bodies than dealing with the live ones.

Speaking of the dead, was that Joe's widow, Delilah, standing outside Althea's shop? It was hard to tell. I was still a few blocks away. The woman kind of looked like her. Then again, from this distance, she also kind of looked like Florence. Whoever the woman in front of the crystal shop was, she glanced up and down the street before opening the still boarded-up door. A moment later she disappeared inside.

My curiosity should have made my feet move any faster. But the closer I got to the shop, the slower my stubborn feet moved. Tears were stinging my eyes by the time I stopped outside Althea's shop. Plywood covered the large display windows that flanked the front door. The pretty turquoise awning had been ripped away. It's twisted and broken frame looked like metal fingers, reaching out from the building in a plea for help. *The First Wish*, the shop's sign that had been painted directly on the building's red brick in purple and blue scrolling letters looked as if someone had taken a sandblaster to it, removing much of the paint. All that remained was the ghostly outline of the words.

Bonbon with the Wind

The walls are still there, I told myself before pushing the door open. A bell chimed.

"We're not open!" Althea called from somewhere in the darkened rear of the shop.

"I'm not here to buy anything," I called. "Unless you have a love potion handy. Trixie asked me to pick her up one of your love potions. Do you even sell love potions?"

With the plywood covering the windows and the electricity still off in the building, the shop's interior was eerily silent and shadowy. Shafts of blue-tinted sunlight streamed in here and there through a blue tarp that stretched across where Harley's office should be and, above that, a roof. My heart twisted. Why had Harley lied to me? There was clearly nothing left of his office.

A breeze rustled the tarp. Its movement made the shadows dance.

"Penn? Is that you?" Althea called. She hurried toward the front of the store where I was standing next to a toppled display shelf. She was dressed in dusty overalls. Her hair was hidden under a tightly wrapped silk batik scarf that had been dyed an explosion of rainbow colors. A tool belt hung around her waist. Instead of hammers, she had an assortment of trowels hanging from the loops.

"You know it's me. Is your mother here?" I asked her, while eyeing the damage. Her shop looked worse than what I'd heard.

"Should Mama be here?" Althea gave me an odd look. "She told me she'd be working at the Chocolate Box all afternoon."

"I...um...she's angry with me," I admitted haltingly. When I saw Althea was about to ask for details, I quickly added, "You're not doing the fix up work all by yourself, are you?"

"Some of it. I want to get the shop open as soon as possible, and it takes forever for the insurance adjusters to do...well, anything."

"Certainly, you're not going to rebuild the upstairs and the roof." It wasn't even Althea's roof to rebuild. Bertie owned the building along with several others in the downtown.

"Mama is working on getting some contractors out here for that. Truth is, many residents in the Charleston area are in desperate need of a contractor and there aren't enough to go around. So, it's hard."

"Was it a tornado that cut through here?" Most of the homes and businesses weren't as badly damaged as Althea's shop. The Chocolate Box had simply needed to be dried out to keep the mold from growing. I'd been told that Althea's cottage, which had been built on top of an ancient sand dune in the middle of the island, hadn't even flooded. But tornados that often formed within a hurricane could tear apart a building while the neighboring structures survived unscathed.

"Yeah, it looks like a tornado did this. The other two shops and upstairs offices in this building aren't nearly as badly damaged as this place. And Harley's office, well, it's gone. We also lost part of the back wall. I'm working on rebuilding it so I can, you know, lock up at night."

"You're building a brick wall? By yourself?" I really should have come by sooner.

She shrugged. "Harley and Gavin have been helping. Some of the other residents have been out here as well. Ethel swept up as best she could. But with the gaps in the wall, the wind keeps blowing the debris around again."

I'd told myself that I was too busy helping others on the island to check on Althea. Harley had seemed happy enough to move his office to his apartment while he waited for what he'd called a few *renovations.*

I felt a spurt of anger at that but, thinking back on conversations I'd had with Harley over the past week, I think he had tried to tell me how Althea's shop and his office had been destroyed, but I hadn't been willing to listen. *I'm too busy, I'm too busy,* I'd kept telling myself—lying to myself. "I'm sorry. I should have—"

"No. You don't get to apologize," she said, her voice sharp. She closed her eyes and sucked in a deep breath. When she opened them, she appeared to be her calm self again. "The damage is more than I'd expected, but it's not something I can't manage. Don't worry after me or pity me. I don't need it." She pulled a trowel from the loop in her tool belt and held it up like a triumphant warrior would raise her sword. "I've got this. Tell Trixie that if I find a love potion when I'm going through the ruins here, I'll bring it by."

"Sure. Okay."

Althea turned to return to her work.

"Uh...wait. I saw a woman come in here a few minutes ahead of me. She looked like Delilah Fenton. Is she still here?" I asked before she could disappear into the shadows again.

"You must be mistaken." She gestured to the piles of broken crystals and damp building materials. "No one has come in here. I'm not open. I won't be open for business for a long while."

"But I saw..." I realized that the bell on her door had chimed loudly when I'd entered the shop. It would have done the same for the woman I'd seen.

Althea looked around the shop. "What exactly did you see?"

"Nothing. I must have been mistaken. She must have gone into a different shop."

Althea smiled as she shook her head. "All of the neighboring businesses are either still closed for repairs or closed because it's Sunday. So, Penn, tell me exactly what you saw."

It wasn't the Gray Lady.

Althea would insist I saw a ghost when I described the woman. From a distance Delilah Fenton looked similar to the woman Althea and I saw talking with Joe on the beach. Who was *not* the Gray Lady.

"I really need to find your mother and apologize," I muttered as I kicked a small pile of sand and insulation on the floor. Something in the pile went clank. A sliver of light had worked its way into the shop through a crack in the plywood covering one of the front windows. It glinted off the metallic object I'd kicked and struck me in the eye.

I lifted my hand to cover my face. "Ow, that's bright."

75

"Unnaturally bright," Althea said.

We bent down at the same time. Our heads knocked together.

"Sorry." I rubbed the top of my head.

"My fault." She reached out and scooped up the metal object that was reflecting the beam of sunlight and sucked in a sharp breath.

"What is it?" I asked.

She dropped it into my hand. "Isn't that the coin Joe found on the beach?"

"Stella found it," I corrected. But Joe had picked it up and identified it. "He'd said it was a Spanish gold coin from the eighteen hundreds."

The coin in my hand was gold. And it did look similar to the one Joe had picked up.

"Are you sure this isn't a toy from something you sell, like a touristy treasure kit?"

"I don't sell treasure kits," Althea was quick to point out. "And I don't sell coins, real or fake. The thought of a lucky coin is a lie." That was the most reasonable thing I'd heard her say in a long time. For a moment I thought that maybe she was coming to her senses and was gradually giving up on all this magic nonsense. But then she added, "Coins are more attuned to holding bad energy than good. I don't even like having them in the cash drawer."

I handed her back the scarred piece of gold and rose to my feet. "It's not the same coin," I said. I dusted sand and bits of her shop off my legs. "Joe was found with that coin in his hand. I saw it."

Her dark eyes widened as she turned the tiny treasure over and over in her hand. "You know what this means?"

"Not really," I admitted.

"Well, we can't be sure, can we? But I bet it means Joe was right. There is pirate treasure on Camellia Beach." She paused a beat before adding with a great big grin, "And apparently the Gray Lady herself not only wants us to find Joe's killer, she also wants us to find the gold."

Chapter 10

Us. **I hadn't** missed Althea's use of the word.

Forget that I was still feeling all bruised and distrustful around her. Forget that I didn't believe in the Gray Lady nonsense. Forget, also, that I'd already told Joe's daughter that I was going to help her find out what happened to him. Forget all of that.

I honestly wanted to draw a line in the sand and start afresh with Althea. It would feel so good to smile easily with her again. Or to pop in over to her house for a glass of her sweet tea.

So, yes, I hung onto how she'd said *us* for a ridiculously long time.

I'd love to go on a treasure hunt with her. She'd spout all sorts of theories of magic and ghosts and probably throw in a fairy or two for good measure. I'd grump and growl while secretly eating up her kookiness.

I wanted *us* to be *us* again.

I should have told her all of that. But I'd been raised in a family where sharing feelings was akin to showing your enemy where you hid your weaknesses. So I'd pressed my lips tightly together and left her shop with nothing more than a promise to be back after I had apologized to Bertie and that I'd bring more help.

As soon as I stepped back on to the sidewalk, I sent another series of texts.

JUST SAW YOUR OFFICE, I texted to Harley. YOU SHOULD HAVE TOLD ME. WE REALLY NEED TO TALK.

WHERE ARE YOU? I texted to Bertie. JUST LEFT ALTHEA'S SHOP. SHE AGREED TO LET ME HELP HER GET THINGS UP AND RUNNING AGAIN. I WISH YOU'D TOLD ME HOW BAD THINGS WERE. YOU SHOULD HAVE TALKED TO ME. I KNOW SEVERAL CONTRACTORS WHO CAN HELP. I'LL CALL THEM.

I stared at my phone's screen while hoping that watching it would cause my texts to get answered quicker. The honking of a horn jolted me back to awareness of the world around me—the constant hammering of roofing nails, the whirl of a saw, and the voice of a man I knew well.

"If it isn't my bad Penny," the man said.

"My name is Penn, not Penny," came my automatic reply, an unnecessary reply. He knew my name and knew I didn't like it when he called me Penny. But it was his way of being friendly. Like a caring father, he enjoyed teasing me.

I tore my gaze from my phone. Detective Frank Gibbons flashed an amused smile in my direction. He trotted down the town hall's front steps. Gibbons worked for the Charleston County Sheriff Department.

Chief Byrd would call in help from the county sheriff whenever he needed more manpower, expertise, or the use of the county's criminal lab. Byrd and Gibbons were friends. That was why, more often than not, Gibbons was the one who'd get a direct call from Camellia Beach's police chief with a request for assistance.

Whether he was in town on business or not, I was pleased to see him. As always, he was impeccably dressed in a dark suit that had been expertly tailored to fit his large body. My fashion-designer half-sister, Tina, had told me again and again that it wasn't the size of the person that mattered, but the clothes the person wore. I glanced down at my off-the-rack shorts that were so poorly cut that they made my hips appear much larger than they should. Those cheap shorts would have made anyone's hips appear big.

I quickly shrugged off the thought. Since moving to Camellia Beach, I'd been learning how to relax more and not stress so much over my appearance or what anyone thought about it. Unlike nearly everyone in my father's side of the family, very few on this tiny beach town were judging me based on looks alone.

"What brings you to town?" I asked Gibbons after giving him a quick kiss on the cheek. "Nothing sinister, I hope. There's too much going on in town as it is."

He gave his head a rueful shake. Up close, his friendly smile appeared strained. I'd known him long enough to recognize that something was troubling him. I held back from jumping to the first conclusion that sprang to mind—murder. Or more specifically, *Joe's* murder. He could simply be fatigued from the aftereffects of the hurricane. The recovery efforts had put a strain on nearly everyone I'd talked to.

"Actually," he said. "I'm glad we happened to meet up like this. I need to talk with you."

"You just came from talking with Chief Byrd?" I glanced back at the town hall.

"Yep."

"Of course you did. There's no other reason you'd go there." I paused, wondering why the police chief had called him. "Byrd told you something, and now you want to talk to me?"

"Yep."

"What did he say I've done this time?" I said with a sigh. I wasn't upset, merely curious.

"Well, for one thing, you found a dead body."

"You sound surprised," I said.

"More perplexed than surprised." His brows furrowed.

"Actually, Stella found Joe's body. Hank told me it was an accidental death."

Gibbons nodded but held his silence.

"I just learned a few hours ago that Joe Davies was an alias. His real name was John Fenton. He had left a wife and daughter behind when he'd run to Camellia Beach. Did you know that?" I asked.

"Yes. Hank did mention that to me."

"I think Joe was murdered." There. I'd said it.

"Hank disagrees," Gibbons said.

79

"He's wrong." Friend or not, I put my hands on my hips prepared to win the argument I expected to have with him.

Only, Gibbons didn't argue. He sighed. "Joe's death—while concerning—isn't why I'm looking for you right now. Nor is his secret life."

"Oh?" I hadn't expected him to say that. "That's a relief." I guessed. "So…you're simply here to check up on me and the shop? That's so…so sweet."

"Yeah, well…" He rubbed the back of his neck. "No. This isn't a social call, Penn. I need to talk with you because you had a private conversation with a Mr. Silas Piper after the billionaire filed a missing person report."

"Really?"

Why does Gibbons care about that?

"Piper and my dad are old friends."

Unless—

"Oh my goodness, his brother *was* murdered!" My heart started to pound. "That's two murders in a short period of time."

"Hold up now." He backed up a step. "I'm not saying anything of the sort. I'm not here to talk about Joe Davies or how he died. And honestly, I don't know where Taylor Graham is. What I want to know is if you're helping Silas Piper in his search for his brother. Are you searching for him?"

I shook my head. "I talked with Piper that morning because I thought I might be able to give him some information about his brother." I told Gibbons about how a stranger wearing a tweed hat had come into the Chocolate Box asking for Joe Davies the day the storm arrived. I also told him how we'd found a tweed hat by the door, and that seeing it had worried me. I finally told Gibbons how I'd asked Silas Piper to send me a picture of his brother.

"And?" The older detective crossed his arms over his chest, and he watched me with what appeared to be mild curiosity. I suspected the patient expression was more practiced than real.

"And I recognized the man in the photo. I recognized his brother."

He nodded as if the news didn't affect him one way or the other. "And yet his brother is still listed as missing."

"Is he?" I asked, all innocent.

"Did you tell Piper that you recognized the man in the picture?"

"No," I admitted. "Did Byrd ask you to come out to the island to search for the missing brother or did Mr. Piper?"

"You already know what a powerhouse Silas Piper is. He makes a call to a politician, and suddenly I find my caseload shuffled to other detectives and told to focus only on locating Piper's brother. That's why I'm here." He drew a long, controlled breath. "I find it interesting that as soon as I started searching for him, the first name that came up associated with Mr. Graham is yours."

"That does seem odd," I agreed.

"Like a bad penny, you do seem to turn up wherever there's trouble."

"Now, you're starting to sound like Chief Byrd."

He chuckled. "Unlike Hank, I understand that you're not the cause of the trouble. You're focused on getting out and helping the community. That will put you in some difficult spots from time to time. I've seen it happen before."

"You have?" For some reason, I felt comforted by that thought.

"It's a story for another time. Right now, I've got a younger brother to find. It seems as if you have a piece of the puzzle. So tell me, is the stranger with the tweed hat Piper's long-lost brother?"

"No." I said with a smile. "I have no idea who that man was."

His bushy eyebrows shot up. "No? But you said you recognized the man in the picture Piper had sent to you."

I started to tell him what I knew about Piper's brother. It wasn't a secret, just slightly troubling.

But suddenly I saw the man (the one who'd lost his tweed hat) walking down the street. He looked left. Then right. And then ducked inside Bunky's, the island's small grocery store.

"Sorry. Can't talk right now," I said and jogged after him.

Chapter 11

"Penn!" Gibbons roared as he raced after me.

"Wait for me at the Chocolate Box," I called over my shoulder. If I was going to help Joe's daughter find any kind of closure, I needed to find out why that man was looking for Joe and if he knew about Joe's secret life. "Tell Fletch to give you some free samples."

I heard Gibbons swear and then the pounding of hard leather on the pavement behind me.

A large hand clamped down on my shoulder. Although Gibbons was old enough to be my father and carried at least fifty more pounds than I did around his middle, the man was fast.

"I need to talk to that man." I tried to twist out of his hold. "He's the man who lost his tweed hat."

His grip tightened. "You said he wasn't Piper's brother."

"No. But he seemed to know Joe. And he is a stranger to town. Joe didn't have any friends from outside Camellia Beach. At least, none that anyone knew about. I need to talk with him." I tried again to break free.

Gibbons was a professional and knew how to keep a suspect or informant from running. "Talk to me first, Penn. I need to put this missing person case to bed. I don't have time to chase after some bigwig's alcoholic brother and drag him home when I finally catch up to him. I'm a busy man."

"But—" I saw his expression and closed my mouth. He wasn't going to let me charm him or use logic to convince him to let me do what I wanted, not today. Like nearly everyone around here, his nerves were strained. Ever since the storm, we'd all gotten stretched like rubber bands on the verge of snapping.

"Where did you see Piper's missing brother?" Gibbons prompted with his hand still clamped on my shoulder. The strain in his voice had softened just a tad.

I considered Gibbons a friend. He loved my chocolates and would tell strangers about my shop like I imagined a proud father would talk up his daughter's accomplishments. He also worried about my safety and was protective. He cursed and complained whenever I'd start poking my nose into one of his murder investigations. He was a man with a good heart, and I truly wanted to help him.

"He came into the Chocolate Box hours before the hurricane hit. I got the impression that he was some kind of professional surfer. He said he'd come to town to catch the big waves." As I said that, I realized that wasn't quite the truth. While I'd convinced myself that Big Dog had been in town just because of the waves, and his appearance at my shop had nothing to do with Joe Davies' death, wasn't what he'd said. No, not really. He'd told Harley that he was in town for another reason—a reason he hadn't disclosed—and that the chance to catch some big waves had been a bonus.

Gibbons' hand slipped from my shoulder. "What's wrong?" he asked. "I don't like that look you have."

"Um…nothing. Really. Nothing. Just a stray thought." A nagging worry gurgled in my stomach again. It had rumbled in my belly like a prickly burr when I first saw the picture Silas Piper had texted to me, the yellowed and slightly blurry photo of Big Dog. I needed to do some research. That was all. There was no reason for there to be any kind of connection between Joe Davies and Big Dog. The two men practically lived on two different planets. Any simple Google search would prove that.

Gibbons watched me. "Nothing, huh?"

"I must have eaten something that didn't agree with me for lunch. Probably lettuce." I patted my stomach and laughed. It was a nervous, inappropriate chuckle. Embarrassed, I tried to make it sound like a cough.

He still appeared concerned, but he didn't seem interested in pressing me about why I was acting so nervous. "Taylor Graham is a professional surfer?" he asked instead.

I nodded with no small measure of relief. "He calls himself Big Dog."

"Big Dog?" He stroked his chin. "If he's a professional, that means Harley knows him. Harley knows all the pros." He began to walk away.

Crap. Crap. Crap.

Even though I really, *really* wanted to get into Bunky's and talk with the mysterious man who'd lost his tweed hat, I chased after Gibbons because I knew what he'd do next.

He'd go and get Harley involved with whatever dangerous thing Big Dog had gotten himself into. It was the same dangerous thing that was eating a hole in my gut whenever my mind focused on the aging surfer and my premonition that his mysterious reason for coming to Camellia Beach was bad news.

I was having premonitions. Wouldn't Althea love to hear about that?

My entire body trembled at the thought of Harley in any kind of danger.

"Don't involve Harley," I begged.

"Why not?" Gibbons stopped long enough to ask.

"Because…because…" What could I say to convince him? "Because he has a son. Please, I'll tell you whatever you need to know."

"You haven't told me everything you know already? I'm disappointed." He sighed. "Okay, I'm listening. Do you know where Big Dog is now?"

"No, but—"

"If Harley is his friend, he might have a phone number or know another way for me to get in touch with him. I won't be asking him to set up an ambush or confront the guy. Besides, this surfer is merely a thorn in my side, not some dangerous criminal," he said as he hurried down the street away from me.

I ran after Gibbons. "I suppose Piper provided you with a copy of the letter from his brother. You did see that letter, right? It said if the letter was sent, he'd been murdered." I drew a shaky breath and repeated that last word in case Gibbons had somehow missed it, "Murdered."

Perhaps it was some kind of post-traumatic stress that had me acting this way, so panicked and as irrational and as superstitious as Althea. But for the life of me, I couldn't stop thinking how I needed to keep Harley safe at all costs. Because of me, Harley had nearly gotten himself killed. And that incident wasn't the first time he'd found himself in danger while I pursued a killer. And simply remembering how close I was to losing him gutted me.

"Don't go to Harley with this," I pleaded. My vision turned all blurry. I blinked. And then blinked some more before everything turned clear again. Dang it, I needed to get my eyes checked. There must have been something wrong with my eyes, because I didn't cry. Not unless I was watching sappy commercials around Christmastime. "Don't get him involved."

"No one has been murdered," Gibbons said in a calm, fatherly voice. It was a voice that lured me into believing him.

"No? Are you sure? Because I'm not."

"Penn—"

I was too wound up to let him try and talk me out of what my subconscious knew to be true. "It'd be easy to kill someone during a hurricane by hitting him over the head, wouldn't it? The flood waters would wash all the evidence away. Everyone would suspect that he'd gotten bludgeoned by the storm. It'd be an open and shut case. No one would question why strangers were in town searching for him or start to wonder about his double life."

"You're talking about Joe Davies," he said.

I nodded.

"I'm not interested in Joe Davies. Not right now I'm not. Not while the sheriff is breathing down my neck insisting I produce instant results for Piper. All I'm doing is searching for a man who has gotten himself misplaced during the storm. I'm betting he dropped his phone into the ocean and has been hanging out at a bar somewhere, blissfully unaware that he's causing me such a colossal headache."

"Or he got washed out to sea while surfing the hurricane," I mused aloud to reassure myself that Big Dog's appearance in town had nothing to do with Joe's murder.

The detective cursed. "Don't say that." He swore again. "I hadn't even considered that. But dang it, you're probably right, and it'll take weeks for me to track down the body…if it ever washes up."

I closed my eyes and pictured the surfer floating under the ocean somewhere beyond the breakers, that easy smirk still on his face. But as much as I wanted to let Gibbons convince me that there was no connection between Joe Davies and Big Dog, my grumpy gut wouldn't allow me to do it.

Piper wouldn't have received such a letter from his estranged brother unless Big Dog had been worried that whatever he was pursuing here in Camellia Beach was going to get him killed. And since this was such a small island town, the chances that there were two deadly intrigues happening at the same time were incredibly low.

I pulled out my phone.

"Who are you calling?" he asked me.

"Nobody. I'm doing a quick Google search." I typed in the search bar "Taylor Graham" and "Joe Davies". While neither name showed up on the same website, after a quick scroll I did find that the two men did have something in common.

"The two men were both from Virginia!" I handed Gibbons my phone. In the list of known addresses, it showed that Big Dog had lived in Virginia. "Joe Davies lived in Virginia before he decided to run away to Camellia Beach to find a new life."

"Virginia is a large state." Gibbons tried to hand the phone back to me.

"It is," I agreed. I pointed to the name of the town—Cedar's Hill—on the phone's screen. "Kind of makes me wonder why two men from the same town both eventually showed up in Camellia Beach. Joe

Davies was from Cedar's Hill too. I wonder"—I tapped my chin—"did they leave at the same time?"

"They left about a year apart," he admitted.

"You already knew there was a connection between the two men?"

He shrugged. I suppose I shouldn't have been surprised that he'd known about it. Gibbons was a thorough investigator. He'd have checked out all the angles before coming to Camellia Beach to talk to anyone. He'd once told me that the best investigators knew the answers to at least half of their questions before asking them. How else would one spot a lie?

"Coincidences are not evidence of murder, Penn."

"Oddly timed deaths might be evidence, though. Was Big Dog in Camellia Beach searching for Joe Davies? And what about the other man?" I glanced over at the door to Bunky's Grocery again. No one had come out. I needed to get in there to talk with him. I'd tell him that I'd found his hat and then try to turn the conversation over to Joe Davies. "Why was he looking for Joe Davies? Why now? What was the urgency?"

"I don't know," Gibbons admitted. "Let's not forget, however, that the Gray Lady had warned Joe. She'd told him to get off the island."

I rolled my eyes so fiercely my head started to ache. "Not you too. There's no such thing as the Gray Lady."

He smirked. "Paranormal investigations aren't part of my job description. Can't say one way or the other if I believe in the otherworld. Nor does it really matter, does it? Joe—or John or whatever name the man cared to call himself—ignored the mandatory evacuation order and paid a steep price for it."

"Dead men can't evacuate," I argued.

"No one at the coroner's office has said that he died prior to Hurricane Avery coming ashore."

"Well, they should be saying that, because that's what happened. I just know it. I feel it right here." I touched my hand to my chest. Oh, wouldn't Althea have loved to see that too? "Joe Davies was murdered."

Gibbons leaned toward me. "I understand what you believe. And you might even be right. But until I find this surfer who calls himself 'Big Dog,' Joe Davies' death is none of my business. The two men might have come from the same town, but they lived in two completely different worlds within that town. Different sides of the railroad tracks. Joe's death has nothing to do with a rich family's missing black sheep."

Chapter 12

The *black sheep* comment stung. It shouldn't have. Gibbons hadn't been talking about me. I knew that. Even so, as I hurried toward Bunky's Grocery I was still thinking about it and feeling sorry for poor Big Dog. Perhaps he'd disappeared because he didn't want to face his family's scorn anymore. Or perhaps he'd written that letter claiming he'd been murdered as a way to test his family. Would they care he was in danger? Would they come to rescue him?

Because I was my family's black sheep, I knew how painful it was to be in such a position in a family.

At least I had a makeshift family here on Camellia Beach who loved me. Just as I reached the grocery store's front door, my phone pinged.

It was a text from Harley. RAN INTO SOME TROUBLE AND COULDN'T GET TO MY PHONE. HAVE TO DEAL WITH IT THIS AFTERNOON. YES, WE NEED TO TALK. TONIGHT?

Trouble?

As in Big Dog trouble?

As in dead body trouble?

As in murderers lurking around every corner trouble?

WHAT KIND OF TROUBLE? I texted.

WANT TO TELL IN PERSON. TONIGHT? popped up on my phone's screen.

OK. TONIGHT, I reluctantly texted while worry brought tears to my eyes. After blinking them away, I added, GIBBONS WANTS TO TALK WITH YOU. BE CAREFUL.

ALWAYS AM. He'd added a heart emoji to the text that made my heart swell. Did that little symbol mean I was forgiven? Did it mean we'd returned to being…um…whatever it was we were to each other?

Why couldn't life in Camellia Beach be as simple as the police chief always claimed it was? The town's newly revised travel brochure had promised the glamour of Miami Beach tucked within the fabric of a friendly small town. The glamour of Miami Beach had been an outright lie. There was nothing glamorous about Camellia Beach. It was shabby. It was charming. And, sometimes, terrifyingly deadly.

I needed to get into Bunky's and find that man who'd been wearing the tweed hat. But instead of rushing into the store, I stared down again at the heart emoji on my phone's screen and smiled.

I was still staring at it and smiling like a goofy teen when the glass door leading into Bunky's swung open. I looked up, expecting to see the man without the tweed hat exiting the store. But it wasn't him. The woman hurrying out of the store nearly collided into me. She held two large paper shopping bags that were stuffed to the top with groceries.

"Bertie!" I should have known she'd go shopping. When she was upset, she cooked. Sometimes she cooked enough to feed the entire island.

"We need to talk," I said to her. "I need to—"

"Not now," she cut me off. She brushed past me. "I'm in a hurry, and these bags are heavy."

"Well, you don't have to do it alone." I tried to take one of the overfilled bags from her, but she stubbornly hugged them both to her chest. "Don't be foolish. Let me help you."

"Don't like how it feels, do you?" she asked as she nudged me out of the way with her hip.

Before I could stammer an answer, Bubba jumped out of a rusty red truck and hurried over to us. He relived Bertie of both grocery bags. Bertie, I noticed, readily released them for him. Then, while balancing the bags in his hands and against one hip, he managed to open the passenger-side door for her. He ran to the driver's side and climbed in, nestling the shopping bags between them. The old engine grumbled and coughed and spit sooty black smoke from the tailpipe.

"Don't move to Florida!" I finally managed to get out. I shouted it, actually, as the truck pulled out of the parking spot in front of the shop and jostled away down the road.

While the apology didn't go nearly as well as I'd planned—as in, *not at all*—I took comfort in knowing Bertie was going to be at Bubba's for the next several hours and not packing for Florida, which would buy me time to go running after Mr. Tweed Hat. The sooner I figured everything out and made sure there wasn't a killer on the loose in Camellia Beach, the sooner everyone could go back to normal.

I marched into Bunky's. By the time I'd gone up and down every aisle, the determination in my step had turned into a frustrated shuffle. The man was no longer there. He must have made his purchase and left when I wasn't watching.

On the way out, I bought a bottle of chocolate milk. As I stood outside the grocery store, I took a long sip of the drink that tasted like chalk. (A hazard of working with fine chocolate was that all ordinary chocolates start to taste like chalk.)

Down the road, I spotted construction workers carrying a large window toward one of the older cottages. A man with a crazed look in his eye was attacking a downed tree with a chainsaw. And an older man was walking toward the beach with a shovel in one hand and a metal detector in the other. Everyone seemed to have a purpose. Everyone appeared busy. And there was no sign of my hatless stranger. But, I told myself, I now knew that he'd returned to the island. And that in itself was a valuable clue.

Chapter 13

After giving up on finding the tweed hat man, I spent several hours at the Chocolate Box working alongside Fletcher. Despite being short on chocolate inventory, absent of our regular shipment of morning pastries, and absolutely out of milk for our popular milkshakes, many of my regular customers returned after Sunday lunch, seemingly happy to order coffee and tea while waiting for any fresh gossip.

The Gray Lady had once again become the hot topic of conversation. As time passed, more and more people came into the shop, giving the copper bell over the door quite the workout. Mr. Tweed Hat didn't return to the shop—not that I'd been expecting he would. The people coming into the shop weren't residents of Camellia Beach. At first I assumed these new people were a fresh influx of construction workers. But then I overheard enough of the excited conversations to realize—much to my chagrin—the strangers were ghost hunters who'd come into town in hopes of catching a glimpse of what people were starting to call a killer ghost.

I suppose the black ball cap with *Charleston Ghost Hunter* stitched in white thread that half a dozen of them were wearing should have clued me in on that sooner. In my defense, I was distracted. As soon as there was a lull in the shop's foot traffic, I planned to visit Bubba's house to apologize properly to Bertie.

About an hour after I saw her at Bunky's, she had called Fletcher to make sure he wasn't swamped at the shop. She'd told him that she felt bad about running out on him since it was her afternoon to work. I took that as a good sign. But she'd also added that she wouldn't have run off if I hadn't driven her insane.

Fletcher had needled me and needled me for details about what I'd done to upset Bertie this time. I would have told him what had happened if he hadn't added the *"this time"* dig.

"You know I-I'll f-f-find out," he stuttered and pointed to his deer hunter hat.

Yes, I did know that. He was a clever guy.

By about four o'clock that afternoon, the traffic in and out of the shop had slowed down. We were out of chocolate and running low on coffee. The ghost hunters, however, appeared rooted to their chairs. Their voices vibrated with the excitement of their hunt.

Fletcher offered to close up. He made a few of his trademark snide remarks after I'd reminded him of the things that needed to be done before he left for the day. "J-just go f-f-fix things with Bertie."

"Sure. Fine," I said as I hung up my apron. I then hurried out the back door, then hopped into my Fiat. Its small engine roared to life.

I was glad to get out of the Chocolate Box. Listening to the ghost hunters' nonsensical musings about how a ghost could cause a man's death—and why a ghost would bother to kill anyone in the first place—had been making me crazy.

"The Gray Lady didn't kill Joe," I shouted as I drove over to Bubba's. I hit the steering wheel with my palm for added emphasis. "Everyone in town has lost their ever-loving minds, that's what's happening here. Island-wide insanity." Having voiced it out loud made me feel better.

It took no more than five minutes to get to Bubba's house, even with having to swerve around the piles of storm debris that lined the road. The debris would remain there until a dump truck came to haul it away.

Bubba lived on the southern tip of the island. To the left of the road, the vacation homes lining the beach were still tightly boarded up. Roofs were missing shingles. A few had been covered with blue tarps. It'd take a while for the absentee owners to receive the insurance money needed to fix them. In the meantime, they sat there—their beautiful landscaping wiped away by the waves—like lonely echoes of happy summer vacations from bygone days.

Bonbon with the Wind

To my right, on the marsh side of the island, development was sparse. The land was low and swampy. It looked even swampier after the hurricane's flooding. Actually, this part of the island looked quite different than it had before the storm. Once, there had been a thick arching canopy over the road. It was gone. Leaves and branches had been violently snapped off the live oak trees. Pools of water encircled ancient scrubby oaks twisted into strange shapes from years of unrelenting wind. Several Palmetto trees were bent over.

I came upon a narrow dirt driveway that met the main road. I stopped the car and stared at the deeply rutted drive for several minutes before I recognized it as the path that led to Bubba's place.

His small house sat atop tall wooden stilts, giving it the look of a boathouse in search of a river. The house's blue paint had peeled off here and there revealing a bright yellow hue underneath. The storm had hacked away at the long wooden dock behind the house that snaked through the marsh and all the way to the salty river beyond it. Huge sections were now missing. It would take quite a bit of work and money to make it safe to walk on again. But everyone in town knew how much Bubba loved that dock. He'd get it fixed before he did anything about the blue tarp covering the rusty metal roof on his house.

I climbed the narrow steps up to his whitewashed front door. Like the dock, the treads needed work. I skipped a few that looked like they wouldn't support my weight while keeping a tight grip on the handrail.

I'd texted Bertie and Bubba to warn them that I was coming over, so I wasn't at all surprised when the door opened before I reached the front porch. Bubba came out. His smile, wide as always, made me feel welcome.

The inside of his house smelled damp—everybody's home smelled damp since the hurricane—but the air was warmed with the savory scents of roast beef and potatoes and all sorts of seasonings that were unique to Bertie's delicious cooking palette. My mouth watered.

Bubba led me to the kitchen where Bertie was standing at the sink, scrubbing a pan. I jammed my hands into the pockets of my shorts and stared at the floor a moment before saying, "I came to apologize. I'm an idiot. I say and do stupid things. You already know that. So please, I beg you, please stay. Don't move to Florida. You know the shop needs you. But that's not the only reason I want you to stay. I'd miss you. I'd miss having you as my roommate."

"Move to Florida?" Bubba howled. "What's this nonsense about moving to Florida?" He stomped around the house—making the entire structure shimmy and shake. The glass stemware in an overstuffed china cabinet next to me clinked and tinkled as if alarmed.

While Bubba stomped and grumbled and sometimes bellowed, Bertie set the pan she'd been scrubbing in the sink. She methodically dried her hands on a dishtowel before turning around. Her lips pressed into a thin line that made her look like a stern schoolteacher. The hard look in her dark brown eyes made me shiver.

"Bubba stop fussing so," she snapped. "And stand still already. I feel like I'm rocking around on a sinking ship."

With her expression still angry, she took a step toward me. Instinctively, I shrank back. "I'm really sorry," I said, holding my hands out in front of me. "Really."

"Honey." Bertie lunged for me and pulled me into the circle of her arms. "You know I was just blowing off steam. This business with the hurricane and the seemingly insurmountable task of getting everything fixed up has been a terrible ordeal. More than half the time, I feel like exploding."

Her arms tightened around me in a great big motherly hug.

While hugs nearly always make me feel awkward and vulnerable—I never know where to put my arms—Bertie's hug felt safe. I held onto her far longer than I think she'd expected. I ate up our body-to-body contact like a starving person who'd just taken a seat at a banquet.

"Does this mean you're not leaving Camellia Beach?" I asked though my face was still pressed into her shoulder.

"Of course I'm not going anywhere, child." She patted my back. She then added sharply, "Bubba, please hush for a moment." Her voice softened again. "For one thing, Penn, I have to get that building of mine fixed. Althea texted that you'd stopped by and saw the damage. I've been calling contractor after contractor. Nary a one has made it out to the building to look things over to give me a quote. They're already swamped with work. I'm just about ready to pull my hair out. It's maddening."

"Someone should have told me about the tornado. I'll be more than happy to make some phone calls. I'm sure I can get someone out there to fix the building right up. You know I know some people. After all, I've been having work done at the Chocolate Box for months now. I'm sure I can hire someone to start next week."

"Oh, no!" Bertie nearly shouted. She jumped out of the hug that had gone on for too long anyhow. "You don't need to do that. Really. I appreciate it, but no. Please, just, no."

Her reaction startled me.

"I—um—okay. I just thought—"

"Have you eaten lunch?" Bertie blurted, speaking much faster than her usual controlled cadence. "Let me fix you a plate. Sit down. Heavens, Bubba, don't just stand there. Show her where to sit down."

Instead of following Bubba to his dining table, I stood there staring at my friend while she piled food on a white china plate. I couldn't help but wonder why in the world she was refusing my offer to help her find workers who could fix up Althea's and Harley's businesses. Did she not trust that I'd help? Did she think I'd use this act of kindness as some sort of leverage against her? My family often did that, but I never would.

Bubba came back over to me. He bent down and whispered, "You'd better do as she asks, you know what I'm saying?"

I knew. You didn't cross Bertie when she was offering up food. I followed him to the table. Like a true Southern gentleman, he pulled out a chair for me to take. As I sat, he said, "While you eat, you can tell us how you're going to solve Joe's murder."

I nearly fell out of my chair.

The mere mention about solving Joe's murder was what had caused the trouble between Bertie and me in the first place. I glanced in her direction. Her hand, gripping a spoon heavy with mashed potatoes, had stopped moving.

"I don't think—" I started to say.

Bertie's eyebrows inched up a notch.

I squinted at her, as if squinting would help me see into her mind and know what she was thinking. Of course I didn't have to do that.

I already knew how she felt about my not telling them that I was investigating Joe's murder. They had to be experiencing the same painful feelings that had hit me like a freight train when I learned that none of them had told me how badly their building had been damaged. The realization that they hadn't trusted me—*didn't* trust me—to help them had hurt like a punch to the gut.

My gut grumbled, interrupting those thoughts. The food Bertie had cooked smelled wonderful.

My stomach rumbled even louder. "If you bring that plate over here, I'll tell you everything I know."

Bertie set her hands on her hips. "I'm not your waitress. You can come over here and get it yourself." Although she sounded fierce, I noticed right away the sparkle had returned to her eyes.

"You did tell Bubba to make sure I sat down," I countered, but I got up and fetched the plate myself. I found a knife, fork, and spoon in a drawer and helped myself to some sweet tea while I was in the kitchen.

In addition to the perfectly seasoned roast beef, Bertie had added collard greens, butter beans, mashed potatoes, and biscuits. Everything was drowning in thick gravy.

"My word, this is good," I said after I'd taken the first bite of the collard greens. No one made collard greens like Bertie.

Bertie took the seat next to me. Bubba sat across from me. He popped open a beer, gave me a salute, and then drained half the bottle. Bertie tapped impatiently on the tabletop.

"It's not the Gray Lady," I said after finishing off the biscuit.

"Of course not," Bertie agreed.

"We don't know that," Bubba said. "They say she's a protector of the island."

"Ghosts don't kill people," Bertie argued. "Least, not so directly."

"Ghosts don't kill because they don't exist," I corrected.

"Then who do you suspect?" Bubba asked.

I cut into the roast beef. "Too soon to tell. Bubba, you knew Joe, didn't you?"

"I hunted the beach with him a time or two," Bubba admitted. "He mostly discouraged anyone from treasure hunting with him. I think he did it because he was afraid that if he found something, he'd have to share it. We'd meet up at the Low Tide Bar and Grill sometimes. He would drink bourbon. I would have a beer. He'd ask me about island lore. He sometimes wanted to know about anyone new who'd moved to the island. He seemed especially worried about you, Penn."

"He did?" That surprised me. "Why?"

Bubba drained the rest of his beer. "I always assumed he was worried that someone else would take up an interest in treasure hunting. He seemed to think that he earned the right to be the man who searched the beach for pirate gold."

"He couldn't have been that protective," Bertie said. "He talked and talked and talked with me about Blackbeard and his treasure whenever he came into the shop."

"Sure, he would talk to everyone about the treasure, but he never said anything of substance," Bubba said.

"That's true. Every time I talked with him, it was the same thing. Blackbeard's treasure was hidden somewhere on Camellia Beach," I said.

Bubba nodded. "He never told anyone anything new. And what he did tell us was information anyone could find on Wikipedia. He'd added that little part that he thought the treasure was on Camellia Beach. Yet, he claimed to have reams and reams of research in his house. Why was that? Perhaps it was because he'd found something important. Perhaps he was afraid someone else might discover whatever secret he was holding onto, so he only told people what they could find for themselves with a simple Google search."

"Wow. You've thought about his treasure hunting far more than I have," I said. "I had assumed it was simply Joe's hobby."

"I suspect it was much more than a hobby with him. Like I said, he questioned me about everyone who came to town. He acted worried that someone else would start sniffing around Camellia Beach. He seemed especially worried about people like you, Penn, who ferreted out people's secrets."

"That's why you can't lock us out, Penn," Bertie said. "We each knew Joe in different ways. We each hold a unique piece of the puzzle."

I shoveled some mashed potatoes in my mouth, so I wouldn't have to immediately say anything, like, "Dang it, you're right." When I'd first come to the island, I hadn't trusted anyone and had tried to investigate a murder on my own. That's how I'd learned—the hard way—that I needed help.

But this time around I wasn't locking them out because of a lack of trust, I was locking them out because I loved them.

"Did you ever suspect he was lying about, well, everything?" I asked once I'd finished chewing.

Bubba shook his head. "People come to Camellia Beach for many reasons. We're accepting of everyone regardless of why they chose our island. We've learned not to ask too many questions. Or think about their reasons for being here too hard."

I chuckled. "You're kidding, right?"

He shrugged. "It's a live-and-let-live island. We're friendly. We're easygoing. We make living here a pleasure."

My chuckle turned into a laugh. "He's pulling my leg, isn't he?" I asked Bertie.

She shook her head. "'Judge not, lest you be judged.'" She often quoted the Bible on Sundays. Attending church services did that to her.

"Camellia Beach is packed full of the biggest, busybodies I've ever met," I said. "The entire town has this unquenchable need to know everything about everyone."

"You're one to talk." Bertie tsked.

"Perhaps that's why I feel so at home here. I fit in." I found it easy to admit. "So, Bubba, tell me the truth instead of feeding me one of the business association's slogans. Did you ever suspect that the story Joe was telling you about his fisherman past wasn't on the up and up?"

Bubba thought about it for a minute. "He talked and talked and talked so much about Blackbeard's treasure, I suppose he never gave me the chance to think about anything else when we were around him."

"He seemed a little scattered at times," Bertie said. "He'd forget things. Sometimes, important things. We've had enough people on the island with early stages of dementia that one starts to recognize the symptoms. I wonder if he didn't suffer some kind of mental breakdown at some point and simply forgot who he was and where he lived. I spent some time with his wife this morning. Delilah seems like a lovely woman. Why would he run away from her?"

Both Bertie and I looked at Bubba.

"Ah, is that how it's going to be?" he said. "Y'all are all looking at me, the dedicated bachelor, and start wondering why a man would leave his wife. I ain't never had a wife, mind you. So how in blue blazes should I know?"

Bertie crossed her arms over her chest. I followed suit.

"A man runs when he's under too much pressure," he finally said. "Delilah might seem friendly, but who knows what pressures she put on Joe or what she'd say to him when they were behind closed doors. We all wear different faces when we're around different people."

"That's the truth. Joe's daughter told me that Delilah married him for the inheritance he'd gotten after his first wife died."

"He had a daughter as well?" Bertie cried.

"Didn't I mention it?" I explained how I'd happened to meet Mary at Joe's burned-out shell of a house. "She is not friendly with her stepmother."

"Clearly, Penn, you need to work on sharing information with others," Bertie admonished.

Since she was correct, I practiced sharing by telling Bertie and Bubba everything I knew about Joe Davies—AKA John Fenton—including how I'd felt a kinship with Mary Fenton and how I'd promised to help her. Opening up to the ones I loved was the first important step toward solving Joe's murder. It also, ultimately, led to one of the worst mistakes in my life.

Chapter 14

Chocolate takes on the flavors around it. Which is a wonderful thing if you set a chocolate bar next to an orange or fragrant lavender flowers. It's not quite so wonderful if you accidentally place a chocolate bar in the refrigerator next to a clove of garlic.

My customers had shown me that people were also like chocolate. They take on the flavors of the place where they live.

Island life here on Camellia Beach must have changed Joe Davies. It had changed me. I don't think I ever knew what inner peace felt like before moving to Camellia Beach. Had Joe found peace here? Or had his relentless search for pirate gold made him even more nervous and anxious? He didn't strike me as one of the relaxed residents. He certainly wasn't like Bubba, with his easygoing take-life-as-it-comes attitude. So, I wondered, as I walked Stella along a trail that wove its way along the marsh that Sunday evening—how had Camellia changed Joe?

The trail Stella and I were following had been battered by the storm. We both had to step over—and in some cases, climb over—fallen trees and an assortment of beach debris. With a happy bark, she scurried under a piece of wood siding tilted up against a rusty freezer.

The sun was just beginning to set over the marsh and the river beyond, turning the sky a rich red that deepened until it disappeared into the distant tree line. As I crouched down to lure Stella out from her impromptu den, a chilly breeze rose up from nowhere. It felt like icy fingers had tiptoed down my spine. I shivered.

This was my first fall in the South, and I was starting to think the autumn season was no different that the Lowcountry's hot and humid summers. Scratch that, fall seemed to be *more* humid. So where had the cold breeze come from?

I spun around, expecting to see...

I don't know what I expected to see.

Mr. Tweed Hat?

Big Dog?

A mad killer frothing at the mouth?

Or the translucent Gray Lady?

Stella, who was still hiding in her makeshift den, growled.

A light flickered between the tangle of broken trees a few hundred feet away.

"Hello?" I called.

The chill I'd felt earlier crawled up the back of my neck.

"Hello?" I called louder this time.

Only the distant sound of crashing waves answered me. The trail seemed eerily still. Stella had stopped growling. She'd crawled out of her den with her tail tucked between her legs. She crouched low and tilted her head to one side, her large ears like radar discs turning this way and that.

I held my breath, listening.

The light in the bushes wavered again. That's when I heard it— a soft scrape. Like the sound of someone digging.

"Is someone there?" I called.

"Just me," came the answer from behind.

I spun around to find a shadowy figure walking toward me. Stella started barking like a maniac.

"Harley. Thank goodness, it's you." The tension coiled in my shoulders relaxed at the sight of him. "Do you see it?"

"See what?" He had to shout the question to be heard over Stella's barking.

"Hush, Stella. That's Harley."

"I think that's why she's barking like that. Your little dog doesn't like me."

"Nonsense." Ignoring my dog trainer's advice, I tossed her a piece of bacon, just to get her attention. "She's simply excited to see you."

"Yeah, excited to get her teeth into my ankle."

I tossed her another piece of bacon, which she quickly gobbled down between barks.

"Do you see that light?" I asked. While trying to get my naughty pup to calm down, I pointed to where the vaporous light had been floating around several hundred yards away.

Harley stopped just out of nipping range and peered into the wooded area. "Sorry. Do you still see it?"

I gave up on trying to calm Stella's snapping jaws and looked for myself. Other than the slight glow of the crescent moon far above our heads, the area was dark.

"There was something there. Someone, I think. Someone digging."

He was quiet for a long moment. "It could have been the moon reflecting in a marshy area." He paused and then turned his face up at the sky. A crisp breeze rushed by us. "Let's get back inside."

With a shiver, I agreed.

"Is a cold front coming in?" I asked as we made our way down the pathway.

"Not until next week," Harley said.

"Maybe it came early." I rubbed my arms. "I'm cold."

"Really? It's probably still close to eighty degrees out. I hope you're not getting sick."

"I never get sick," I announced.

By the time we reached the back steps that led to the second-floor apartments above the Chocolate Box the chill had vanished.

The lamp at the top of the stairs had been blown off by the hurricane. Replacing it was on my to-do list. The recessed lights in the covered second-story porch's ceiling provided a soft welcoming glow as we climbed up to our apartments.

"Your place or mine," I asked as we reached my apartment door. I could hear Trixie and Barbie arguing about whether to watch Matlock or NCIS.

"Definitely mine," Harley said. Was it my imagination or had his voice suddenly tightened? "We need to talk."

His door wasn't locked, which was odd. He always locked his door. Even if Gavin was home, he would lock the door. But Gavin was at his mother's house for the rest of the week.

"What's going on?" I followed him inside his place. Stella pulled the leash out of my hands to charge into the apartment, barking like a vicious attack dog.

"I have an unexpected guest," he said with a nod to the man sitting at Harley's old wooden kitchen table. The man barely glanced in our direction. He was too engrossed in peeling shrimp.

"Big Dog," I said, immediately recognizing the bearded surfer. He still looked like a rogue pirate. "Your brother is looking for you."

"So are the police," Big Dog said right before dredging the shrimp he'd just eased from its shell through a deep red cocktail sauce. He chewed before adding, "And I can't let them find me."

Chapter 15

"You can't harbor him, Harley. You're a lawyer and an officer of the court," I whispered after I'd pulled him to the far side of the living room. But Harley's apartment was as small as mine, and there was nothing wrong with Big Dog's hearing.

"There's not a warrant out for my arrest," the surfer answered before Harley could. Big Dog tossed Stella an oversized shrimp and instantly won my dog's admiration. The little traitor was wagging her tail at one of my main suspects for Joe's murder and flirting with him with her big brown eyes.

"You do know that Detective Gibbons is looking for him?" I asked Harley.

"Yeah, I know. I talked with Frank this afternoon." He then quickly added, "But Big Dog is correct. A person has every legal right to go missing from their family. There's no reason I should feel compelled to hand him over to the authorities. He's not wanted for any crime. Joe's death is still classified as accidental."

"Why would you mention Joe?" I demanded. With my hands on my hips, I spun to toward the surfer as he dipped another freshly peeled shrimp into a cocktail sauce that smelled like Heaven. "What have you done?"

"Nothing!" Big Dog said. "Honest."

"Well, that's not exactly true," Harley said with a sigh. "Why don't we sit down and have some dinner while we get everything out in the open?"

Dinner consisted of a large bowl of boiled shrimp in the middle of the kitchen table next to an equally large bowl for the shrimp shells, and a roll of paper towels. No side dishes. No plates. At least Harley provided me with my own soup bowl filled with cocktail sauce. He opened three Palmetto Ale beers and handed one to Big Dog and one to me.

Harley was such a bachelor. When his son wasn't around, his dinners were often simple affairs like this one-bowl wonder. And because of my fondness for shrimp, I peeled one and nearly swooned at the sweet and spicy flavor of the cocktail sauce before demanding Harley explain why he was hiding Big Dog in his apartment.

"It's good, isn't it?" Harley said as he watched me with a warm smile.

"It was your Granny's recipe," Big Dog told me. "She shared it with me the last time I visited." He leaned toward me and whispered, "The secret ingredient is chocolate."

My eyes widened. *Chocolate?* I ate several more shrimp while Big Dog told me about the fresh tomatoes, the brown sugar, fat cloves of garlic, the chili powder, and of course the cocoa powder that went into the recipe.

I'd peeled another shrimp when Harley cleared his throat. "I hate to interrupt when you're obviously enjoying the dinner I've prepared." His friendly eyes sparkled with pleasure. "But we do need to talk."

"About keeping the other person in the loop about what's going on?" I asked as I pulled the tail off the shrimp. "I saw your office today. Or perhaps I should say I saw where your office used to be. You should have told me."

His tanned cheeks darkened. "Yeah, about that. I didn't want to worry you. It's not like I was keeping information about a potential murder to myself."

"Perhaps I didn't want to worry *you*," I said.

"Do the two of you need a moment alone?" Big Dog pushed his chair away from the table and began to rise.

"No," both Harley and I said.

Stella yipped until Big Dog sat. He handed her another piece of shrimp. I shook my head at how quickly she'd trained the tall surfer.

"We need to talk about why you're here in town," I said to Big Dog. "I know you and Joe are both from Cedar's Hill in Virginia."

"Yeah, I lived in Cedar's Hill for a time." Harley's surfing buddy no longer looked so friendly. He glared in my direction. I didn't let it rattle me. After all, I'd been glared at by Chicago society matrons who had honed the art of the fierce stare into a finely sharpened weapon.

"So you knew Joe when he was John Fenton." Not a question, but a statement I was pretty sure was correct.

"No," he snapped. "I didn't know him."

"Really? You didn't know him?" I found that hard to believe. "But you came to Camellia Beach because of him."

Big Dog's hard gaze remained locked on me as he sipped his beer.

"If you want to stay here, you need to be honest with Penn," Harley told his friend. "This apartment has now become an honesty zone. For all of us." He winked at me. "You told me you came to Camellia Beach to clear your name. You said you sent that letter to your brother because you thought your life might be in danger. Tell Penn how this involves Joe Davies."

"It's a long story," Big Dog said. He took another long drink of his beer. Stella barked for him to give her another shrimp.

"I learned from Frank just this afternoon that Big Dog is Silas Piper's missing brother. But you already knew that, Penn," Harley said when his friend didn't start talking. "You should have told me."

I bit my lower lip. He was right. I should have told him. "I didn't want you to get involved. You have a son to think about. And"—I spread my hands—"these kinds of things have a way of turning dangerous."

"Which is why you should have—" he blurted. He then shook his head. "Big Dog is here. And there's trouble aplenty that we need to sort out before we start picking apart what's wrong with this part of our relationship. But right now and from here on out, no secrets. No lies."

"I have never lied to you," I protested.

He raised his eyebrows. "Omission can be considered a kind of a—"

"Okay, okay. You didn't tell me about the damage to your office and Althea's shop. I didn't tell you about recognizing Big Dog in the picture Piper had sent me. We both were wrong."

"I agree."

"Good." I didn't like that Big Dog was sitting in Harley's apartment. I didn't like that I felt guilty for trying to protect Harley. And I certainly didn't like this feeling that I needed to apologize for it.

Harley frowned at me for a long moment. It looked as if he wanted me to say something. When I didn't, he sighed. He then turned to Big Dog, who was watching us and smirking. "Tell us what happened to make you tell your brother that you thought your life was in danger."

The surfer grunted. He didn't make any effort to hide the resentment in his voice. "My perfect older brother—the brother with the good half of the genes—thought I was wasting my life as a professional surfer. He never approved of anything I did, and that included my birth. My mother had me after she left Silas' dad. She ran off with the Piper estate gardener. But after a year living off a gardener's income, she returned to her marriage. Silas and I never did get along. I was the gardener's son and a bastard." He slumped down as he said it. "But his dad, out of love for my mom or guilt or an old-fashioned sense of duty, provided for me. I lived off a generous allowance. Not that he ever let me forget I wasn't a Piper. The old man denied me the family name. After he died, Silas told me he'd stop sending my allowance if I didn't do his bidding. That's how I ended up taking a break from the surfing circuit and going to work—in a suit—as bank manager for the Consolidated Bank of Cedar's Hill. Worst. Job. Ever. Everyone around me was so mind-numbingly dull."

"You stuck with it, though," Harley said with an encouraging nod to his friend.

Big Dog gave a long, slow sigh. "I admit I wasn't paying that much attention. As I said, it was the worst job. But it was my job, so in a way, I guess it was my fault when assets went missing."

"Someone was embezzling at the bank?" I asked.

Big Dog shrugged as he opened another Palmetto Pale Ale. He then handed Stella another shrimp.

"Big Dog served five years in prison for the crime," Harley said.

"Silas assumed I was guilty. He didn't come and talk to me. He told my dad, who still works as a gardener at the estate, that he'd expected something like this would happen. Blamed it on my bad breeding. Breeding? Like people are dogs?" He sucked in a deep breath. "Without consulting with me or letting me try and figure out what had happened, Silas deposited enough money into the bank to cover the millions in losses and then hired lawyers who railroaded me into taking a plea deal. It was his way of sweeping the scandal under the rug before the media got whiff of any of it. Google it and you won't find anything anywhere about my going to jail. Ever."

"Big Dog hasn't seen Silas since this happened," Harley added. "Isn't that right?"

Big Dog nodded. "I didn't see Big Bro while it was happening. He couldn't be bothered. So why should I reach out to him now? I got out of prison and decided to never go crawling back to him for anything. He didn't ask me if I was innocent. He'd assumed that since I was a world-class screw-up, I must also be an embezzler. Oh no, I don't need that in my life. I'd starve on the street before accepting a dime from him."

Clearly, Big Dog wasn't starving. He sat at Harley's table dressed in a Brooks Brothers polo shirt and Tommy Bahama khaki shorts. Not the most expensive clothes, but not cheap either. This guy wasn't living on a shoestring, which meant he had money stashed away somewhere. Embezzled money?

"This is an honesty zone," I pointed out. "That goes for you too, Big Dog."

"I'm not lying."

"But you just said you wouldn't ask your brother for any kind of help, and yet you sent him a letter, warning him you were in danger."

"She has a good point," Harley said.

"He was only supposed to get that letter if I was dead. You know, dead. As in, over my dead body. If the embezzler killed me, I wanted Silas to go after the bast—*erm*—the guilty party. If I was dead, I'd have no hope of clearing my name and shoving my innocence into Silas' smug face. If I wasn't around to do it, I'd need him to connect the dots for me, you know?"

"Say we believed that." I didn't. I put down the shrimp I was peeling in order to cross my arms over my chest. It was my turn to practice my skills at cutting a glare. "What are you doing here in Camellia Beach? Why now?"

"I followed Sammy Duncan here. He'd just been sprung from prison. You see, I wasn't the only person caught in the net the feds cast over the illustrious Consolidated Bank of Cedar's Hill. Another worker, a bank teller, was convicted of the crime. They called him a co-conspirator. I think they called me the linchpin and kept looking to me to tell them where I'd stashed what Sammy had taken. But I couldn't tell them that because I didn't have it. The feds stopped asking after brother-boy repaid what had been lost. They stopped asking about anything. My guilt was a fait accompli. Silas' interfering with my life has always caused me trouble. There was this one time in college when—"

"Tell us about Sammy Duncan," Harley interrupted to say.

"Right. Sammy. He worked as a teller at the bank. I didn't really know him, because I didn't pay that much attention to the people who worked under me. It was an awful job. So boring. I wish I'd paid a little attention though. This Sammy guy must be a real stupid creep. The feds had no trouble proving he was responsible. Because he didn't have the lawyers I had, and because he didn't take a plea deal, he served a much longer sentence. He was released a few days before the storm hit. I followed him from the prison. Drove everywhere he drove. That's how I ended up here."

I looked over at Harley and asked, "Do you think Sammy is the guy with the tweed hat that came in looking for Joe?"

Harley shrugged. "I got to the Chocolate Box after he left, remember?"

"Shoot. That's right." I looked over at Big Dog. "Does this guy wear a tweed hat?"

"I don't know," he said.

"And you weren't the least bit suspicious that Sammy Duncan came to a town where you just happened to have friends and had visited many times in the past?"

He shrugged. "No one was more surprised than I was when he ended up here. Pleasantly surprised, if truth be told. Did you see the size of the waves that day? The beach, a hurricane, big waves. It's a surfer's wet dream," Big Dog said. He flashed his devil-may-care grin.

I'd known Harley long enough to know that surfers were single-minded in their pursuit of the perfect ride.

"The stolen money was never recovered," Harley supplied.

That wasn't hard to believe. For someone who was cut off from any kind of funding, Big Dog seemed to be living quite comfortably.

"He plans to prove his innocence," Harley added.

"And you believe that?" I expected better from Harley.

"I've known him for years. He's a good guy."

"No offense, Big Dog—Taylor—whatever your name is, but your story doesn't work. How will finding the money prove anything? You could have easily been in on the embezzling and let your friends Sammy and Joe hide the money while everyone forgot about the crime."

"I swear I didn't know either of them!" Big Dog shouted.

I swung my attention back over to Harley. "He might seem like a *good guy* on the surface, but…" I left the rest unsaid as I waved my hands in the surfer's direction.

Harley knew about my past and how I'd learned to harden myself against even the most trustworthy of friends.

"I trust him," Harley said, his voice gentle. It melted my heart a little.

"Before the two of you get into an argument over me, how about I tell you what I think is going on, and, Penn, you can choose to believe me or not. I can't stop you from going to the police, but I'd rather you didn't."

I sat back in the chair. He was the black sheep of the Piper family. For that reason alone, I supposed I needed to give him the chance to tell his side of the story. Once branded a black sheep, one was rarely given a chance to explain, well, anything.

"Okay. Sure, tell me what's going on," I said before I started to peel another shrimp.

He looked surprised. "I…really?"

"Yeah, why shouldn't I listen to you? Are you going to lie within our honesty zone?" I asked.

"No, I just—" He looked down and smiled into his bowl of cocktail sauce as he shook his head. "I expected that since you'd talked with the police and know that both Joe and I are from Cedar Hill that you would have already formed your opinions about me."

"I may have." I wasn't going to lie about that. "But that's not going to stop me from hearing what you have to say."

"That's decent of you." He looked over at Harley, who was watching the two of us with an expression that looked like an equal mixture of amusement and pride. "You were right about her. Penn is someone worth getting to know."

"You said that about me?" I asked Harley.

"Of course I did."

I was touched. I reached across the table and squeezed his hand.

"Again, I ask," Big Dog said with a wicked grin taking up much of his pirate face, "do the two of you need some time alone?" He waggled his pirate brows. "Or perhaps lots of alone time?"

"Um…" Did Harley and I need a moment to ourselves? "No. We need to focus on figuring out what's going on." I glanced over at Harley and my heart fluttered. He was watching me in a way I'd never seen before, like he was a hungry coyote on the prowl and he saw me as a tasty bit of prey. Oh my, that look was having a heady effect on me. But this wasn't the time or the place. "We…um…need to focus," I repeated.

Harley drew a shaky breath. "Yes, we need to figure out why your brother and the police are so keen on finding you, Big Dog," he said. "And if this has anything to do with Joe's murder."

"You actually think he was murdered?" I asked. That surprised me.

"*You* think Joe was murder, Penn, and I trust your judgment. We're a team, remember?" Harley said. "So, let's get this business sorted."

A team. I don't think two words had ever sounded as sexy as those.

"Where do we begin?" Big Dog asked.

"I suppose we should start with your brother. Silas Piper told me he was looking for you because of that letter you sent via your friend, the one telling him you'd been murdered," I said.

"Oh, that stupid letter." Big Dog groaned. "I wish I'd never written it."

"Well, you did. And he has it. But he made no secret that he thinks of you as the black sheep of the Piper clan, or perhaps more accurately, the albatross hanging around the necks of the Piper family. So, I'm wondering if he came to Camellia Beach because he is truly concerned for your welfare or is there something else about what you're doing here that's worrying him?"

"Wait, my brother is actually here? In Camellia Beach?" Big Dog asked. "You didn't simply talk to him over the phone? He-he didn't send someone? He came...in person?"

"He was here a week ago," I told him. "He went to the city police department to report your murder. He seemed upset, but I did think it odd that he came to the island personally and so soon after the hurricane had blown through. He could have just as easily hired someone to quietly look into the matter for him."

Big Dog pressed a shaky hand to his lips. "He didn't visit me after I was arrested. Not once. He wouldn't even take my calls."

My heart ached for him. I knew what he was feeling. It was never a good sign in a black sheep's life when a family member went from ignoring your existence to taking a personal interest.

"Let's get back to the money," I said. "Why do you think your accomplice...*er*...Sammy Duncan would come here?"

"If I knew that, I'd already have retrieved what he'd taken from the bank, now wouldn't I?"

"Okay." I needed to get things straight in my head. I started ticking off the points we knew. "Joe was murdered. Probably before the storm. His house burned to the ground. Had someone deliberately burned the house down to cover up his murder? A few hours before the storm hit, a stranger wearing a tweed hat came to the Chocolate Box and started asking where he could find Joe. Shortly after he left, you arrived at the shop. Were you following the stranger who visited the shop? Was he Sammy?"

"Um..." Big Dog smiled sheepishly. "I had some serious surfing to do that morning. I kind of lost track of Sammy. Haven't been able to find him since."

Gracious, no wonder Silas had wanted to keep his brother on a short leash. He seemed quite helpless. Or was that helpless guy routine an act?

I looked over at Harley. Was he buying his friend's story?

"Can you get me a picture of Sammy?" I asked. I needed to find out if he was Mr. Tweed Hat.

He pulled a cell phone from his pocket and started to swipe on the screen. It was the latest model and nearly as big as a tablet. "Just a minute." He tapped the screen. Waited. And then tapped the screen some more. "Here's Sammy Duncan," he said and handed me his phone.

Although the guy in the picture wasn't wearing a hat—the picture was from a newspaper report that included Sammy's mug shot taken shortly after his arrest—I recognized him right away. He was Mr. Tweed Hat.

"Did Sammy go anywhere else after being released from prison? Or did he come straight here?" I asked.

"He visited his mother for a few days. She threw a huge welcome home party. All the Cedar's Hill church ladies came out with their best covered dishes. The entire block smelled delicious," Big Dog answered. "After the party, he hopped in his mom's ancient Subaru and drove here."

"How do you know that?" Harley asked.

"I was sitting in a car outside, watching his house. I didn't want to miss anything he did."

"Do you think Joe had the money?" I asked.

"I don't know," Big Dog answered.

"Did Sammy and Joe know each other back at Cedar's Hill?" I asked.

"I don't know," Big Dog repeated with a rueful shake of his head and sideways smirk that made me want to scream at him. "I didn't know them."

Do you know anything?

While he had provided me with a name and information about my mystery man, the rest of what he'd told us created more questions than answers. Part of me wanted to pick up the phone and turn him and that smirk of his over to Detective Gibbons.

But then I looked at Harley.

Even if Big Dog reminded me of a smarmy pirate, he was Harley's friend. Harley had made the decision to hide him in his apartment. It'd be up to Harley to call Gibbons—or not.

"You don't happen to know anything about Blackbeard's treasure, do you?" I asked.

"What?" Big Dog wrinkled his nose. "I haven't had an interest in pirate stories since I was eleven or twelve."

"How about the Gray Lady?" Harley asked, much to my chagrin. "Have you heard about her?"

"You know I've heard about her," Big Dog said with a snort. "Everyone is talking about how the ghost killed Joe Davies." But then he leaned toward me and said, "If you ask me, I think his death was cosmic retribution, especially if he ran off with the goods and left me and Sammy behind to take the blame."

"I see." I wiped my mouth and fingers with a paper towel. "Thank you for the shrimp," I said as I stood.

Harley jumped to his feet while Big Dog remained slouched in his chair.

"Do you have to go?" he asked. He grabbed hold of my hand. "I was kind of hoping we could talk more."

I glanced over at Big Dog who was peeling another shrimp. "I think we've talked enough for tonight." Big Dog was only going to feed us the information that he wanted us to know and nothing more.

I called Stella over to me.

She didn't budge from where she was sitting at Big Dog's side.

"Stella, come." I snapped my fingers and clicked my tongue.

Still, nothing.

"Bacon," I sang and waved a small piece of it in the air.

She sniffed.

Slowly, reluctantly, she climbed to her feet and dragged herself away from her new favorite person. I handed her the teeny sliver of bacon, patted her head, and then picked up her leash. "I'll see you tomorrow?" I asked Harley.

He twined his fingers with mine as he walked with me toward the door. The contact felt intimate and comfortable. He followed me out to the porch then closed the door behind him. "This wasn't how I wanted tonight to go. His showing up like this changed all my plans." He turned toward me with the most adorably frustrated frown. "But what could I do? He's my friend."

"You did exactly what I'd expect." I pushed a lock of hair away from his face. "You're a nice guy, Harley. You do what's right. That's why I like you so much."

"Is that what you think of me? That I'm nice?" He braced his hands against the wall on either side of my head and moved so his warm body was pressed against mine. "If you could hear my thoughts right now, you'd know I'm not all that nice," he said, his voice low, sexy. "There's nothing nice about me right now."

A stuttering heartbeat later, he kissed me. His mouth, hungry and demanding, gave me everything I never knew I needed from a man. When our lips finally parted, I was literally breathless. I didn't realize a kiss could leave a person breathless. I'd thought that was a fantasy woven by romance writers.

His lips on mine had left my legs trembling and feeling rubbery. I put my hand on his chest to keep me from sliding to the porch decking. The rapid thump of his heart beat against my palm. Clearly, he'd been just as affected by the kiss as I'd been.

Gracious, his expression looked fierce.

I realized suddenly that up until now, we'd been playing at dating. Playful kisses. Harmless date nights. Solving a few murders with him playing the role of my sidekick. They'd been games. No expectations. No danger—*except for the chasing after murderers part.* My heart had remained safe.

But this kiss, oh my…

It made me want things that scared me more than a deranged killer ever could.

"I'm done playing nice, Penn," he said. "If you want to be in a relationship, no more pushing me away. No more secrets. If you're going after a killer, you tell me. We go forward as a team. Or we part ways."

Uncertain if I could talk without my voice cracking, I nodded.

He kissed me again. Gently, this time.

I wrapped my arms around him and lived in the moment…for the moment.

Slowly, we both pulled away.

He was breathing faster than before.

So was I.

He pressed his forehead to mine.

"Tomorrow?" I said, lamely.

He nodded.

"Breakfast?" I said.

"I'd like that." He stepped further away from me. That odd chill that had plagued me earlier returned.

"Are you sure a cold front isn't coming through?" I rubbed my arms to chase away the goose bumps.

"The weather is supposed to hold steady until Friday. Tell Bertie I've got the insurance papers ready for her to sign. I'll bring them with me in the morning."

"Yeah, I'll do that. See you in the morning then," I said. Lame parting words, but I couldn't come up with anything romantic. I opened my apartment door. Stella darted inside. The theme song to the Mary Tyler Moore Show was playing on the TV in the living room and spilled out into the night.

I stood there at the threshold, thinking how wonderful it felt to have Harley in my life. I wanted to say something—something not hokey—that would let him know I was ready to go all in on our relationship. I searched for the right words. But if there were right words to say in such a moment, I didn't have a clue to what they were.

"You put up with me," I said instead. "That must make you one of the nicest guys in the world. And I love that about you."

Before he could answer, before I could see how he'd react to my accidental use of the *L*-word with that compliment, I stepped inside my apartment and slammed the door closed behind me.

Just in time too. My wobbly, romance-stricken legs gave out on me, and I ended up leaning against the door. A long, happy sigh escaped my lips.

"Hot date night with Harley?" Barbie asked.

"Looks like she got that love potion from Althea's shop and used it on herself," Trixie said with a tsk. "I needed that potion."

"You need to take a cold shower," Barbie said.

I wasn't sure if she was directing that comment at me or at her sister.

With a happy yip, Stella ran over to where the two sisters were sitting on the sofa. She then ran back to me, circled my legs, before returning to the sisters with their endless supply of snacks. With her adorable black nose to the carpet, she started to sniff around for cheese crumbs.

I, on the other hand, headed straight to my bathroom to take that cold shower.

Chapter 16

Judging by the size of the crowds visiting the Chocolate Box the next day, an outsider would have thought it was the Fourth of July weekend, not some random October Monday. Between the hungry ghost hunters who'd spent the night on the beach with all sorts of questionable-looking ghost-detecting equipment and the treasure hunters who had rolled in early with their more expensive (but just as questionable-looking) metal-detecting equipment, the shop's meager stock was nearly sold out by ten o'clock.

Ethel Crump had returned and was telling everyone that she had sensed an evil presence on the morning wind. "Mark my words"—her voice scratched like dry leaves—"the storm may be gone, but the Gray Lady isn't done."

After her warning, the murmurs in the shop grew louder until the copper bell over the door chimed. Everyone fell silent as they turned toward the shop's entrance. My customers all held themselves stiffly as if expecting the Gray Lady herself to waltz into the shop.

Killer ghosts, indeed. I snorted.

The woman who walked through the door wasn't the Gray Lady. She was younger than a century's old hag. Her long red hair had been pulled back into a high ponytail. She was comfortably dressed in jeans and a scoop-neck T-shirt in a faded blue hue that suited her pale complexion.

I smiled and waved to Mary Fenton. She'd come to a jolting halt just a step inside the door.

"Good morning," I called to her. "Come in. I think there's some coffee left in the urn." I crossed the room to join her, and then added so only she could hear, "Your stepmother isn't here."

Her tense shoulders dropped. A sigh of relief relaxed her bright red lips. "Thank goodness. This is a small island, and I really don't want to talk to her. I have nothing to say to that woman. Well, nothing polite. If you don't mind, I'd appreciate it if you didn't mention to her that I've been talking with you."

The buzz in the room returned to its normal level. The ghost hunters went back to playing with their electronic equipment and the treasure hunters went back to studying maps of the island.

I poured Mary a mug of coffee. I stirred into the cup a small square of Amar chocolate that melted immediately. "It's on the house," I told her.

"I couldn't accept," she protested.

I held up my hand and insisted.

She thanked me before taking a sip. When the hot drink touched her mouth, she closed her eyes. A spread across her lips with a look of pure pleasure. It was an expression I'd experienced myself every time I tasted the rich and almost magically healing flavors of the special chocolates we made at the Chocolate Box.

"Oh, my," she said, still smiling. "That is exactly what I needed. Thank you."

We found seats at an empty table in the middle of the shop. She tapped the coffee mug. "This is the best thing I've ever tasted. You should be selling your chocolate nationally."

Many people in the past several months had urged me to take the Amar chocolates to a national market, which was why I was well practiced with my answer. "I enjoy running a small shop. And the cacao beans we use to make the chocolate come to the Chocolate Box in extremely small batches. I honestly wouldn't have enough for national distribution."

She shook her head in amazement. "If you handled things correctly, you could be rich."

"There's more to life than money."

"Not much that I can think of," she grumbled.

I understood why most people might think I'd lost my mind when it came to my attitude toward money. But I grew up in a family with an excess of riches and a shortage of kindness. Living on this small island while making chocolate candies by hand gave me something that no amount of money could ever buy—happiness. I didn't want to work as head of a factory. I didn't want to live my life in a sterile office. "I'm comfortable with how things are," I explained.

She shrugged. "Have you learned anything new about my father's death? I heard he was found with a gold coin in his hand. Do you think he'd found Blackbeard's treasure?" She sat forward in her chair. "I want to make sense of why he left Cedar's Hill and why he died. I don't understand anything about what's happening. Why was he obsessed with gold anyhow? It's all so confusing."

I wasn't sure what I could tell her. Should I share with her what Big Dog had told me about the embezzled money from the bank? I wasn't even supposed to know where Big Dog was hiding. And although I truly wanted to help Mary, I didn't know if I could trust her.

I reached across the table and gave her hand a squeeze. "I'm still asking around," I told her. "I think in order to understand what happened here, we need to understand why your father disappeared from his old life."

"I agree," she said shakily. "I've always assumed he was running from *that* woman. But thinking about it now, I suspect my anger over their marriage, and what she did with my mother's things, colored how I saw the situation. If he'd wanted to get away from her, he could have moved to another house. He didn't have to run away from me."

That made sense.

"Now that you're seeing what happened six years ago in a new light, can you think of any new reason why he might have left?"

She shook her head. "No, I keep thinking about it and thinking about it. I can't imagine what he could possibly be doing living here. He left a nice house and a stable job to live in a tiny shack of a house that he rented. Why?"

I thrummed my fingers against the table and decided to give her a breadcrumb from what Big Dog had told me. "Did your father know Sammy Duncan?"

Her face paled at my mentioning his name. "Mr. Duncan? His daughter was my age. Kylie and I were cheerleaders together in high school. That was years ago. Didn't he get in trouble with the police about something?"

"I believe he did," I said. "Did your father know him?"

She shrugged. "I suppose they might have talked at the cheerleading competitions. My parents would come to watch. Kylie's parents came too. So did most of the parents of the cheerleaders for that matter."

"There was no special connection between your father and Sammy, though?"

"Not that I knew of." She leaned closer toward me. "Why?"

"I'm trying to figure out why your father abruptly left Cedar's Hill. Does his leaving have anything to do with his obsession with Blackbeard's treasure? Or did he leave because of something that had happened in Cedar's Hill? Was he running away or running toward something?"

"I don't know," she said softly. She jotted two phone numbers on the back of her business card. "If you find out anything, you can reach me either on my cell phone or at my friend's house where I'm staying in downtown Charleston. I expect to be in town for a few more days. Even though *that* woman is making all the funeral arrangements, I don't want to leave before the police release Dad's body."

It wasn't until she left that I turned the card over and saw where she worked. Just like her father, she sold cars at Cedar's Hill Imports.

"You saw her," one of the ghost hunters accused. He'd sauntered up to me a few minutes after Mary had left. He appeared to be about my age—mid-thirties—lanky, with dark stubble covering the lower part of his face. His nose bent to the right and then to the left, looking as if it'd been broken more than once and had healed poorly each time. He was dressed all in black, which really wasn't a great clothing choice for working at the beach. The putty-colored sand dusting him, and his clothes, stood out in stark contrast.

"You mean, Mary?" I gestured toward the door.

"No, not *that* woman." He shook a grainy, shades-of-gray photograph of the beach and what appeared to be someone's smudged fingerprint in one corner at me. "*Her.*"

I frowned at the photograph. "Is that supposed to be the Gray Lady?"

"Yeah. She's right there, as real as anything."

As real as nothing.

He wasn't the first ghost hunter to come up to me, wanting to hear the story about what I'd seen on the beach. I told him what I'd been telling everyone. "I saw Joe talking to a woman several hundred feet away from where I was standing. He claimed he'd spoken with a ghost. I'm not so sure." I pointed to his photograph. "What I saw wasn't that."

He sniffed, and then carefully slid his photograph into a protective plastic sleeve. "They say everyone who sees the Gray Lady experiences destruction. Joe talked with her and died. Your friend lost her shop." He tilted his head to one side. "What happened to you?"

"Nothing. Nothing at all, because it's nonsense." I tried to walk away from him. I needed to get back to the display case and front counter. After all, I had a shop to run.

"Nonsense?" He stroked his stubbly chin as he stubbornly followed along beside me. "You're one of those, are you?"

"One of what?"

"A nonbeliever." He made it sound like an egregious sin.

"I suppose you could call me that. I don't believe in the Gray Lady. Joe didn't want to tell us who he met on the beach, but it was clearly someone who'd upset him. Ghosts don't exist." I then

126

remembered how arguing with the customer wasn't good for encouraging return visits. "I mean, I understand that you disagree with me on that. I don't mean any disrespect."

He laughed. "Honey, everyone in these parts knows you're not a believer…in anything. I'm Brett Handleson." He stuck out his hand for me to shake. He had a firm, but sandy, grip. "I also heard that you aim to get to the bottom of things with regard to Joe's untimely death."

"Not by myself," I said. "There's a group of us who've decided to ask around about it. We're concerned residents, that's all."

"But you're the driving force."

I shrugged. "We're working as a team."

He leaned forward and whispered, "Even when it comes to the treasure?"

I jerked back.

"They say Joe found the gold, and that's why he ignored the Gray Lady's warning to leave the island before the hurricane. That's why he was killed."

"It's a popular opinion around here," I said without agreeing or disagreeing. It wasn't my place to argue that ghosts were bunk to people who clearly devoted their lives to finding proof that they existed.

"Does that mean you *are* looking for the gold?" he leaned toward me and whispered.

"I'm looking for answers. Where the search takes me"—I spread my hands—"is anyone's guess."

"You saw the Gray Lady. Your date with disaster might still be waiting for you. You'd better watch yourself." With a nod toward his friends who were still sitting in a far corner, he left the shop.

"The kooks are thick in here," Ethel hobbled up to me to say. "I think they're hoping Stevie McWilson is going to come back."

"Is that why you're here this morning?"

She rarely came into the shop on Mondays, the day she went to the hairdresser, which for some reason was a full-day event for her and her friends. They said it was a Southern thing. I wasn't so sure it was true.

"I heard Stevie McWilson is hoping to interview more people who saw the Gray Lady. They're going to do an exposé that might get picked up nationally. Can you imagine that? Little ol' Camellia Beach being featured on the national news, that would be quite the boon for us."

"It would," I had to agree, even though I didn't like it. I'd much rather a reporter did a story on the plight of the sea turtles or how the town managed to preserve its maritime forest or even about the small, locally owned businesses that survived despite sharp economic downturns. But ghosts? What was next? Fairies and goblins? I shuddered to think how the business association would try to spin it.

Would my shop always be crowded with ghost hunters? Was this my new normal? I guessed if it was, I couldn't be too upset. They seemed to be a hungry bunch.

Ethel hobbled back to sit with her friends. After clearing another table, I managed to return to the front counter. Ethel's friends were all dressed in their best dresses, wearing more makeup than usual, and keeping a close eye on the door. Ethel had caught the interest of a couple of the ghost hunters. One of them was waving a handheld electronic device as if he were scanning her. It made all sorts of odd beeps and tweets that seemed to please the rest of the ghost hunters.

I heard several of them whispering that they'd found the Gray Lady. And she was drinking her coffee black.

I stood at the counter, watching this while I sipped my coffee (with plenty of cream.) My thoughts kept going back to the gold coin we'd found clutched in Joe's hand. Why was he holding it when he'd died? Why hadn't he put the coin in a pocket?

We'd also found a similar gold coin in Althea's shop. Were they pieces of Blackbeard's missing treasure? Oh, I wished Althea could help me with this end of things. In addition to being an expert on things that went bump in the night on the island, she also possessed an encyclopedic knowledge about the island history and lore. I supposed history stories and ghost stories did go hand-in-hand.

Joe's obsession with Blackbeard's treasure confounded me. If Joe had—as Big Dog had suggested—taken the embezzled millions and run off with it, why would he be so obsessed about searching for gold coins that he'd risked his life for them? If treasure hunting had simply been a hobby, he wouldn't have stayed on the island during a hurricane to look for the coins. Especially not after the Gray Lady had warned him to leave.

Fudge, had I *really* just included the Gray Lady in my list of clues?

Ghosts? Bah.

Someone had upset Joe. Someone he didn't want us to know about. And instead of telling Althea and me who he was talking to on that fateful morning on the beach, he'd lied and claimed he saw the Gray Lady.

But who was he talking to?

It was a woman. That much was clear.

Oh dear, the circumstances surrounding Joe's death didn't add up. There had to be something missing from this story. Or some*one*.

Why would someone want to kill a rather feeble old man?

Embezzlement.

Pirate treasure.

Ghosts.

"Penny for your thoughts," Detective Frank Gibbons said.

It startled me to find him standing on the other side of the counter. I'd been so wrapped up in the puzzle surrounding Joe's death that I'd totally missed him coming into the shop. I hadn't even heard the bell ring. He wore a warm smile. Instead of his everyday work suit, he was dressed in khaki pants and a light blue polo shirt.

"Are any of the golf courses around here even open again yet?" I mused aloud.

He nodded. "A few."

"I never pictured you as a golfer. Actually, I never really pictured you doing anything other than your job and going to church." He and Bertie sang in the same church choir.

He chuckled. "I do have a life, although Connie might disagree with me on that." His wife had once complained to me that she didn't appreciate the midnight calls I'd sometimes made to him. "I have a rich life outside of work."

"And part of that life is golfing? Really?" I'd never seen the allure of the sport. My father golfed every free moment he had. Of course, living in Chicago limited the months where he could golf locally. Here in the Charleston area, golfers could get out on a course twelve months a year. "I'm not buying it, especially considering that your polo shirt is so new it still smells like a department store. As you can tell, I'm running low on chocolate. Do you want a coffee?"

"Actually, I'm here for another reason." He sighed as he gazed lovingly into the glass case. "Am I reading that sign correctly? Are you selling pumpkin seed bonbons?"

"I am." I reached in and pulled out the last one for him to eat. "Here. They're good."

He bit into it and moaned with pure pleasure. "Good is an understatement, Penn. I've never tasted anything like this. It's like a peanut butter cup, but one hundred times better."

I beamed like a proud parent. "It's the honey and the pumpkin seed. They're a match made in chocolate heaven."

"Text me when you get more in stock. I need these in my life."

"I do too," I agreed. "They are addictive, which is probably why I can't keep them in stock. I keep eating them." I drew a long breath. "If it's not my chocolate that has you visiting me, what's going on?"

He scanned the room. It was something he did often. I figured that it came with the I'm-a-cop territory. But there was something in his action today that made me uneasy.

"Do we need to talk privately?" I asked.

He sighed. "It might be best."

"Ethel? Can you watch the front for me? I'll be back in a minute." Bertie was running errands and Fletcher had asked for some time off, which was why I was on my own this morning.

"Sure thing, honey. Got some detecting to do?" Her eyes twinkled with amusement.

"No," Gibbons barked the same time I sang, "May-be."

I led the way down the narrow hallway and to the back door that opened onto my stone patio. As soon as we'd stepped outside, I regretted bringing him out here. How could I have forgotten? Harley was harboring Big Dog upstairs. Well, not *illegally* harboring him, but still...I hated lying. If Gibbons asked me directly if I knew where to find the flighty surfer, I had no idea what I'd tell him.

Before he could ask me anything, I held up my hand. "Let me try my hand at this detecting business. And you tell me how I'm doing."

"I don't know—" he started to protest. But because he also looked amused by my idea, I didn't give him the opportunity to talk himself out of playing along.

"You've been golfing with Silas Piper. He didn't invite you to walk the links with him for fun. You were there to provide him with a progress report."

"I shouldn't encourage you," he grumbled.

"Am I right?"

"You're right. But that's not what I'm here about."

I glanced up at the porch above us before asking, "Okay, shoot. What's going on?"

"I heard from Hank that you're convinced Joe Davies was murdered, and that you're investigating."

"I wish the police chief would stop tattling on me. I'm an adult. And I'm not breaking any laws or even interfering with an investigation since no one in town or the county is investigating Joe's death," I complained.

"Penn, how many times do we have to go through this? How many times are you going to risk your neck before you realize the danger isn't worth it?"

I shook my head. "No one in law enforcement thinks Joe was murdered. If that's the case, my poking around shouldn't matter at all."

"It shouldn't." He walked away from me and then abruptly spun back around. "It shouldn't matter, but there's that." He pointed to the shop. "The treasure hunters are out in full force. And they think Joe knew where the gold is. I've seen this before back in the eighties. Someone thought they'd found the location of the gold and silver coins Confederate soldiers had stolen from the Union payroll. The treasure was purportedly worth more than $100,000 back during Civil War and believed to have been buried along the banks of the Santee River. There were multiple gunfights and a few suspicious deaths as well. The archeologist who claimed to have located the treasure died in a tragic car accident before she could begin an official excavation."

"This is Camellia Beach," I said. "And Joe has been talking nonstop about the treasure for eight years now."

"He'd only talked about treasure. He'd never found a gold coin before the hurricane hit."

"He was still clutching the coin when we uncovered him," I said. "If a treasure hunter killed him, the hunter would have ripped the coin from Joe's hand."

"*If* he was murdered, which we know he wasn't. The storm surge overtook him. And now that word is out about that coin, you're overrun with treasure hunters."

"Okay. Consider me suitably warned," I said with a smile. "You're not the first one to warn me. Not more than ten minutes ago, one of the ghost hunters told me practically the same thing."

"Really?" Gibbons drew out the one word as he stroked his chin. "A ghost hunter warned you about treasure hunters? That seems...odd. And troubling. Did you get his name?"

"I did. But, hey, I thought you weren't investigating anything that had to do with Joe's death."

"I'm not." He shook his head. "I'm not here on official business. I'm here as a friend. And as a friend, I'd kind of like to know who threatened you so I can check him out."

Even though he sounded angry, I was touched. Gibbons had fussed at me more times than I liked. But he had always done it with love.

"He told me his name is Brett Handleson. He was irked that I didn't believe in ghosts."

"Never heard of him," Gibbons said. "Is he from around here?"

"I don't know. I didn't ask."

"I'll check him out when I get a chance to make sure he's not dangerous."

I brushed a kiss on his cheek. "Thank you. That'll make me feel much safer as I move forward."

"That wasn't my intent. I'm not here to encourage you to take risks."

"I know. I know. You're worried about my safety, and I appreciate it. I truly do. If I promise to keep you in the loop as well as Harley, Bertie, and Bubba, will that make you sleep better at night?"

"No," he grumbled. "You need to promise me that you'll stay away from paranoid treasure hunters. Actually, what you need to do is accept that the hurricane killed Joe. Can you do that? For me?"

"Sorry, Gibbons. I've promised Joe's daughter that I'd help her find out what happened to him. I can't go back on my word. If her father was murdered, she deserves to know the truth. It's not like the police are doing anything about it."

"That's because his death was an accident! It was—" He was about to say something else but stopped abruptly and looked up. "What's going on? Why do you keep glancing at the upstairs porch with that guilty look on your face?"

"Guilty? Me?" I struggled to keep my gaze on him when it kept trying to float back up to the underside of the porch.

"It's all over your face, Penn. I'm a professional. I've been trained to read body language. And right now, you're telling me quite a tale with those glances up to the second floor. So tell me—what's going on?"

"Oh. Nothing. I'm only wondering if Bertie is home yet." Not exactly a lie. I *had* wondered more than once when I could expect Bertie. "We're having a devil of a time sourcing the necessary ingredients for our chocolates. The suppliers are all backed up thanks to the storm. And without ingredients, we can't make chocolates to sell." Again, not a lie.

He narrowed his eyes and leaned in closer to me. My cheeks burned with guilt. I worried he could read my face as easily as if my secrets were printed in big, bold lettering across my searing hot forehead.

"For one thing, we're all out of pumpkin seeds," I said before I cracked under the pressure and blurted out that Big Dog was hiding out upstairs. I liked and respected Gibbons. And it was killing me to keep this secret from him. He had suffered through a golf game and I was sure plenty of admonishments to get the job done. "Do you know where I could buy some? Pumpkin seeds, that is? I want to make an extra-large batch of the pumpkin butter bonbons this afternoon."

He relaxed. I suspected he was remembering how much he'd enjoyed eating the bonbon I'd given him. They were really very tasty and—thankfully for me—easy to make. "Text me if you manage to get the ingredients, and I'll be on your doorstep when you open tomorrow morning to buy the lot of them."

"There won't be any new batches until I can find a way to restock my pumpkin seeds and honey, which has been proving close to impossible right now."

"Well, then, I'll ask around for you. Contrary to what some people think, I do happen to be pretty good at finding hidden things." He began to walk away.

I slumped against the wall of the building and breathed out a sigh of relief that he hadn't suspected there was another reason why I kept looking up toward Harley's apartment.

The ruse had paid off. That was, until he turned around abruptly. "Don't think you distracted me with your pumpkin seed siren song, Penn. I want you to come clean about what's going on up there." He pointed toward Harley's apartment. "I'll see you tomorrow morning. I hope you'll have those bonbons for me. And even if you don't, I'll expect you to give me the answers you've kept dodging today."

Chapter 17

At the end of the day, I flipped the *open* sign over to *closed* and went straight to the chocolate stash I kept hidden in a small drawer underneath the cash register and found a bar of pure Amar chocolate. After eating the chocolate bar bursting with the fruity flavors of the rain forest, I texted Harley and told him about my visit from Gibbons. Harley was busy filing papers for insurance claims. He returned my text, saying that he was still in downtown Charleston. We made plans to discuss everything that evening.

With that handled, I spent the rest of the day on the phone with suppliers from all over the region, desperate to get someone to deliver the ingredients we needed in order to run a chocolate business.

"Sorry. Really, sorry, ma'am. But there's nothing I can do." The man I had on the phone did sound rather distraught. He was a representative from the thirteenth company I'd called...and the last one on my list. "We won't be able to get any deliveries out to your area for at least another week. We lost nearly our entire stock when Avery took off our warehouse's roof. It'll take time to restock. We're having to ship in supplies from sources around the country."

"I see." I bit my bottom lip. The pantry's shelving in front of me was empty. No ingredients meant we couldn't rebuild our inventory of truffles and bonbons. We were even out of coffee, which meant unless Bertie had had better success on her shopping run we wouldn't be able to open tomorrow. Or the day after that. Or the day after that.

After hanging up with the supply company, I mumbled several inventive curses (most involving fudge).

"What's that?" Bertie asked as she came into the kitchen. She had a paper grocery bag in each hand. Neither looked terribly full.

"There won't be any deliveries of goods to our area for at least another week. Please tell me you had better luck than I did."

Bonbon with the Wind

She placed the shopping bags on the counter. "Unfortunately, no. The shelves are awfully bare in the grocery stores. I suppose they're dealing with many of the same suppliers you've been talking to." She pulled out two vacuum sealed bags of coffee. "Since I paid retail prices for all of this, we might not make any money on anything we sell."

I nodded as I helped unload the bags. In addition to the coffee, Bertie had purchased organic peanut butter, a couple of jars of maraschino cherries, even more jars of condensed milk, a few quarts of heavy cream, a bag of powdered sugar, a bag of brown sugar, and a bag of organic crispy rice cereal. It gave us enough ingredients to make some of our more popular chocolates.

"It's a good thing we didn't need bread or plain milk," Bertie said as she handed me several receipts. "All three grocery stores I visited are plum out of essentials."

I looked at the receipts and my eyes bugged out. She hadn't been kidding about us not making money on anything we sold. But the good news was that if we made chocolate candies from the supplies Bertie had found, we'd be able to stay open for a few days. After that, well, I wasn't sure what would happen.

I was going to have to talk with Bubba about one of those emergency business loans he'd mentioned when we'd first returned from the storm. Without considering my own situation, I'd loaned out nearly all the inheritance money I'd set aside for building repairs and unexpected business costs. The bulk of the money had gone to residents who'd needed ready cash to pay for repairs while waiting for the insurance company to send out checks. As a result, both the business and my personal bank accounts were looking rather slim. And I'd already exceeded the quarterly amount of money I could withdraw from my trust fund. Grandmother Cristobel, from my father's side of the family, guarded it like a fierce bulldog.

"I'm not sure I'm going to be able to pay for more ingredients at this price," I said. "The Chocolate Box doesn't have the reserves in the bank for it."

Bertie nodded. She knew about and had approved of the loans I'd made over the past week. "If supplies can't get into our region, doesn't that also mean farmers around the area might be having trouble getting their goods out?" She already had her cell phone in hand. "I know a few people who might be able to get us enough substitutes at wholesale prices. That'll help us stock at least a partial inventory."

"You can do that? You're a gem." I kissed Bertie on the cheek. "While you're making those calls, I'll call a few of the contractors I had make repairs on the Chocolate Box and I'll call my painter, Johnny Pane, too. I'm sure they'll all be glad to get to work on rebuilding Althea's shop and Harley's office right away."

"No!" Bertie barked so loud that I jumped back and knocked over one of the chocolate grinding mélangers.

Fletcher ran into the kitchen wielding an umbrella like a sword. "Is-is everything o-okay in here? I-I h-heard a c-crash."

"Just me being clumsy," I admitted. "What are you doing here? We're closed."

"I-I c-c-came in to help clean up," he said, his gaze avoiding mine.

"Huh…" I bit my lower lip. My gaze went back to the umbrella he still held at the ready. "Fletcher, what if there was a killer back here with us? What did you plan to do? Whack him over the head with that thing?"

"It-it g-g-gets bigger when you o-o-open it," he said as he waved the tiny accessory around with a flourish.

"But it's not open." I worried about the young man. If he charged into a truly dangerous situation armed like that, he was liable to get himself killed.

"Of course it's not open." Joe's estranged wife, Delilah waltzed into my kitchen. She came into my space as if it were the most natural thing in the world to do. "Everyone knows it's bad luck to open an umbrella inside a building."

Not everyone believes in stupid superstitions.

Bonbon with the Wind

I locked my teeth together to keep myself from saying that aloud. I still couldn't decide what it was about Delilah that made me want to crawl out of my skin, so I tried not to let my feelings toward her affect how I acted toward her. Instead of saying something childish, I let the kitchen's calming aroma of the Amar dark chocolate fill my senses.

Today, Delilah was dressed in a pale lavender pantsuit. Her silky blonde hair was perfectly styled. Everything about her—from her highly polished pumps to the way she tilted her chin up in the air just so—screamed sophistication. Perhaps that was what bothered me about her. She was too much like my father's side of the family—the judgmental ones who lived in Chicago.

"Can I help you, Delilah?" I asked, proud of how calm I sounded. "I'd offer you some chocolates, but unfortunately, we had to close early."

"That's all right," she said with a chilly smile. "I don't eat sweets. I only eat healthy, whole foods." Her lips thinned as she looked me up and down. "You might not know this, but sugar is not good for your complexion. Prematurely ages your face."

It wasn't her, I reminded myself, but my irrational reaction to her that made my nerves prickle whenever she opened her mouth. I was hearing echoes of my family in her voice, tainting my opinion against her. I doubted she made puppies into winter coats. And with that thought, I forced myself to smile. Being nice to her wasn't simply the decent thing to do. Earning her trust could save lives.

Delilah knew all about Joe and his life in Cedar's Hill—likely better than anyone else, including his daughter. She could very well be the key to helping me figure out why Joe had created a new fake life here on Camellia Beach and if that double life of his had gotten him killed. Hopefully, we'd be able to figure it all out before anyone else on Camellia Beach got hurt.

"Perhaps we could help each other," I said to Delilah. "I have a few questions about Joe's—I mean—John's life before he moved to Camellia Beach."

"I...um..." Her gaze flew over to Fletcher. "Thank you, but your assistant is already helping me sort things out. He's quite the detective. I've been impressed with his ability to see what's at the heart of these horrible goings on."

"And what's at the heart of it?" I asked. I wasn't too proud to pool our resources.

Fletcher cleared his throat several times before answering, "Clearly, Joe told some of his friends back in Virginia about how close he was getting to finding Blackbeard's treasure. One of his friends may have spoken out of turn and caused a killer to come looking to steal the treasure from Joe. Or maybe one of his friends is a greedy killer himself. We haven't been able to decide yet."

Delilah clutched her hands to her chest and sighed with delight. "Doesn't he have the loveliest speaking voice? It's so musical."

"Um...yes," I said.

"I've been trying to convince him to join my church choir," Bertie said with great enthusiasm. "He's got a rare, strong voice that any church would be proud to feature."

Fletcher adjusted his deer hunter hat and blushed.

"Did your husband know a man by the name of Sammy Duncan?" I asked her. She'd hooked her arm with Fletcher's and had moved toward the door.

She froze. Her shoulders stiffened. "Sammy Duncan." Her voice was almost a whisper, but the way she said the name it sounded like a threat.

Not willing to be cowed—even though she still intimidated me terribly—I persisted, "Cedar's Hill isn't that big of a town. Did your husband know him?"

She shook her head slowly. "That's the man who went to jail for stealing quite a fortune from the Consolidated Bank. John wouldn't get involved someone like that. He might have sold cars—and that can sometimes give a man a bad reputation—but he was honest when it came to money. He liked to tell me, 'Delilah, if you do business with a slick businessman, you deserve what you get when he takes all your money.' He didn't just say it, he lived by that rule. Always careful with his money."

"Are you saying your husband didn't know him?" I asked again.

"Of course he didn't know him. I just said that." She tugged at Fletcher's arm, as if anxious to get away from me.

"Then why do you think Sammy Duncan came into the Chocolate Box a few hours before the hurricane hit desperately searching for your husband?" I asked.

Fletcher sucked in a sharp breath. "The-the m-m-man with the tweed h-h-hat?" His head whipped around to watch Delilah's reaction.

Oddly enough, she didn't react. Not really. She drew a few slow breaths before saying, quite calmly, "I assure you I have no idea."

And that was all she would say about that.

Chapter 18

"It's louder than the county fair in here," Bertie complained later that evening as she picked up the ringing phone. "Don't mind me. I'll take this in my bedroom." Her hairless kitty darted into the room ahead of her.

Contestants on the Wheel of Fortune were shouting out letters on the TV, making it hard for anyone in the living room to hear. We'd all gathered at my apartment to decompress after a long day.

It was half-past seven. Harley was sitting on one of the armchairs. Since Trixie and Barbie were taking up most of the sofa, I perched on the chair's overstuffed arm. Althea had picked the twin to the armchair I was sharing with Harley and sat there smirking at us. She'd been describing how repairs were going at the shop. Bertie, after refusing my help, had finally been able to hire a few workmen. They'd begun work on rebuilding the damaged back wall that afternoon. Althea had read their auras and seeing that they were pleasant shades of blue had deemed them trustworthy.

"If their auras had been a cloudy green"—she shook her head—"I would have been forced to fire them on the spot. I'm so glad I didn't have to do that."

Thinking she was making a joke, I laughed.

"You can never be too careful with hiring construction workers you haven't dealt with before," she admonished.

"You could—*oh, I don't know*—ask to see their business license and bond," I said.

"Mama did that. I did one better."

"She's been reading auras forever," Harley said. He rubbed his hand up and down my back. "When we were dating, she'd decide on whether or not to go out to dinner with me based on the color of my aura."

"He used to have a volatile aura."

"You used to sneak out of the house to see me," Harley said. "And your parents terrified me."

"Yes, and you were a wild college boy." She laughed. "Don't worry, Penn. His aura has settled down considerably now. It's usually a calm shade of indigo."

I looked back at Harley and winked. "That's good to hear."

"I said *usually*. Right now, Harley, your aura is a vibrant red." She waggled her fingers at us.

"And that means?" Harley asked.

"It means Penn could soon be a very happy woman."

"I can only hope that's true," Harley whispered in my ear, making me tingle all over and wish yet again that Big Dog wasn't hiding out in Harley's apartment.

We all turned serious when Bertie returned to the living room. She looked upset.

"What's wrong?" Althea asked.

"What now?" Harley asked.

"Who died?" I asked.

Bertie hesitated before turning to me. "That was Gibbons. He said someone threatened you today?"

Trixie and Barbie cheered. I think they were cheering the winner of Wheel of Fortune and not my misfortune. The young man on the TV had just won a new car.

Harley tensed. "Someone threatened you? Who? How?"

"It wasn't really a threat. More like a warning," I said. "It wasn't much different than what Gibbons had said not ten minutes later. Both men warned me to be careful around those treasure hunters."

"A stranger came up to you and warned you to be careful? That sounds like a threat to me," he said.

Althea nodded.

"Who was it?" Harley asked.

"One of the ghost hunters, Brett Handleson." I couldn't understand why everyone was acting so concerned.

Harley shook his head. "I don't know him."

"I don't either," Bertie said.

"It doesn't matter," I told them. "Gibbons said he'd run a background check on the guy to make sure he's not a troublemaker. To tell the truth, so much has been going on today, I really didn't give Brett or his photograph of the Gray Lady much thought until now."

Althea jumped out her chair. "He had a picture of the Gray Lady? Really? And you saw it?"

"I saw a smudge on a photograph that looked more like someone's thumb than a visitor from some other plane of existence."

"Oh." She dropped back into her seat.

"Penn," Harley said in his deceptively calm lawyer voice. "I won't lie and tell you I'm not worried. Everyone knows you're asking around about Joe's murder. Maybe we need to turn over everything we know to Hank and walk away."

I understood Harley's concern. Heck, I shared it. "But we can't walk away. For one thing, I have a reputation. Even if I climbed up on the roof and shouted to world that I was going to stop trying to protect the residents of Camellia Beach from a killer, no one would believe me."

"She's right, you know," Althea pointed out.

"I wouldn't believe anything different," Trixie said. "Penn, we love you to pieces, but we all know you can't help yourself when it comes to poking your nose into other people's business."

"You say that like I'm the only one who does that around here," I complained. "Talking about your neighbors and trying to figure out who's doing what is an island-wide obsession. There are no secrets in this small town."

"Except the ones people are willing to kill to keep," Barbie said with a nod.

"Yes, I know that only too well." Just a few months ago, when asking around about Cassidy Jones' murder, someone had sent me a threatening note, warning that I'd die a horrible death if I continued to ask questions. The note, I later learned, hadn't come from the killer, but from someone else in the community who was willing to kill me if I happened to stumble upon whatever secret they were hiding. Had Joe sent that letter? I twined my fingers with Harley's. "I don't want to do anything that will cause anyone to get hurt."

We all nodded in agreement. Trixie and Barbie nodded and hummed along to the opening music of Jeopardy.

"Speaking of worrying things," I whispered in Harley's ear, "where is Big Dog tonight?"

"He thinks he knows how to find Sammy Duncan," he whispered back. "He left about an hour ago to follow up on it. I expect he'll be back and hungry in a couple of hours." He then kissed me. It was chaste, and quick, and shouldn't have made my toes curl, but it did.

"The two of you loving up on each other is sweet and all," Althea said, "but it's not going to help us figure out what happened here during the hurricane and why things are still dangerous."

"I can answer your second question," Barbie said without taking her eyes off the TV. "Whoever killed Joe still hasn't been able to find the treasure." With her next breath, she correctly answered a Jeopardy question before the contestants could even hit their buzzers.

"She's right," Althea said. "I think we need to find out as much as we can about this treasure and what Joe knew when he died."

"Sounds risky," Harley said. "There are other issues at play as well. We could follow alternative lines of questioning first."

"Like what?" Althea asked.

"Well, for one thing, we should figure out why Sammy Duncan came to town looking for Joe," I said and then explained what we knew about him and the stolen bank money that had never been found.

"We can't forget about the Gray Lady," Althea said. I gave her a hard look of disapproval. She held up her hand. "If your theory is correct, and the lady we saw wasn't a ghost, we need to find out who contacted Joe before the storm and what she told him that frightened him half to death."

"You're—surprisingly—right," I said. "But with all these threads"—I counted them off on my fingers—"pirate treasure, stolen money, secret identity, and the Gray Lady, that we need to follow, where do we begin?"

"I don't know," Bertie said. "And we're not going to figure anything out on an empty stomach. Dinner is ready."

Bertie, Trixie, and Barbie had all taken turns in the kitchen this afternoon. There had been a few minor arguments over spices. Whatever they'd made smelled absolutely delicious. Althea and I raced each other to the kitchen table. I laughed when I won. Harley came in a close third. (I think Althea tripped him.)

"Where's Bubba?" I asked after we'd all found our places around the linoleum-topped table for dinner.

"I didn't invite him." Bertie carefully placed a big tureen filled with butternut squash soup in the middle of the table along with a plastic container of sour cream. The soup's spicy aroma reminded me of autumn in my native Midwest—the cooler weather, the crunch of dry leaves under your feet, the smell of burnt firewood in the air.

"You didn't invite him?" I asked after I'd recovered from the rush of pretty memories. "I thought everything was going good between you two."

"It is," she said. She ladled soup into our bowls.

"Then…?" I prompted.

"He doesn't need to be haunting me every minute of every day," she said with a sly smile. "He's not earned that yet."

I glanced over at Harley. He'd earned the right, and then some, to follow me around anytime he wanted. In the past year, he'd put his life on the line for me more than once. And he believed in me when no one else had.

"I'm thinking the same thing," he mouthed.

We both chuckled.

"What?" Althea asked.

"Sorry." I wiped my mouth with a napkin, hoping to wipe the silly smile off my face. I didn't even know why I was smiling.

"She took the love potion that she was supposed to pick up for me. That's what's going on," Trixie complained. She folded her arms across her chest. "And now she and Harley are behaving like two hormonal teens. Next time you come over, if you could bring more of that potion, I can really use it. Must be super potent that stuff of yours."

Althea turned to me. Her eyes were bright with mischief. "It's the most potent potion you could imagine."

"Althea! You know I wouldn't take a love potion," I protested.

"No? Look at you. And Harley." She shook her head while I sputtered.

"I didn't cast a spell on Harley. That wouldn't be fair to him...or to me. We're simply—"

"Exactly," Althea said. "I've been watching the two of you all night. Anyone with a brain in her head can read the signs. The two of you have fallen in love. And love has got to be the best kind of magic, don't you agree? It makes you feel all giddy, and also a little sick."

Gracious, whenever I was around Harley, I did feel both giddy and queasy. Was that love?

"Excuse me." I pushed my chair from the table and then set my napkin beside my half-empty soup bowl. "I...um...need to get some air."

"Do you want me to come with you?" Harley asked as he started to stand.

Yes, I wanted to say. *Yes, I'd love for you to come with me and kiss me and help me pretend that I'm not scared to death because there's something going on in my heart that's making me feel as fragile as spun glass.*

"No," I said. "Stay here. Finish your dinner. I'll be back in a minute."

I hurried outside where the cicadas were singing to the last of the sunset and the silvery Spanish moss on the ancient oak trees was swaying above Camellia River's rippling waters. Stella had darted out the door with me. She sat with her warm, tiny body pressed against my leg. I closed my eyes, breathed, and thought about Blackbeard's lost treasure while pushing all that vulnerability and queasiness deep, deep down where it couldn't bother me.

While I knew I needed to go back inside, I couldn't seem to convince myself to move.

"Bertie was sure I'd find you downstairs working with your chocolate," Harley said after he came out onto the porch.

Stella growled.

"Hush, sweet puppy," I said without turning away from the darkness of the marsh and the wide Camellia River beyond it. Stella jumped up and took a bacon treat from my hand, but I could feel her excited energy as she stood next to my leg. "I didn't know where to go. I need to be inside with all of you so we can talk about what we need to do next."

"That can wait until morning," Harley said.

"I can't talk about us. Am I in love with you? I-I can't talk about it, or think about, or even—"

He took my hand and gently turned me around so I was facing him. "We don't have to talk about anything. I get it. I have my own baggage, remember?"

With the silence of the marsh, the hum of the cicadas, and the nearness of the man I may or may not have fallen hopelessly in love with, this was turning into one of the most romantic moments of my life. I put my hand on Harley's strong chest and leaned toward him. He leaned toward me.

And...

Stella bit his leg.

"Son of a—!" Harley shook his leg. I could see he was being careful to avoid kicking my dog who'd just put new holes in yet another pair of his suit pants.

"Sorry! Stella, naughty girl." I scooped her up. She wagged her tail and looked quite pleased with herself. "I don't know why she keeps doing this to you."

"I keep tell you that she doesn't like me," Harley grumbled as he put a finger through one of the tooth holes in the cuff of his pants.

"Did she hurt you?"

"No, just my pants."

"I'll get you a new pair." *Again.* "Well, I suppose I should get inside and help clean the dishes."

Before I could escape, Harley put his arm across the apartment door. "You know I'm letting Big Dog use Gavin's room. And I'm sure he's not returned from his search for Sammy. Plus, when he does get back, he's more than capable of finding his own way to bed when he comes in." He swallowed. "I hate thinking of you next door to me, sleeping on a sofa that's not nearly long enough. Besides, the sisters are talking about staying up late to watch a Newhart marathon. It'll be hours before you'll be able to get any sleep."

"What are you saying?"

"I'm saying come to my apartment and share my ridiculously oversized bed with me."

"It's a queen-sized bed. That's not ridiculously big by any standard." My heart started beating a little faster.

"Well, it's still lonely in a bed designed for two." He held out his hand. "No pressure. No expectations for tomorrow. Just you and me and whatever happens between us."

If I had taken my time and thought about it, I'm sure I would have come up with hundreds of reasons to not share his bed. So I didn't think. Not about Joe. Not about greedy treasure hunters. Not even about what my heart might or might not be feeling. Instead, I reached out my hand and let him lead to way to his apartment.

Sleeping in a bed for the first time in over a week felt like heaven. Make that heaven double dipped in dark chocolate sauce.

Chapter 19

Bertie and I came into work early the next morning to make peanut butter cups, crunchy chocolate crispy rice bars, dark chocolate cherry bonbons, and our best seller Bertie's dark chocolate sea salt caramels. I wore a silly smile on my face. And hummed.

I never hummed. But this morning I hummed. This aberration from my normal behavior amused Bertie to no end. She teased me in her kind, motherly way.

Despite our hard work, by opening time we'd only managed to fill less than half of the display counter. I hoped I was wrong, but I suspected we'd run out of candies and have to close early again today.

At least it was a Tuesday, our slowest day of the week.

Bertie, satisfied that the shop was all set for the day, returned upstairs to help the Baker sisters. Since the coffee was brewed, I poured myself a cup and stirred a couple of squares of Amar chocolate from my secret stash, and then unlocked the front door. Over the next hour, I served a couple dozen sleepy ghost hunters who had spent another night on the beach hoping to catch sight of a specter. I was surprised Brett Handleson wasn't among them. I'd overheard several of the ghost hunters commenting rather dejectedly on how they were giving up on finding the gray ghost.

I was also surprised that Ethel Crump and her friends were nowhere to be seen. I hoped their absence meant Stevie McWilson and his news team were planning on staying away as well.

As he'd promised, however, Gibbons walked into the shop a few minutes after nine o'clock. He'd ditched the brand-new polo this morning and had returned to wearing one of his starched white suit shirts. A dark gray suit jacket, which matched his pants, was slung over his arm. A serious expression made him look rather fierce.

"I'm sorry to have to disappoint you, Detective," I said. "Although Bertie was able to find a source for pumpkins and pumpkin seeds, I won't be able to get them until Thursday afternoon."

"I'm not surprised." He dropped a heavy paper bag on the counter with a thunk. "These were dang hard to get my hands on."

I peered in the bag. "Hulled pumpkin seeds?"

"Three pounds worth," he said with a sharp nod.

"H-how? Where?" I stammered. I couldn't wait to whip these seeds into pumpkin butter. "You didn't use your official position with the sheriff's office to shake down some poor farmer for these, did you?" I joked.

He tilted his head and gave me a look that made me wish I hadn't joked about the gift. "My wife's nephew has a farm in Awendaw."

"Please thank him for me. How much do I owe you for them?" I asked while I folded the sides to construct one of our gold to-go boxes.

"It's on me," he grumbled. He pulled a card from his pocket. "Here's his contact information. He said you can call anytime to discuss what else you might need."

I nodded. "Thank you. That's very kind of you."

Instead of seeming pleased that I'd accepted his gift, his eyes narrowed and the muscles in his cheeks tightened. "I consider you a friend, a friend I care for. What do you consider me to be to you?"

"A friend, of course. You've helped me more times than I can ever repay." I patted the bag of pumpkin seeds. "You're one of my dearest friends. I don't know why you feel the need to ask that."

"You don't, Penn? Really?" His frown deepened.

He didn't say anything else. It was part of his detective training. He let silences work for him.

I knew what he wanted me to say. He'd warned me that he'd return this morning. He expected me to tell him why I was acting so cagey yesterday. I was no good at keeping secrets. But this was a secret that wasn't mine to tell.

I sighed.

Did I talk or stay silent? Whose friendship did I betray? Gibbons' or Harley's? Why couldn't there be a clear-cut answer to these kinds of questions?

I started to blindly put chocolate candy after chocolate candy into the to-go box for Gibbons.

Last night, I'd fallen asleep before Big Dog had returned to Harley's apartment, and I'd left to work at the shop before he'd gotten up this morning. I could truthfully tell Gibbons that I hadn't seen the man in the past twenty-four hours. But by doing that, I was, in a way, betraying the rules of friendship.

I folded the ridiculously overstuffed box closed and held it out for him.

"You can't bribe me into ignoring whatever secret you're keeping from me," he said, even though he took the chocolates and did look pleased to get them. "Also, you're giving me too much."

"Share them back at the station." I'd give him every chocolate I had in my case if that would make things right between us. I took a deep breath and closed my eyes for a moment. "If it means anything, I do want to help you."

"Then help me. I've been chasing my own tail looking for this guy. And all I keep hearing is that he's been seen around your shop. Someone saw him last night climbing the back steps up toward your apartment."

"He's not staying at my apartment," I said in a rush. "Honest. I'm not hiding him from you. I would never do that."

"But you know who is."

"Yes," I admitted.

"It's Harley?" he said sounding like he couldn't quite believe it himself. He then slammed his hand against the counter and cursed. "He's a lawyer. He should know better."

"I didn't say anything about Harley. Why would you even think he'd do something like that?"

"Because I believed you when you told me Big Dog is not at your apartment." He turned on his heel and marched toward the door.

"Wait!" I yelled.

He didn't stop. The bell over the door clanged like a warning chime as he left the shop.

My first thought was to rush after Gibbons, but he wouldn't shirk responsibility simply because I'd asked him to. Besides, I didn't trust Big Dog. Despite everything he'd told us about Sammy and the stolen money and his protestations of innocence, niggling doubts sparked and danced in my head whenever I thought about him and his reasons for wanting to talk to Joe Davies.

The coroner had ruled that Joe had died from blunt force trauma to the head. The police had concluded that flying debris from the hurricane had killed him. But my instincts were telling me that he was murdered. If Joe had helped Sammy rob the bank, Big Dog had a powerful motive to kill him. Because of those two men, Big Dog had spent years of his life in jail.

GIBBONS IS ON HIS WAY UP, I texted to Harley. SORRY.

NO PROBLEM. BIG DOG DIDN'T RETURN LAST NIGHT. I'M WORRIED, Harley texted back. LET'S REVIEW ALL WE KNOW. I'LL COME DOWN AFTER GIBBONS LEAVES.

I took a sip of my coffee while wishing I was upstairs providing Harley with whatever emotional support I could. Fletcher came running in from the back door. His deer hunter hat was tilting at such a precarious angle it looked like it might slip off at any moment. And there were twigs and leaves stuck here and there to his jeans and his Chocolate Box T-shirt. Mud was smeared across his cheek.

"Are you okay?" I asked, more than a little alarmed.

He nodded.

"What are you doing here? You're not scheduled to work today." Since we were short on inventory, and the inventory that we did have on hand had been awfully expensive, I'd asked Fletcher if he would mind taking this week off and possibly the next. He'd readily agreed. I'd wondered about that at the time. As a rule, he didn't agree to anything I suggested so easily. "What's going on?"

He breathed hard for a long time. He clearly was trying to calm himself enough so he could talk without having his stutter get in the way. "I need you to come with me," he sang.

"I can't leave." Gibbons was with Harley. I couldn't go anywhere until I knew what was happening between them. And besides which, Bertie was upstairs with the Baker sisters. They were going through Bertie's clothes. The hurricane had destroyed most of Trixie and Barbie's wardrobes, and they were both about the same size as Bertie. Later in the afternoon, if the shop still had chocolates to sell, Bertie and I had planned to switch positions. Bertie would work at the shop while I took Trixie and Barbie to Charleston to shop on King Street for new outfits.

Fletcher tugged even harder on my arm. "Y-y-y-ou…" He glanced at the door.

"Why do I have to come?" I demanded.

He grunted then glanced at the door again.

"If it's so dire and such an emergency, you need to call Hank or Gibbons or EMS or the fire department. Gibbons is upstairs talking to Harley. You could ask him to come down." *And take the heat off Harley for a bit.* "I can't just run off and leave the shop unattended. And I'm not a detective. Neither are you."

"C-c-come." He closed his eyes, cleared his throat several times, and then heaved a deep breath. "You must," he pronounced with knife-edged precision. "I can't call the police. I'm already in over my head."

154

Stella barked.

I'd brought my little papillon along with me as I followed Fletcher down a thorny trail at the Southern end of the island. I hadn't planned to take her with us, but when I'd gone upstairs to ask Bertie if she could take over at the shop, I'd found Stella sitting on the sofa between Trixie and Barbie. The two women had taken a break from sorting through and trying on Bertie's clothes to watch an episode of Law and Order. They were snacking on pretzels filled with peanut butter while giving Stella nearly as many as they were eating. Poor Stella was already looking rounder in the middle since the two sisters had come to live with us. I had to get my tiny dog out and give her some exercise before her belly started to drag on the ground.

When I had tried to put the leash on her, she'd growled. Comfortable sofa? Steady stream of snacks? Or outside in the humidity tromping through the mud and briars? I understood her reluctance.

I hated leaving Harley alone with Gibbons.

Fletcher drove to where the island road ended and a county park capped off the island's Southern tip. He parked along the side of the road near Bubba's house.

Before leaving the car, I texted Harley, telling him where I was, who I was with, and that something was wrong.

He didn't text back right away. That worried me.

Before I could send Harley another text, Fletcher hurried me out of the car and down a narrow swampy trail. Thick clouds of mosquitoes swarmed around our faces and buzzed in our ears. The trail seemed to curl back on itself several times.

"We-we're nearly there," Fletcher promised, not for the first time.

"Are you sure we're not lost?" I asked him. A thorny bush scratched my leg, leaving a bleeding gash.

"N-nearly there," he repeated.

We had to climb over downed trees and jump over puddles so large they supported sea life. Just as I was beginning to give up hope that we'd ever escape this confounding trail, we emerged from the canopy of palmetto, pine, and live oak trees where the land met the marsh. While I'd thought we were going around and around in circles, I could now see that we'd in fact traveled a fair distance down the island. Where we were standing, I could see Camellia's southern tip.

But it wasn't the geography that caught my attention, it was the sight of Delilah Fenton. She was dressed in an outfit someone might wear on safari through the African plains, complete with pith hat with mosquito netting draped down around her face. Fletcher and Delilah made quite a pair with their silly hats. But then I swatted a mosquito biting the tip of my nose and wished I had her hat.

It wasn't her choice of headgear that puzzled me, though. Or the fact that we'd found her, here, at the end of a ridiculously twisty marsh trail. It was the fact that she was kneeling next to a man who was lying face down in the marsh's tall spartina grass and pluff mud.

Fletcher cleared his throat.

Delilah jerked her head in our direction, her eyes jumpy and as frightened as a startled rabbit's. Was she trying to figure out the best way to run away?

"What happened here?" I asked while Stella, bless her, sat glued to my side, not even barking. This was my pup's second encounter with a dead body in as many weeks. Her tiny body trembling as she remained pressed against my leg.

"I found him like this," Delilah said.

"And why didn't you call the police?" I reached into my pocket to do that right away.

"We can't!" She lunged at me to grab the phone. "We can't tell anyone!"

I held my phone out of reach. "Why not?" The two of them had told *me*, for heaven's sake. Something I wished they hadn't.

I could just imagine how Gibbons was going to fuss and cuss when he found out about how many people had walked around his crime scene before he got out here. Was the body in the marsh Big

Dog's? Harley had said his friend was missing. It was probably him, which only made things worse. "We can't just leave him in the marsh."

Stella barked as if she disagreed. She jumped up and tugged on the leash, urging me to go back the way we'd come.

"I..." Delilah held up her hands and looked over at Fletcher.

"S-s-she tampered with the murder victim," Fletcher said.

"Hold up now." This kept getting better and better. "How did we go from finding a dead body in the marsh to tampering with evidence?"

Stella tugged at the leash even harder. I was starting to agree with her. This wasn't a place I wanted to be. If not for Fletcher's look of complete horror, I might have let Stella take the lead and run away with her.

"S-she h-handled the m-murder weapon." He pointed to a large pipe smeared with blood on one end that had been tossed into the bushes growing on high ground.

"If you picked up the murder weapon, why did you throw it so far away from the body?" I asked Delilah.

"I didn't throw it. Fletch did. I could have never thrown it that far. It's too heavy."

I turned to Fletcher. "You handled the murder weapon as well? Are you crazy? Have you learned nothing from all of those mystery novels you read?" He'd read dozens and dozens in the past few months as *research*.

"I-I-I p-p-panicked." By the way his upper lip was quivering he was clearly still in a full-blown state of panic.

"So, let me get this straight. Both of you have handled the murder weapon, and that's why you don't want to report the murder to the police. Is that correct?" I asked.

Fletcher gave a tight nod.

Delilah glowered.

"Not wanting to call the police doesn't make a lick of sense," I said. "You tell Byrd or Gibbons or both of them. They might be upset that you messed up their crime scene, but they'll understand. It's not like you have a motive to kill some random guy you just happened upon when walking in the marsh." Even as I said it, a sick feeling twisted and gurgled in my stomach. "Oh, my goodness. This isn't a random guy you found. And you weren't just taking a stroll in the marsh. You were here for a reason."

"T-t-tell her," Fletcher ordered. Despite the stammer, he sounded quite forceful.

"It's Sammy Duncan," she wailed.

I didn't know if I should feel relieved or horrified. "You mean the guy you didn't know?"

"I..." Again, she looked over to Fletcher.

"She knew him," he said.

"I see." There was very little I loathed more than being lied to. My desire to help them cooled even more.

Honestly, I was feeling quite put out. On the short car ride to the end of the island, I had tried to get Fletcher to explain what was going on. But he'd stammered. Stella had barked. And I'd given up, figuring I'd find out soon enough. Now, however, I wished I'd insisted he had prepared me that we were on our way to see a dead body and that the dead body was the same Sammy I'd been hoping to find...alive...and willing to talk about why he'd come to the island in search of Joe.

If I'd known the truth, I wouldn't have joined them out here, helping them muck up a crime scene, while knowing that Delilah had lied to me. Instead, I would have insisted he called the police and had them join him on this hike through Camellia Beach's thick maritime forest.

"We're calling the police," I said. I started to bring up the screen for my phone's quick dial list.

"Wait!" Delilah cried. "There's more. I touched the body. I..." She held up a piece of paper. "I took this from his pocket."

"Were you here when this happened?" I knew Fletcher was young and delusional about his detective skills, but I couldn't believe he could be this sloppy.

Fletcher looked down at his feet. "I-I w-w-wasn't here."

At least there was that.

"I called him after I found Sammy," Delilah explained.

"Did you kill him?" I asked her.

"No!" She lunged at me again. Before I could react, her wet, muddy hands were on my shoulders and she started shaking me. "No! I followed him. I had to. He had the map."

Stella, bless her, did what Stella does best. She jumped up and bit Delilah on the knee.

Delilah shrieked and released me. "Did your dog just bite me?"

"Probably. She's protective, so I suggest you don't attack me again." I attempted to brush the mud off my shoulders. The pretty turquoise and purple batik sundress Althea had given me for my birthday looked stained beyond repair. "Please—and without grabbing me and making me think you go around assaulting people, and maybe even killing them—tell me why you followed Sammy. And what you think is on that map?"

Did I expect her to tell me the truth? Not really. Still, I wanted to hear what she had to say. But before I let her answer, I picked my phone off the ground and pushed the quick dial button for Detective Gibbons. As bad luck would have it, it went to voice mail. I left him a message that there was trouble down on the Southern end of the beach and that he needed to call me ASAP. I then pushed the quick dial button for Camellia Beach's police department and reported that there'd been a murder and gave the location.

It was a sad commentary on my life that I had not one, but *two* police departments in my short quick dial list.

"Okay, now talk," I said to Delilah. "Was Sammy alive when you found him?"

"No! How many times do I have to tell you? I didn't kill him."

"She didn't," Fletcher answered.

"How do you know?" I asked him without tearing my gaze away from someone who could be a real danger in front of me.

"She called me in a panic, and I believe her," he sang.

"That's not good enough for me. A person could panic after killing in a fit of rage." I then asked Delilah, "So, you found him. Was he lying in the mud on his stomach like that?"

I still hadn't taken a good look at the body, and I really didn't want to.

"No." She cleared her throat. "I rolled him over when I was checking his pockets. Since he was in the water, I was worried that the map would get ruined."

"And what was so important about this map?" I asked.

She tightened her lips. At first, I thought she wasn't going to tell me. "It was John's map," she grudgingly admitted.

It took me a moment to realize she was talking about Joe.

"Is it a treasure map?" I asked.

Delilah tucked the paper into a pocket. "They're all after it. But they don't deserve it."

"Who is after it?" I asked.

"Who isn't looking for it?" she said and gestured around us.

"Blackbeard's treasure?" I asked.

Instead of answering, she barked a sharp laugh.

At the same time, sirens wailed.

Her eyes widened. "You can't tell anyone about the map," she said in a harsh whisper. "No one can know I have it."

"No, I'm not doing that," I said. "I'm going to tell Byrd and Gibbons everything I know."

"Then get out of my way." She shoved me. I managed to catch myself before falling into the marsh next to Sammy. She ran down the path toward the approaching police officers, I presumed.

"W-w-w-hat d-d-d-did you do that f-f-for?" Fletcher stammered. "Y-you scared her off."

160

"I'm doing what is right because this is a murder investigation. *Two* murder investigations. And the only thing I know about this woman is that she lied to me when she told me that her husband didn't know Sammy. I'm not going to cover for her when, for all we know, she killed her husband and then killed Sammy to get that map she just ran off with. Is it a treasure map to Blackbeard's gold or to a stash of stolen money?" I asked him.

He shrugged. His lips quivered. I couldn't help but wonder if he was lying to me as well. I hated to think he might be.

A few minutes later, several uniformed officers plus Marion Olrich with one of her assistants stepped out of the woods. The ghost hunter Brett Handleson followed them. He remained at the edge of the forest while the police rushed over to the body in the marsh.

"What are you doing here?" I demanded of Brett.

"I heard the call go out on the police scanner and thought I should follow along and check it out. You know, in case the Gray Lady has struck again."

They'd taken the same path as Delilah had run down. But when I asked if anyone had seen her, no one had, which was odd. As far I knew, that was the only path from the marsh back to the road.

Where did she go? Joe's widow had disappeared.

"*Like a ghost,*" Brett whispered.

Chapter 20

"Delilah is a ghost," I mused.

"What's that?" Brett asked.

"Delilah is the Gray Lady." I don't know why I hadn't realized it earlier. That was why she'd looked familiar the first time we met. It was because I *had* seen her before.

"Charity Penn," the county detective interrupted us. He walked over to where I was standing at the edge of the marsh. After jotting my name into his notebook, he introduced himself as Detective Jerome Prioleau. It was the same kind of notebook Frank Gibbons used. But that was where the similarity to the two men ended.

Unlike Gibbons with his hands-on approach, Prioleau had declined to go near the body. Instead, he'd let the crime scene techs take charge. He was much younger and thinner than Gibbons. He had a hungry look in his eyes that unnerved me. "Interesting that I'd find you near a murdered man who—"

"I called it in," I pointed out.

"Hmmm," he said without emotion as he wrote some more in his notebook. He then flipped back through its pages while silently reading his notes. "You were also the one who discovered Joe Davies' body?"

"My dog found him," I corrected. "I think she'd followed the smell."

"Interesting." Prioleau flipped through his notebook one more time before adding more notes to it. "You seem to be on hand whenever someone is murdered in this town."

"Where is Gibbons?" Gibbons knew me well enough that he wouldn't be treating me like a suspect.

"*Your* friend has been assigned by the sheriff to find some rich man's missing brother," he said. "*I'm* the one the Sheriff has assigned to figure out what's really going on out here in Camellia Beach. Good thing, too. I pulled several cases Detective Gibbons has worked on lately—all out here on this beach of yours. It's interesting how there have been so many murders on such a small island in the past year. Very interesting. And somewhat troubling, don't you agree?"

He stared as if expecting me to confess to something. Since I had nothing to confess, I kept my mouth shut.

"You and Detective Gibbons have developed a friendship, haven't you?" The way he said it made our relationship sound suspect.

"I consider nearly everyone who comes to my shop a friend," I said stiffly. "That's the kind of community Camellia Beach is. Friendly."

"But you're new to the area. You moved to town less than a year ago and then a friend of yours was murdered."

"No. I moved to town *after* my friend was murdered."

He didn't say anything for quite a long time. Was he waiting for me to say something else? Well, if that was the case, I hoped he was prepared to wait forever.

Finally, he said, "Interesting."

No, it's not interesting, I wanted to tell him. It was sad and tragic, and I still blamed myself for my friend's death. But I didn't say any of that since none of it was related to the murdered man lying not ten feet away, and I didn't want him to think it was.

"Why would you want to move here? This town must hold bad memories for you considering how one of Camellia Beach's residents killed a friend of yours."

"My grandmother left me the family chocolate shop in her will," I ground out. "And if you know everything else about me—as it seems you do—you must know that as well."

A muscle in Prioleau's jaw twitched. He looked down at his notebook again. I wondered what he had in there that he found so fascinating. "I've heard that there has been a sharp increase in suspicious deaths since you've moved to Camellia Beach. I wonder why."

"You've been talking to Police Chief Byrd?" I asked.

"Perhaps. I've also heard that you've been asking around about Sammy Duncan. Why?"

"Because Sammy was searching for Joe Davies before the hurricane, and I was the unlucky one to find Joe after the hurricane," I said, working extremely hard at keeping my anger from flaring. "I feel like you're trying to goad me into saying something that would prove to you that I had a beef against Sammy and killed him."

"Did you?" he jumped in and asked. His eyes glittered with that hunger I'd noticed earlier.

"I called the police about his death. I wasn't the one who found him in the marsh. Delilah Fenton found him. She called Fletcher, who called me. And for your information, I want to find out why Joe was murdered and do whatever I can to keep anyone else from getting hurt. Yes, I wanted to talk to Sammy. I wanted to know why the first thing he did after getting out of jail for robbing the bank where he'd worked was to drive to Camellia Beach in search of someone he supposedly didn't know that well. And yes, when I called the police, I called thinking I was going to cooperate and share everything I knew. But the way you've been talking to me, I wonder if I shouldn't shut up now and call my lawyer."

He flipped through his notebook some more, jotting notes down here and there. Once he was done, he looked up at me again. "Yes, now would be a good time to call your lawyer."

"He was trying to rattle you," Harley said.

"Well, it worked." I sipped the glass of buttery smooth merlot wine Harley had ordered. After I'd called him from the crime scene, he'd directed his secretary, Miss Bunny, to cancel his afternoon schedule. He'd then met me at the Southern end of the island. After having a few words with Hank Byrd and then with the unfriendly Detective Prioleau, he took me to the Low Tide Bar and Grill. On the way, he'd called everyone in our little posse, telling them that we needed to talk about what had happened.

"Before we talk about that," I said. "I need you to tell me what happened between you and Gibbons."

"I told Gibbons everything," Harley admitted. "I told him that Big Dog had been staying in Gavin's room. I told him about the stolen money and Big Dog's plea deal. And I told him that Big Dog has been missing since last night."

"Big Dog is still missing?" That wasn't good news. "How did Gibbons react?"

"Not well." Harley grimaced. "I kept my head, though, and reminded him that Big Dog wasn't formally wanted by the police. He wasn't breaking any laws by avoiding his brother."

"Poor Gibbons. The sheriff has put him in a difficult spot. I wished he'd assigned Prioleau to search for Big Dog so Gibbons was free to investigate Sammy's murder."

"I suspect Gibbons would agree with you about that. He was eating those chocolates from your shop like an ex-smoker chews gum. I don't think I've ever seen him so jittery."

"I just hate that he's upset with us. He's our friend. I hope you didn't overdo your lawyer voice. I know it can drive me crazy when you use that tone on me."

Harley smiled wanly at that. "It's not like he could disagree with me. But don't worry. I didn't push things too far. I even promised him that I'd give him a call the minute I heard from Big Dog."

"You did?" That both pleased and surprised me.

"I did. This farce has gotten too dangerous. We need to get everyone together and talking."

I agreed.

"Wait. Something just occurred to me that doesn't make any sense," I said. "Gibbons said someone saw Big Dog coming up the back stairs toward your apartment last night."

"He told me that as well," Harley said, shaking his head. "I tried to get him to tell me who told him that. It can't be right. Big Dog didn't sleep in Gavin's bed. And I'm a light sleeper. I would have heard him come in."

"You don't think your friend is responsible for what happened to Sammy?" I asked.

"No," he answered without thinking about it. "No. He wouldn't kill anyone. That's just not who he is."

"Are you sure?" I asked.

"Yes." Again, he answered very quickly. "What would killing Sammy do for him? He's in town to prove his innocence. Killing the only man who might be able to do that would be insane."

"I've always thought revenge often came from a kind insanity. Isn't that what writers such as Edger Allen Poe and Stephen King have taught us?"

"That's fiction, Penn. Not reality," he countered. But I'd made him smile. Seeing it made my stomach feel all fluttery. Gracious. This love thing felt awfully like coming down with the flu.

"Still…" Even though Harley trusted his friend completely, I wasn't ready to blindly accept Big Dog's innocence. I also didn't want to argue with Harley about it, so while I kept Big Dog at the top of my suspect list, I quickly changed the subject. "Why couldn't Gibbons be the detective investigating Sammy's murder? I thought he was kind of like the sheriff's department's permanent liaison with Camellia Beach."

"It doesn't work that way. Investigations generally get assigned on a rotating basis," Harley explained. "It's been our luck that Hank trusts Gibbons and requests for him by name. But with Gibbons being subbed out to do Silas Piper's bidding, the sheriff assigned the first available detective."

Bertie and Bubba joined us at the table.

"So that's how we got stuck with Detective Friendly-Pants?" I asked.

"I'm afraid so," Harley said.

"Stuck with who?" Bubba asked as he took the chair next to mine.

We told Bubba and Bertie about Detective Prioleau and how he'd interrogated me.

"Who is Jerome Prioleau?" Bertie asked as she squinted at the card the detective had given me.

I'd lived in Camellia Beach long enough to know she wasn't asking us to explain again that he was the detective heading up the murder investigation. She was asking about his family. She wanted to know where he came from. Was he from the Charleston area? Or had he moved here *from off*? Who were his kin?

"Never heard of the guy," Bubba said with a shrug.

"I wasn't asking you." Bertie swatted him on his arm.

"Hank said he's new," Harley said. "From what I can tell, he's ambitious. A real go-getter. I've never worked with him personally."

"Who's his mamma?" Bertie asked somewhat sharply. I imagined she'd taken that tone since the others at the table had apparently missed the point of her original question.

"I can try and find out," Harley offered. "As I said, I've never worked with him and only met him when I drove out to make sure he didn't hold Penn any longer than he needed to."

Bertie nodded seemingly pleased to know we'd all soon know about Prioleau's family history, which in the Lowcountry could be an amazingly powerful tool.

"We need to watch that detective," Fletcher interjected from across the room. "He's a treasure hunter."

Instead of joining us at our table, Fletcher went straight to the bar and ordered a shot of whiskey. He swallowed the shot, wiped his mouth with the back of his hand, and then tapped the bar top, signaling he wanted another. The bartender refilled his cup.

"How do you know he's a treasure hunter?" I called to him.

He drained the glass a second time before answering. "He kept asking me about what I knew about Blackbeard's treasure. L-l-like a d-d-dog with a bone, he was. He kept pressing me about the treasure instead of asking me about Sammy. It was unnerving. Oh, he also asked quite a lot about you. Sounded to me like he thought you had a reason to want Sammy dead, like he thought you went around killing people in the town."

"And exactly what did you tell him, young man?" Bertie stood and propped her fists on her hips.

Fletcher snorted. "I told him the truth—that P-P-Penn has a temper."

I wanted to scream at him that I didn't have a temper. But that would have been counterproductive. "I now know why this detective thinks I'm guilty. Thanks for that, Fletcher."

"I only t-t-told him the t-t-truth."

"You made our girl here look guilty as sin," Bubba said.

"I told the t-t-truth." Fletcher growled. "Wh-wh-what else d-d-d-do you think I'd do?"

"You know Penn would never hurt anyone," Bertie said.

Fletcher shrugged. "*Do* I know that?"

Harley squeezed my hand. It was a gentle reminder to not make a scene in such a public place. I nodded in agreement.

Fletcher was the best employee I'd ever hired, but he'd come to work for me with a massive chip on his shoulder. While he often did things before I needed to tell him what to do, he acted offended whenever I'd tell him to do something around the shop. Bertie had suggested that he behaved that way because he was young and still thought he knew more than the rest of the world.

He certainly thought he knew more about sleuthing than anyone else.

Was that the problem? Had I offended him when I'd suggested Delilah Fenton might be guilty of murder? He's been spending quite a lot of time with Delilah lately. And I'd all but accused her of hitting Sammy on the back of the head and killing him in a fit of anger.

"We've been both working on this problem from different angles," I said to Fletcher. "Perhaps it's time we pooled our knowledge so we can figure out what's really going on."

Fletcher downed another shot of whiskey. "Y-y-you chased h-h-her away. And n-n-now you n-n-need me to f-f-find her. I-I'll n-not let you u-u-use me like that." He slammed the glass down. Without even glancing in our direction, he marched out of the bar.

"Delilah is an interesting piece of the puzzle," Harley said, as he frowned at the closed door.

"She's an interesting piece of something else to Fletch." Bertie touched the side of her nose. "But if you ask me, I think she's using him for something other than his youth."

"You don't actually mean they're romantically involved?" How had I missed that?

"When Bubba was driving me home Sunday evening, we saw her step outside of Fletch's cottage dressed in nothing but one of his Chocolate Box T-shirts."

"Don't know why the cub would be interested in an old woman like that." Bubba shook his big head with dismay until Bertie smacked him on the arm. "I mean, it's not my place to judge." She smacked him on the arm again. He turned to look directly at Bertie. His mouth spread into such an alluring smile that even my stomach flipped. "I mean, my love, that woman has to be at least twenty years older than you."

Bertie harrumphed. At the same time, the corner of her mouth turned up just enough to show she wasn't immune to his charms.

If I had to guess, Delilah was in her early fifties. Bertie, on the other hand, was somewhere in her mid-seventies. Like many women in the South, her exact age was a closely guarded secret.

It wasn't Delilah's age that got me wondering, though. What I wanted to know was what she was doing with Fletcher. Was she honestly attracted to him? Despite his prickly nature, I supposed he wasn't a bad catch. It was Delilah's timing—so soon after learning of her husband's death—that made me think she might be using him. But for what purpose?

She claimed she wanted justice, but she was acting more like a jilted lover than a woman mourning a man she'd loved and genuinely missed. And I couldn't help but think about what Joe's daughter had said about Delilah. Mary had painted her stepmother as a cold-hearted, money-hungry harpy.

"Delilah is the Gray Lady," I told them.

"What?" All three of them asked at once. Harley grabbed my hand.

"Are you…feeling okay?" he asked gently.

"I'm not losing my mind," I assured them. "More like coming back into my right mind. It was Delilah I saw talking with Joe on the beach that last day anyone saw him alive. I'm sure of it. Which means she's been lying to us. She knew her husband had changed his name and moved to Camellia Beach. And she spoke to him before he was killed."

Did she kill him? As I sipped my wine, I had to admit that it would be wrong to jump to conclusions. During my childhood, my father had gone through a succession of wives. Some of them had been horrible. One, I'm still convinced was the devil herself. But most of his ex-wives had been vilified mainly because it was easier to blame them for the failed marriage than my father, who we'd all still had to live with and love—kind of. Had Mary done something similar to her stepmother?

"Delilah told me she followed Sammy out to the marsh," I told my friends. I ran my finger along the edge of the wineglass, making it sing. "I bet she was hoping he'd lead her to the treasure."

"Or perhaps she simply wanted to hit Sammy over the head with a metal pipe," Bubba said.

"A blow to the head—that's also how Joe died," Harley mused aloud.

I turned to him. "You're right! The two men died the same way. And I suspect after we find either Delilah or Big Dog, we'll learn enough about the events leading up to the murders to be able to prove which one is a killer."

Chapter 21

"It's not safe out here for me. It's not safe for anyone," Joe had warned. Althea and I had thought he'd been talking about the hurricane. But what if he'd been talking about something else?

Delilah had claimed she didn't know where Joe had been living until she saw the photograph that ran with his obituary in the local newspaper. At the time I'd believed her. But now I was convinced that she had confronted Joe on the beach the morning of the hurricane.

Why had she lied about it? And what did she tell him that had upset him so much that he was shaking by the time he'd reached us? Was it about the map?

Delilah had also claimed she didn't know Sammy. Another lie.

Thinking about Delilah's lies made me think about Althea. There was an empty chair at our table. I missed her advice and knowledge of the island, especially whenever there was a lull in our discussion. It was almost as if we were all falling silent at the point in a conversation when she would talk.

"Where is Althea?" I asked. Had no one invited her?

"She had her hands full at the shop this morning. I didn't want to disturb her," Bertie said.

"I'll have to go talk with her this afternoon. She might have some insights about things that we're not seeing," I said.

Bertie smiled at that. "Child, that would make her day."

After eating a hearty po' boy sandwich that was overflowing with tangy coleslaw and fat pieces of fried shrimp and talking through everything we knew about Joe's death and Sammy's murder, I felt drained. Coming across dead bodies still upset me. I don't think I would ever get used to the shock of it. I needed time alone to pull myself together. I needed to smell the sweet scents that I could only find in the Chocolate Box's kitchen.

Bonbon with the Wind

Harley understood. He drove me back to the shop. Before we parted, he gave me a long kiss. "I'll be upstairs working on my computer. In shouting distance, if need be."

Bertie had offered to join me in the kitchen. While I appreciated the offer—we did have an entire inventory of chocolates to make before tomorrow—and I did need all the help I could get, I asked her to wait a few hours. She hurried off to help Althea with the hurricane clean up. Bubba went with her.

Trixie and Barbie had told me not to worry about taking them shopping for clothes today. They'd even volunteered to walk Stella. Though discovering dead bodies wasn't something many people had experienced in a lifetime, everyone around me seemed to understand that I needed time and solitude to recover from the shock.

Since we'd sold out of inventory that morning, Bertie had closed the Chocolate Box shortly after I'd left with Fletcher. The lights were off. I moved quickly through the back hallway, heading straight for the kitchen, where I turned on every light. The overhead florescent lights hummed loudly. The background noise drowned out the imaginary ghosts whispering in my ears about murder and treasures and to *watch out*.

After silently scolded myself for getting so worked up, I pulled down a large metal mixing bowl from an open shelf. It still amazed me how spending time in the kitchen working with my chocolate made me feel so calm. If Althea had been here, she would have told me it wasn't the chocolate but the spirit of my maternal grandmother Mabel Maybank, watching over me and placing her hand on my shoulder, that allowed this feeling of peace to pass through me.

I, in turn, would have told Althea that she was delusional. And then I'd wonder why my thoughts kept going back to ghosts. Althea would have suggested that the universe was trying to tell me something important and that I should listen.

I sighed. I missed my friend.

I wanted to do something nice for her.

While I'd always been a disaster in the kitchen, I did have a handful (a tiny handful) of recipes I'd mastered over the years. Stepmother Number Two, who'd tried to mother me for the short time she'd been married to my father, had taught me her family's secret brownie recipe. The deliciously simple ingredients included sweetened condensed milk, graham crackers, and of course chocolate chips. I hadn't made the recipe since I'd moved to Camellia Beach, but thinking of Althea and how hard she'd been working to rebuild her crystal shop, made me think about Stepmother Number Two and how patiently she'd worked to teach me this recipe. The secret to having the brownies come out right was not to overwork the batter.

Since I didn't want to give Althea brownies with the same rock-hard structure as the bricks they were using to rebuild the shop's back wall, I found a large wooden spoon in a drawer. I used it to mix the ingredients by hand. And because this was something special for Althea, I pulled down the large ancient wooden box that held the rare and wonderful Amar chocolate bars. These bars of chocolate were worth more than their weight in gold. As I chopped up two of the bars and added them to the brownie mixture, the deep, tropical scents of the rich dark chocolate made me dizzy with pleasure.

The oven timer beeped. I dropped the bowl I'd been washing back into the sink and hurried over to the oven. One of my downfalls when it came to baking was that I often forgot to take the food out of the oven before it turned into a charred mess. When I was cooking with inferior ingredients, the loss of a tray of brownies would be an inconvenience, at best. Adding the Amar chocolate to the batter upped the stakes considerably. It'd taken the combined efforts of a village to grow, harvest, and ferment the beans used to make the chocolates I'd mixed into the brownies. Burning them would be a crime.

I was just pulling the pan out of the oven when there was a sharp tap-tap-tap on the kitchen window. Startled, I nearly dropped the hot brownies. As it was, I ended up burning my fingertips when I caught the hot pan with the hand not wearing the oven mitt. I made sure to set the brownies safely on the stainless-steel countertop before turning to investigate the window tapping.

"Mary?" I said with a gasp.

Joe's daughter was standing at the window. Everything about how the stiff way she held herself to how her wide eyes darted left and right scared me. She waved rather frantically when she saw I'd spotted her. I rushed over to the window and opened it.

"Mary?" I repeated. "What's going on?"

"I need to talk to you."

"About what?"

"About my father's murder," she said. "Can I come in?"

I glanced around the kitchen. The brownies needed to cool in the pan for at least fifteen minutes before I could cut them. The mélangers were grinding cacao beans. The batch of pumpkin seed butter balls I'd rolled were cooling in the fridge, waiting to be dipped into dark chocolate. Now was a good time to take a break.

"Just a minute," I told her. "I'll be right out."

On the way to the back door, I texted Harley and let him know that I was meeting Mary on the back patio. An hour ago, such a text would have seemed silly and totally unnecessary. Now, after staring at Sammy's dead body in the marsh, I wanted to put on a suit of armor before stepping outside to talk with anyone.

"I heard my stepmother killed Sammy Duncan," Mary said in place of a greeting. She was breathing hard. "I heard you confronted her about it."

I nodded. I shouldn't have been surprised that someone had already told her about Sammy's murder and Delilah's role in finding him. While the residents of Camellia Beach rarely gossiped to outsiders, I could understand why an islander had told Mary. The matter, after all, did concern her and her father's death.

There were so many suspicions and clues I could have told Mary. Her large guileless eyes seemed to plead with me that I confess everything I knew. And yet, even though I was working on becoming a better person, I still had trouble trusting...well...anyone. Even someone who appeared as innocent as Bambi in the woods.

"Why do you think Sammy was murdered?" I asked her.

She dabbed a tissue to her damp cheeks. "He must have known something about the money. That's all my stepmother cares about—money. She'd lie, cheat, steal, and apparently kill for it."

"The money? Do you mean the money Sammy stole from the bank he worked for in Cedar's Hill? Or the pirate treasure? If it's the stolen goods she's looking for, why would she or anyone think your father had it? How in the world would he have ended up with it?"

She shook her head. "I've been thinking about that quite a lot, you know? Dad disappeared shortly after Sammy was arrested. And as soon as Sammy got out of jail, someone killed my father. Did Sammy kill him? Or did my stepmother? If only we could find the money Sammy took. I'm sure it would explain what happened to my father. Wouldn't it?"

She was watching me with those big vulnerable doe-eyes as if expecting me to have the answers she needed. My heart ached for her. She'd not only lost her mother to cancer, her father had run away, presumably, because he loved riches more than his family. And she'd found him only to discover he'd been murdered.

But there was something about Joe's history that didn't sit right for me. Joe had lived like a man on a tight budget. His rented cottage was small. He never purchased new clothes. His treasure hunting tools were all secondhand. And when he'd come into the Chocolate Box, he'd only buy one chocolate at a time. That wasn't the lifestyle of a man with a fortune at his fingertips. Nor was it the lifestyle of a man who loved money more than family.

True, his search for Blackbeard's treasure had been an obsession. He'd acted desperate to find...something.

"What if your father didn't have the stolen money?" I wondered aloud.

Before she could answer, Harley came down the stairs. He'd changed out of his business suit and was wearing a pair of black board shorts and a gray T-shirt that pulled tight across his muscular chest. The sight of him in his surfer gear made me sigh with a mixture of attraction and irritation. No matter what that man wore, he always looked irresistible.

"You must be Mary Fenton," he said and took her hand in his.

"Um...I...am..." she managed. Her cheeks turned pink. "And...you...are?"

"He's my friend and lawyer," I said, again wishing for a word to describe our relationship that didn't sound as juvenile as boyfriend or as vulgar as lover. I was also wondering why he was still holding onto her hand. Mary was petite, and soft, and very pretty. I didn't feel jealous of her appearance until I saw how she was looking at *my* Harley and how he was touching *her* hand.

"I'm Harley Dalton." Was it my imagination, or had his voice gotten deeper as he spoke his name? At least he'd finally released her hand.

"Pleased to meet you." Mary's already pink cheeks blushed a shade pinker.

"I told Mary that I'd help get some answers about her father's death," I told him, rather needlessly, since we'd already discussed Mary and her family quite thoroughly.

"I am sorry for your loss. It must have come as quite a shock to you to simultaneously learn your father was living here under an assumed name and that he'd died during the storm."

She looked down and nodded. "It's...hard..."

"Mary and I were discussing the possibility that her father didn't have the stolen money. Perhaps Sammy thought he did. Perhaps others thought the same. But, as I explained to Mary, her father didn't live as if he had access to riches at all."

"That's true," Harley agreed. "The residents out here on Camellia Beach aren't a wealthy lot, and your father was living at about the middle-range of our general lifestyle. We'd all assumed he'd retired with a tiny retirement fund. Many professional fishermen put so much of their income back into their boats and equipment, there's rarely much left over for retirement. And that was how he lived."

"But he was never a fisherman, professional or otherwise," Mary pointed out.

"No," Harley agreed. "He wasn't."

"What's more," Mary said as she fidgeted with her tissue, "he'd always enjoyed having nice things. Well, he did before he ran from *that woman*. Do you think he'd experienced some kind of attack, like a stroke that affected his mind?"

"It didn't seem as if his mind was addled," Harley said. "He was quite the local expert on Blackbeard and his treasure."

But was that correct? I didn't want to say anything about it in front of Mary. She was already dealing with enough hard truths about her father. But according to Bertie, Joe Davies had shown signs of memory loss. Was it dementia? Or Alzheimer's? It wasn't something the coroner had checked for in trying to figure out a cause of death, so we might never know.

"Then perhaps he simply wanted a break from his old life." Mary's shoulders sagged. "Maybe he finally learned he couldn't find happiness in the lavish lifestyle his wife had wanted to live, so he came here to see what it'd be like to live a simpler lifestyle. Perhaps he wanted a clean break from his former life, a break"—she sniffled— "even from me."

"As hard as it might be to accept, that could be the case," Harley said using his calming lawyer voice that when directed at me often made me want to scream. "He wanted peace and a break from the business world. It's common around here. In fact, that description fits over half our population."

Mary smiled wanly. "I hope he found a paradise here." She gazed out over the marsh. "But what if he did have the money? What if he was waiting for Sammy?"

The tall spartina grasses were in the process of turning gold. By winter they'd be a soft brown. It was rather stunning to look at, with the deep blue water and the flecks of silver and golden sunlight dancing on the river's ripples. I don't know if the stooped-back Joe, with his quest for pirate treasure, ever slowed down long enough to fall in love with the island's natural beauty. But for me, this place was a heaven on earth.

"Can't you do something?" she pleaded. "First my father and now Sammy. I feel like I'm living in a nightmare, and I can't wake up. I want to wake up and have them alive again." She grabbed Harley's arm. "Please, please help me find out what's happening. Please, help me make this nightmare end."

Harley, with the gentlest voice I'd ever heard him use, promised he'd do his earnest best, which seemed to placate her.

After she'd left, I turned to Harley.

"She's pretty," I said, feeling a pinch of jealousy. I didn't have a good track record when it came to relationships. In the past, I'd dated a man who'd wanted my father to hire him, a man who'd cheated on me with his secretary the entire time we were going out, and a man who'd wanted me dead. While I knew I should trust Harley, part of me couldn't.

"I suppose you could say she's pretty," he said, "if you like small and mousey. Personally, that's not the kind of woman who revs my motor. She acted awfully upset about Sammy's death. And yet, she claims she barely knew him. And her grief feels a little overdone, don't you think?"

"I imagine it's her anger at her stepmother that's driving her emotions. She thinks the woman is ruining everything in her life."

"Well, then, I suppose our next step will be to figure out if she's right. Did Delilah drive Joe away? Or was she in on Sammy and Joe's embezzlement scheme?"

"And," I added, "we need to figure out what happened to the money. Like Mary suggested—find the money, and we'll find the killer."

With Sammy dead, I worried our treasure hunt would lead us straight to Big Dog, who was still missing. If that was the case, part of me hoped we would never find a dime or solve this one. Harley trusted Big Dog.

My sweet, big-hearted beau had been hurt too many times in the past because he'd trusted the wrong people. I hated to think what yet another crushing betrayal would do to him. Would the discovery that he'd trusted yet another murderer turn Harley into someone different, someone I could no longer love? I hoped not, especially now that I'd finally found the perfect word to describe my relationship with Harley that was neither childish nor vulgar.

Harley was my beau.

My beau.

What a perfect Southern term.

I prayed our relationship would last long enough for me to be able to use it.

Chapter 22

Harley followed along as I carried the plate of brownies to Althea's shop. He'd said he was accompanying me because he wanted to taste one, and I hadn't let him. But I suspected he was worried and wanted to keep close. I shared his worry. Not for myself, but for his safety.

Yet again, a snake lurked in my paradise.

"Has Big Dog contacted you yet?" I asked.

"No." His jaw tightened. "It's been radio silence with him. But I know my friend. Despite everything that's happening, he'll still want to find the stolen money before he puts himself under his brother's control. I'm sure that's why he's staying away. Even from me."

"You said he was out last night, searching for Sammy. This morning, Delilah finds Sammy dead in the marsh."

"Yes?" Harley's tone turned guarded.

"I understand that he's your friend." I made sure my tone was gentle.

"He took me in after Jody betrayed me. He helped build my confidence back up. Jody had tried to take Gavin away from me...completely. Her anger and lies had crushed me. I might not have fought so hard for shared custody if Big Dog hadn't pushed me to do it."

"I understand that he's your friend," I repeated, slowly, carefully. "I hate to even suggest it, but with Sammy dead, you have to agree that we're running out of suspects. Big Dog was in town before the hurricane hit, and—by his own admission—he was searching for Joe."

"No." Harley was emphatic.

"You can't tell me his actions don't appear suspicious. I mean, he's living without any money from his brother, with no real job, going from beach to beach to catch the best waves. And yet, he wears fairly expensive clothes. Where does his money come from? Is he knee-deep in debt? Was he in town searching for Joe because he wants to prove his innocence, as he claims? Or was he in town to get the money from Joe before Sammy could? Seems to me an infusion of cash would make his life easier."

Harley stopped walking.

"I'm sorry," I said, truly meaning it. I. Was. Sorry. "But you were the one who required we don't keep secrets. Wouldn't you rather I tell you what I'm thinking instead of pretend I think Big Dog is some kind of free-spirited saint?"

He swallowed and gave a sharp nod, a *noncommittal* nod.

"Could you say something?" His silence was killing me.

"Big Dog is not without means." His flat tone sounded hollow. "He's a top surfer on the circuit. He's signed with three corporate sponsors who make sure he's never without. He doesn't need his family money. And he certainly doesn't need to kill for money."

"Oh." Corporate sponsors might explain why he was wearing designer clothes. "Still, you cannot discount that he followed Sammy from the moment of his release from jail all the way to Camellia Beach and now Joe and Sammy are dead. You told me yourself how determined Big Dog can be. And now he is hiding from the police and his brother so he can do whatever he's here to do."

"Yes, I know all that. I'm not stupid. And I did talk to Gibbons, remember? Because I'm worried."

"Because you do agree with me."

"No, Penn. I don't agree with you. Not about this. Despite all the stupid things he might do I know my friend wouldn't kill anyone. Ever. He's not the killing type. But he is the kind of guy who would do something stupid that might get himself killed. That's why I'm worried."

I tightened my hold on the plate of brownies. Harley was a good man. A kind man. An honest man.

Why couldn't I trust him when he told me he believed Big Dog?

Harley must have read the distress on my face. "I get it," he said, his voice low, his tone still stiff. "I'd be lying if I said it didn't hurt. But I understand why you won't believe me when I say helping Big Dog is the right thing to do."

I tried to smile. The muscles in my face trembled. "Why can't Big Dog step out of the shadows already? I mean, he's causing everyone so much trouble. Gibbons is busy with this silly search for a rich man's brother. He needs to go back to solving murders. I, for one, would be awfully glad if I never had to talk to Detective Prioleau again."

"It doesn't work that way," Harley cautioned. "Even if Big Dog reconnected with his brother this afternoon, this most recent murder investigation still belongs to Detective Prioleau. Like it or not, we're stuck with him."

I groaned.

"Well, at least there is one thing about Big Dog we can agree on," I said, desperate to smooth things over with Harley.

"What's that?" he asked.

"We both want to find him. We can work toward that goal together. And I promise to try and trust your instincts about him."

"Thank you," he said softly. "That's all I ask. For you to try."

The bell chimed on the door of Althea's ruined crystal shop as we entered. The workers Bertie had found were nearly finished rebuilding the back wall. Althea was packing up her inventory in boxes while Bertie pushed sand into piles with the broom.

"It looks like things are coming along nicely," Harley said with a satisfied nod toward the new wall.

"That's why I'm sweeping," Bertie said. "The only way sand can get in now is through your office."

"Did the insurance adjuster show up today?" he asked.

"He did," Althea said. "Thank you for lighting a fire under him, Harley. He said I was originally scheduled for a visit next month."

"Glad to be able to do it. I've been spending most of my time on the computer and the phone these days trying to help everyone in Camellia get the help they need. Plus, getting the ball moving here helps me too." He pointed to the ceiling. Blue-tinted sunlight streamed in through gaps in the ceiling, reminding us all how Harley's office had been completely destroyed.

"Well, he took tons of pictures," Althea said. "Now that everything has been documented, I can box up the inventory and store it someplace cool and dry. Hopefully, I'll not lose my entire stock."

"The crystals should be okay," I said. "They're just rocks."

Althea glared at me.

"I mean, that's something, right? Something you won't lose. I know some of them are worth quite a bit of money. But they're tough." I began to sweat a bit. Ever since the rift between us, I seemed to constantly say the wrong things around her.

Althea continued to glare.

I held up the plate in my hand. "I brought brownies."

Althea leaned toward me. "Brownies?"

"I baked them."

"You baked...?" She sounded disappointed. Everyone on the island knew my limitations in the kitchen. I'd burned enough baked goods to stink up the shop and half the island.

"I can bake brownies," I assured her.

"They smell delicious," Harley added. "But she won't let me taste them. She said they're all for you."

The corner of Althea's mouth tilted up. She set aside the waterlogged book she had in her hand. "Is that so?"

"She was quite adamant," he insisted, which made me blush.

I didn't want her to think I'd gone too far out of the way for her. I didn't want her to think... Well, I wasn't sure what I didn't want her to think. I'd simply wanted to bake her brownies. As a treat. As a small act of kindness.

"You made these? For me?" she whispered.

She took the plate and breathed in the scent of Amar chocolate blended with the rich, creamy sweetness of the brownies.

"They don't smell burnt," she said.

"Don't tease her," Bertie scolded from across the room. "Penn might not give herself enough credit, and her talent in the kitchen might be raw and untrained, but at times it rivals Mabel's."

I gaped at Bertie. Was she serious? My grandmother was a freaking artist in the kitchen. True chocolate connoisseurs used to travel from across the country to taste her truffles and bonbons.

What did I say to that? Compliments made me wary. People gave compliments—otherwise known as lies—when they wanted something from me.

Bertie didn't want anything from me.

Tell her, thank you. Just say thank you already, a voice in my head shouted.

"Um, thank you," I muttered.

Bertie gave a satisfied nod.

By this time Althea had the plastic off the plate. She bit into one of my brownies. And moaned with pleasure.

"Good gracious, Penn," she said as she chewed. "Why have you been hiding these from us? They are amazing."

"I make them whenever I need a pick-me-up. And I thought you might need one too," I said, feeling exceptionally pleased to see her enjoying them.

She reached for another one.

"Can I have one?" Harley pleaded. "Please, Althea. I need a pick-me-up too. My office isn't even there anymore."

She chuckled and pretended to horde them before relenting and handing him one.

He took a huge bite before she could change her mind. He closed his eyes and smiled. "Heavens, Penn, this is good. Why haven't you been selling these in the shop?"

Bertie, still holding the broom, came over and took one from the plate. Althea, by this time, had eaten four and was about to bite into her fifth. Harley had also reached for another one. It was a good thing Bertie had taken one. At the rate Althea and Harley were devouring them, the plate would be empty in no time.

"They're right," Bertie said in a no-nonsense tone. "You should be selling these in the store. They're good."

"But they're not part of Mabel's recipe book," I protested.

"When has that stopped you?" Bertie asked. I struggled whenever I tried to follow any of my grandmother's recipes. Much to Bertie's chagrin, I spent most of my time combining different flavors instead trying to master any of the shop's most popular recipes.

I shrugged as if their praise meant nothing. "Once we get a wholesaler making deliveries again, I'll add the ingredients to our order."

On the inside, my heart danced a crazy jig while also banging a jazzy drumbeat against my chest.

"Go ahead, Penn," Bertie said after she finished the brownie. "Smile and enjoy it. No one is going to take our praise away from you."

"That's right," Harley said. He tossed an arm over my shoulder. "We all think you're amazing."

Part of me wanted to smile and enjoy the moment. But the old part of me—the part that would probably always be broken—put the brakes on that.

"If you think I'm so amazing, why won't you let me help you get workers in here? Why do you fight me when I have contacts with contractors and workers?"

Harley's arm around my shoulder tightened. "Honey, we do love you, but you have to agree you don't have a good track record when it comes to hiring workers."

"I don't have a good track record? W-what do you mean?" I stammered. How could Harley suggest such a thing?

"Well, you don't," Bertie said bluntly.

Before I could react, Harley quickly added, "You have a good heart and you want to help people, but when it comes to finding the best person for the job, you're not very good at it. Maybe it's because of that sweet heart of yours. I don't know."

"You're crazy." I spun around, planning to walk right out of Althea's shop. They'd lost their minds. All of them. If they didn't want my help, fine by me. No, it wasn't fine. I stopped and turned back toward them. "I hired Fletcher. He's the best chocolate shop assistant anyone could hope to find. He does things before I even ask him."

Harley cleared his throat. "You hired him only because you thought he was guilty of murder, and you wanted him close so you could gather evidence against him."

Well, I had done that. "But it turns out he is priceless in the shop. And he hadn't killed anyone."

"How about the assistants you hired when I was out of commission with a broken leg?" Bertie asked. "There was the young woman who nearly burned down the entire building. The young man who thought sugar and salt were interchangeable. The older fellow who had no trouble helping himself to *samples* from the cash register. The silly girl who—"

"Okay, okay. A few bad apples." I interrupted. She was right. Those temporary workers had been horrible. "But that doesn't mean I'm incapable of helping."

"You want me to hire Johnny Pane." Bertie threw her hands in the air in a spurt of frustration. "Johnny Pane, for goodness sake. He still hasn't finished the Chocolate Box's paint job. And he's been painting in there for months."

"He's meticulous," I pointed out.

"He's slow," Bertie said.

"He's steady. And reliable." How could they not see that?

"I'm an old lady, Penn. I'd like to see my building repaired before I die."

"You're not that old," I scoffed.

"But Johnny Pane is *that* slow." She wagged her finger at me.

Well, shoot. She was right. Johnny Pane was the slowest painter on the planet.

"I do want to help." I sincerely did. "But you don't want my money. And you don't want me to get people out here to help rebuild. I don't know what else I can do other than bake a few brownies, and that's not nearly enough. Tell me how I can help."

"You can keep coming around," Althea said. "You don't have to prove your worth to us. You don't have to buy our friendship. You already have it."

Harley nodded his agreement. "However, I could use some help with decorating as soon as we get all the walls up and the roof rebuilt."

"I can do that." The tension in my shoulders eased just a bit.

"As soon as I get everything boxed up," Althea said as she reached for another brownie, "we can start searching for Blackbeard's treasure in earnest."

I liked how that sounded. It was as if things were finally normal between us again.

"After all, Penn," she added, "the Gray Lady has made it clear that we should be the ones to find it."

Yep. Normal.

Chapter 23

"Don't get upset with me," Althea said in place of a greeting that night when I opened the apartment door and found her standing on the other side. It was a warning that would have had me putting up my hackles if I were a dog. As if sensing my discomfort, Stella leapt down from her comfortable perch between Trixie and Barbie and charged my friend as quickly as her swollen little belly allowed her, growling and snapping her tiny jaws.

"Um…why should I be upset?" I scooped up Stella before she could sink her teeth into Althea's ankle. "You know I'm a pretty laidback person. Very little upsets me."

Althea laughed. "Good one, Penn. I hope you keep that sense of humor when you see who I brought with me."

"Who did you bring? You mean"—I drew a long breath—"you brought a date for dinner? Of course I'm not upset about *that*." Althea acted more gun-shy about dating than I used. "Your mom took a quick trip to Bunky's to pick up a few extra things for dinner. She should be home any moment. You know how she always cooks more than enough, so one more won't be a problem." I poked my head out the door. "Who is he?" I searched the empty porch some more. "*Where* is he?"

"I didn't bring a date." She took a long breath. "I…um…it's about the Gray Lady. I've been thinking some more about that woman who you saw coming into my shop on Sunday, the woman who disappeared as soon as she came inside. And then we found the gold coin." She pulled the coin from her pocket. "I think the Gray Lady left it there for us to find, like a clue. Like she wants us to find the treasure."

"I suppose she also left the stinky dead starfish at my shop's door. I wonder what kind of clue that was meant to be," I snapped, completely contradicting my claim of being slow to get upset.

189

She patted my arm. "Come on. He's downstairs." Without waiting for me to agree, she jogged down the stairs.

I followed her. Of course, I followed.

"This is Penn," she said to the tall African American man standing at the base of the stairs.

He wore his silver hair in long dreadlocks that were tied back in a red-and-white bandana. His jeans were worn through at the knees. His plain white T-shirt looked so crisp it must have come straight from the store. And he had no shoes. The lack of shoes made me wince. The ground around here was littered with sharp sandburs just waiting to attack the bottom of an unsuspecting foot.

His soft brown eyes seemed to see through me. He tilted his head to one side. A kind smile pressed to his lips. "Ah lawd, she is the spittin' image of her gran'," he drawled.

"Penn, I've been telling Uncle Kamba about Joe Davies and the Gray Lady and how you might have seen her outside my shop. And how my shop was gutted, but nothing happened to your shop even though you saw her that morning on the beach too." Althea had said this all in a rush.

Uncle Kamba was a root doctor, which, I'd learned from Althea, were the local equivalent to a voodoo priest or witch doctor. I didn't know much more beyond that, because I hadn't listened too hard when Althea had tried to explain it all to me. Honestly, I preferred to think of her uncle as someone who specialized in tree diseases than someone who sold voodoo dolls and love potions.

"I didn't see the Gray Lady," I said, sounding surprisingly reasonable. "I saw *Delilah* talking with Joe Davies. He was the one who'd lied to us and told us that she was a mythical ghost."

While Althea rolled her eyes, Uncle Kamba hooked his hands behind his neck and nodded.

"Besides which, Harley's office was destroyed, and he didn't see the Gray Lady. How do you explain that?" I asked her.

190

"There's no way to control a tornado," Althea said. "It couldn't wipe out my shop without taking Harley's office with it too."

"No way to control a tornado—that's exactly my point," I said a little too triumphantly. I calmed myself before adding, "The storm caused the damage, not a ghost." Stella, who I was still hugging to my chest like a security blanket, nipped my hand. My dog trainer had told me more than once that my little dog needed to feel in control, she needed to have her feet on the ground instead of restrained in my arms. Even though she wasn't on a leash, I set her down. It was do that or risk having her turn into a little alligator chomping at my hand.

"Don't bite anyone," I told her and handed her a little piece of bacon as an incentive to behave. She swallowed the bacon whole, barked at Althea a couple of times, and then barked even louder at Althea's uncle.

With an odd expression on his face, he crouched down to get closer to eye level with Stella.

"Um, I wouldn't do that," I said at the same time Althea warned, "She bites!"

"This lil' bit? She's got the fire of hades in her, don' she?" He made a soft shushing sound and held out his hand.

I clicked my tongue and clapped my hands, hoping to catch her attention before she nipped one of his fingers off.

Stella ignored me. Her wild-eyed gaze was latched on to her latest prey. She jumped toward him. And—

(Now, I don't believe in magic. Of. Any. Kind. However, if I were to start believing in the supernatural this would be the moment it happened.)

Instead of nipping at Kamba's outstretched hand—a game Stella thoroughly enjoyed—she rubbed her head against his open palm and licked his thumb acting like she was a friendly sort of dog who enjoyed greeting strangers.

"Did you smear bacon grease all over yourself before coming out here?" I demanded, only half-joking.

"Nah." He looked up at me and smiled the same wide grin I'd often seen Althea give me when she wanted me to believe the unbelievable. "I speak dog, tho. She jus' needed to know I weren't no threat nor a giant oaf who'd accidentally trip over her fragile body." He patted the ground. "Come. Join me. I'll teach you what I'd done."

Since I honestly wanted Stella to lick hands instead biting, I crouched down beside him.

"Well"—Althea backed toward the stairs—"I'll leave the two of you to talk."

"I don't believe in ghosts or magic," I warned him. "But I do want to know how you bewitched my dog."

"Eh, she's a small soul trembling in a large world. All I did was show her that we're all small souls. Now, she and me, we're on the same level."

None of that made sense, but he was looking at me as if it should. Sometimes Althea would do that too. And whenever I'd pressed her to explain herself, she'd spouted some mumbo-jumbo nonsense that would make me cranky. Since I was already at the edge of crankiness, I simply nodded and reminded myself that I was working with a talented dog trainer and making strides in improving Stella's behavior.

"I suppose you also want to tell me that the Gray Lady is real," I said instead, getting to the heart of why Althea's uncle had left his small island home that could only be reached by boat.

"Don' matter what I say. I can tell you're not going to listen," he said with a ghost of a smile. "So let's talk about something else, like your mother. You've been communicating with her." He said it as a statement of fact.

I shook my head. "No. My mother doesn't want anything to do with me. I've been giving her space. She's not been in my life...ever...so it's not like I'm really missing anything."

"Is that so?" He tilted his head to one side. "But she's reaching out to you. Texting you?"

I shook my head. "Peach has been texting me." I'd received several texts from her just that morning. "She wanted to make sure I was safe during the storm. And then she checked up on me after the storm to ask about the shop." The niggling thought that perhaps Florence had asked Peach to send those texts returned.

"I see," he said. "Unfinished business, that. One day, you'll have to face it."

"There's no rush. It's not as if I've been pining away for a mother. And it's not as if Florence has a maternal bone in her body. It might be for the best that she hasn't been part of my life."

He scratched Stella behind the ear. "She's a pretty little one. They tend to get too much attention, them pretty ones. It makes them quail from all that attention."

Was he talking about Stella or Florence, or both? I could see how Althea was so taken with her uncle and talked about him so much. While I didn't like that he claimed to be magical, his knowledge of how people, and creatures, thought was something I craved for myself.

"Tho I know ya' don' believe in her, are ya' ready to hear what I came to tell you about the Gray Lady?" he asked, the soothing cadence of his voice had captured me in an invisible snare.

"I know she doesn't exist," came my automatic reply, but my voice didn't hold any of its usual bite.

He moved closer. His lips nearly touching my ear. "That's right, child. The worst of the dark spirits don' ever exist." His whispery voice sent a chill down my spine. "That's what gives them the most power, now don' it?"

I rubbed the goosebumps that had risen all over my arms. "That makes no sense."

"If they was real, you could examine them," his voice was as light as the wispy clouds traveling across the dark sky far above our heads. "The Gray Lady ain't real. So that means she can't be watched or measured or explained. She jus' is. An' that's what makes her dangerous."

"You mean because people believe in the story they create troubles for themselves if they think they've seen her even if they only saw a woman on the beach in the dim morning light?"

Kamba leaned back on his haunches and smiled at me. My shoulders relaxed with a bit of relief.

"Whether you believe or not, now, none of that matters. I came down here because I thought you'd be well armed if you knew the origin of the tale," he said.

Intrigued, I said, "Go on."

"The Gray Lady was once a flesh and blood lady, now wouldn't that be the case?"

"I suppose."

"Now, this is the part of the tale your family worked hard to hide." He drew a long breath. "She was a Maybank."

"Somehow that doesn't surprise me. I suppose that's why Althea thinks her shop was destroyed while the Chocolate Box was spared. My ghostly ancestor is supposedly protecting the place?"

"Althea don't know the tale. Not many alive do. Mabel took it to the grave. Didn't breathe of word of it to anyone, not even to Bertie. Ethel might know. That old crone knows much about everything." He chuckled. "Perhaps even more than me."

"If it's such a big secret, how do you know about it?"

"Perhaps the Gray Lady told me?" He smirked.

"I get it. How you know doesn't matter. So, tell me, why is her family name a secret? I suppose there's a scandal behind the tale."

"Scandal aplenty. Verity Maybank was Mabel's great-great aunt. The youngest daughter in family. The Maybanks had moved to Camellia Beach from Charleston in order to open the chocolate shop. This was at the very end of the eighteen hundreds, mind you. Speculators were believing this small island would bloom into a tourist haven for them folks up north. Shops and resorts and restaurants would be needed. The Maybanks were one of the first families to invest in Camellia Beach's future."

"But the boom never came," I guessed.

"Not as they'd expected. No resorts. No hordes of tourists. Jus' locals."

"I suppose this left my ancestors in financial trouble."

"No. Them Maybanks have always had money pouring out their pockets. They kept the shop and stayed in Camellia because something about the island had crept into them, like a vine, but not a deadly strangling one. Verity, a young sixteen, missed the whirl and excitement of Charleston society. The island vine growing through them Maybanks did feel strangling to her."

"What did she do?" I asked.

"Young and foolish as a raccoon pup, she ran into the arms of a villain. Her parents should have warned her, pulled her away from the man she'd chased. But they didn't stand in her way. Perhaps they decided she needed to learn her own lessons. Perhaps they figured that she'd made her own troubles and had to live with them. Perhaps they jus' lazy. I don't know what drove them to turn their backs on their young'n. He didn't marry her. She lived as his mistress for about a year in Charleston, shunned by society and dependent on the crumbs her lover would throw at her. When he married, he gave her one of his new wife's cast-out dresses. That was the last straw. She threw the dress back in his face, stole his horse, and rode like the devil was chasing her back to Camellia Beach. Oh, lawd, the wind was whipping around on the ocean. The rain pelting the island like the heavens were crying for her. She went to her parents. They thought she'd finally come home. But that night with the storm still raging, she stood out in the surf dressed in nothing but a sheer nightgown, with her arms outstretched, and let the ocean take her."

"She drowned herself? Over a man?" I pressed my hand to my mouth. "What an idiot."

Kamba shook his head. "Not because of a man. Because of love—the most fearsome power in the universe. Wielded poorly, it can consume, as it did with Verity. It ate the child from the inside out."

"In time she would have gotten over him," I said.

"Do you really believe that?" he asked. "I hear tell you keep your own heart so tightly wound up I wonder how it to manages to beat. Perhaps part of your DNA remembers Verity's heartache. Perhaps that's why you and the rest of the Maybanks are how they are. Makes one speculate, don't it? The Gray Lady, she's your kin. Her bones are your bones. Her sins are your sins. She warns the living of impending doom before the rage of the storm. You seek to bring answers to victims after the storm. Now, I'm wondering. Now that you know, what you goin' to do with that knowing?"

"You do realize he has a PhD in psychology," Bertie said as she walked by the two of us crouched in front of Stella. She was carrying a load of groceries in each arm. "He sounded like everyone else at his ivy league school before he moved out to that hammock of his and started living like one of Peter Pan's Lost Boys."

I jumped up and grabbed one of the overstuffed paper bags. What had she bought at the store? Bricks?

"You jus' jealous, Sista'," he drawled. "You still pretendin' and not letting that soul of yours sing like it should. It's our heritage. We can't ignore it."

Bertie laughed as she continued up the stairs to our apartment. "Not our heritage. Our parents didn't speak like that."

"Don' change who I am."

"You sound silly," she snapped.

He nodded sagely as he watched her climb the stairs. After scratching Stella behind the ears, he slowly unfolded his long legs and stood. "She jealous," he declared with another slow nod.

"Join us for dinner," I said. I adjusted the heavy bag I had to hold with both arms while I followed Stella up the steps. When he didn't answer I peeked over my shoulder. He was gone.

That night, I dreamed of storms, lost maps, and broken hearts. When I woke up the next morning, the first words out of my mouth were, "That girl was a world-class idiot."

Bonbon with the Wind

Harley grunted in his sleep and rolled over.

Chapter 24

After spending several pre-dawn hours melting dark chocolate squares to pour into molds that looked like old coins, I grabbed Stella's leash and my large straw hat and headed out toward the beach.

As soon as we crested the dunes, Stella tugged on the end of the leash. Her little paw scratched at the sand. She gave a happy yip when a ghost crab emerged from its tiny hole and scurried away. Her yips turned more frantic when I didn't let her chase after it.

"Hush, now. We have serious work to do," I told my little pup and tossed her a low-calorie green bean seasoned in beef broth. Bertie had cooked up a batch of the snacks last night after seeing how much Trixie and Barbie had been feeding Stella. "I need you to dig up more of those gold coins, not tiny crabs."

Stella looked up at me and yipped. I suspect she was asking for another green bean instead of answering me. I'd eaten some of the green beans last night. They were delicious.

"Argh, matey." Althea's bubbly personality filled the air with joy as she hurried toward me. She had a shovel slung over her shoulder. A purple pirate hat sat at a jaunty angle on her head. It perfectly matched her flowing maxi dress. Stella took one look at her and started barking. "If you don't shut your trap, beastie, I'm going to make you walk the plank," Althea growled playfully.

I don't know if it was the strange hat, or the shovel, or her growly voice. Stella, her eyes going wide, halted mid-bark and sat down.

"Good dog," Althea said. She turned to smile at me. "Are we ready to go hunting?"

"Just about," I said. I wasn't sure how searching for Blackbeard's treasure—which may or may not exist—would help catch the killer. Just this morning, feeling more than a little frightened by my string of nightmares, I called Althea and told her about my dreams and how they'd included a map, a map that must have been a reflection of the one Delilah had flashed at me. After describing the details of the map, Althea had insisted on meeting me.

"I don't know why either of us think we'll find this treasure when there is an island full of professional treasure hunters scouring every inch of sand." I gestured toward the small crowd of beachcombers waving metal detectors all around us.

"For one thing, we have the Gray Lady on our side."

I rolled my eyes, which seemed to be a signal to Stella that she should bark.

"Also"—Althea held up her hands to stop me from protesting—"my master's thesis was on the history of this island. I know its secrets better than anyone, save for Uncle Kamba. And if that map you described to me is correct, those hunters are searching in the wrong places. I think I know how to find the place on the map that you described."

She turned on her heel and headed toward one of the few remaining wooden walkovers that scaled the dunes.

I hurried to catch up with her. Stella's tail wagged wildly as she joined in the chase.

"Why did you have me meet you on the beach if that's not where we're going to look for the treasure?" I asked.

"Because I wanted to see the sunrise," she said without slowing her stride. "The front beach is too volatile, too unstable. A pirate would never bury anything in these shifting sands, especially not on Camellia. The sand we're standing on today will be on a beach somewhere in Florida by the end of the year."

"Really?"

She nodded.

"Joe did extensive research on pirates and treasure. Why wouldn't he know this?" I asked.

Althea shrugged.

"And what about the professional treasure hunters?" I pointed back to the hordes we were leaving behind us.

199

"Professionals?" she snorted. "Those are hacks. The professional treasure hunters would laugh at anyone suggesting Blackbeard had even landed on Camellia. Actually, if you look at the facts, it is kind of laughable."

"Then why was Joe so convinced he'd find the treasure? Why was Sammy and Delilah after his treasure map?" I asked. I had to jog to keep up with her, which was amazing considering how my legs were nearly twice as long as hers.

"No clue," she said. "Has Big Dog contacted Harley?"

"No. He's still missing."

"Harley must be worried as all get out."

"He is. I wish there was something I could do for him. I'm starting to hate Big Dog for doing this to Harley. Harley keeps insisting Big Dog is his friend and that he's completely trustworthy, but I don't see it."

Althea slanted a glance toward me.

"What?" I said. "If Big Dog was so trustworthy, he wouldn't keep Harley in the dark like this."

"I'm sure he has his reasons," Althea said.

"Yeah, like he killed Sammy?"

"Or he's scared he'll be blamed for Sammy's death. Remember, his brother didn't support him the last time he was wrongly accused of a crime. Spending several years in jail because of that would make anyone jumpy."

I pressed my lips together. She had a point. Still, I was worried. It seemed rather convenient that the two men who he claimed were responsible for stealing from his bank were now dead. I wondered yet again if it wasn't vindication that Big Dog was searching for, but revenge.

Bonbon with the Wind

We needed a car, to get where Althea had planned to search. She drove us in her yellow Honda Civic to the Northern end of the island where the abandoned red-and-white striped lighthouse kept silent watch over the shoreline. After parking, she led the way down a narrow path that led through the maritime forest on the marsh side of island. Throughout the walk, she lectured me on the history of Camellia Beach, its settlement and how it had sometimes served as a refuge for pirates and criminals. And root doctors.

The hurricane had left the trail she led me down littered with broken limbs, seaweed, sea grasses, and swarms of mosquitoes. We had to slow our pace in order to make our way through the detritus. I picked up Stella, worried she might cut her foot.

The trail took an abrupt turn and narrowed even more.

"Is it much further?" I asked before swatting at yet another flying bloodsucker. Stella nipped at the air to catch the one circling her head.

"If what you described with that map is correct, we're almost there," Althea said without slowing her pace.

"Why aren't you swatting at the mosquitoes? I think if another one bites me I'm going to die from blood loss."

She glanced over her shoulder at me. "Really?"

"Aren't you getting eaten alive?" I slapped my thigh, managing to kill three at once.

"I suppose I've been bit a few times. I really haven't noticed."

"Not fair," I muttered. "Perhaps you could mutter an incantation to keep them away from me." I was joking. Mostly. If she could banish these buzzing creatures, I might accept her claims to magical powers. Well, for just this one time.

She chuckled. "Once we clear the trees, it should get better."

A few yards later, she led the way through a narrow opening that didn't look like a path. Not. At. All. We had to duck and weave through the thick brush before we emerged from the trees and climbed up an ancient sand dune that looked out over the marsh. True to her word, a breeze from the river did keep the mosquitoes from following us.

With the shovel propped on one shoulder and her hand on her hip, Althea turned a complete circle. "If I were a pirate, this is where I'd bury my treasure. It's high land that's protected from flooding. It's not easy to reach. The marsh is deep here. So the area is difficult to access even with a small boat. And the path leading out this way is nearly impossible to find. I stumbled across it when I was a child. Even Uncle Kamba who swears he knows every inch of this island was surprised when I told him about my little hideaway." Her eyes glittered as she added, "He told me fairies kept it hidden."

"Fairies?" I scoffed. Stella barked.

"He could be wrong. It could be a pirate curse or a ghost." She laughed. When she said things like that, I never knew if she was serious or not. "Should we start digging?"

"I suppose." Pirate curses, fairies, the mention of anything supernatural made my skin itch. I set Stella down and rubbed my arms. "It is odd, though. There are no signs of digging here. Those treasure hunters have dug up every undeveloped inch of the island."

"That's true."

"Of course, Blackbeard might have buried his treasure somewhere that's been developed. It might be paved over and we'd never know," I said.

"Could be," Althea agreed. But something about the way she agreed—the lilting and almost dismissive tone, perhaps—made me wonder if she was only humoring me.

"What?" I demanded.

"Feeling prickly? You shouldn't. I agreed with you. We might never find the treasure."

"But..." I said when she didn't. "There's a silent *but* in what you're saying."

"You don't want to hear it," she said.

"Maybe I do."

"You already know what I'm going to say," she said as she scouted the area for a place to start digging. "I've already told you."

"You didn't. I would have remembered."

"The Gray Lady wants us—" She hesitated and looked at me.

I groaned. "You're right. You already told me this. And I don't want to hear it. My ancestor is dropping gold coins for me to find because she wants us to find a lost treasure that wasn't hers and isn't mine. And then I say, '*You're crazy.*' And because I'm still having trouble with this trust business, things get weird between us again."

Althea dropped the shovel and spun toward me. Her jaw had dropped open. "*What?*" she screeched.

I looked behind me before realizing she was reacting to what I'd said. "I don't mean to upset you, but you have to agree that our friendship isn't back on solid footing yet."

"Yes, yes, that does upset me." She marched over to me. "But…but…" She shook her head and tugged on an ear before she drew a deep breath. "There has to be something wrong with my hearing this morning. It sounded like you just said that the Gray Lady is your ancestor."

"I did."

"The Gray Lady is a Maybank?"

"That's what your uncle wants me to think."

"Uncle Kamba wouldn't lie to you."

I shrugged. How could I know that? I'd just met him. And besides which, "It's all a moot point. The Gray Lady doesn't exist."

Althea started to protest but then stopped herself and held up a hand. "Let's just dig." She turned around and jammed the shovel randomly into the ground. After several minutes of digging there was a loud clank.

My heart stopped for several moments before it took off racing that same way it would whenever I spotted the last piece of chocolate in a candy dish.

203

"Is it—?" I asked. Finding the treasure couldn't be that easy, could it?

Althea looked back at me, her eyebrows raised, clearly as surprised as I was.

"Well, what are you waiting for?" I asked. "Start digging."

I stood next to her as she dug around whatever it was the shovel had clanked against. By the outline that her efforts seemed to be producing, the hidden object seemed to be the size of a treasure chest.

It's going turn out to be an old log.

But as we took turns shoveling sand and muck away from the object hidden beneath the ground, the more it became clear that this wasn't a log or a rock or an artifact from the Civil War.

It was a box.

A heavy steel box.

It took both our efforts to lift the box from its hole. Panting, we dropped it on the damp marshy ground. Writing was etched into the top of the black metal box.

Althea wiped the lid with the hem of her skirt.

The letters had been worn away over time, but there was still enough left to be able to make out the words, *Cedar's Hill Consolidated Bank.*

"Well, well, well," Althea said, as she sat back on her heels and stared at the heavy box. "This wasn't what I was expecting."

It was more than I was expecting. Much more.

"This must be the—" I began to state the obvious.

Something in the woods rustled. It might have been a small animal. But with two people already dead because of this treasure chest, our position suddenly felt terribly open and vulnerable.

"It's locked." Althea looked around for something to use to break it open. "There has to be a stick we can use like a crowbar around here."

The last thing we needed was to find a blunt object that any passing murderer could use to bludgeon us. I put my hand on her arm. "We need to get this out of here. *We* need to get out of here," I said.

She glanced out at the thick growth of vegetation that could easily hide a person and then nodded in agreement.

Together, we lifted the extremely heavy bank box. With Stella leading the way, we began the long, slow trek through the thick maritime forest and (I hoped) to safety.

Chapter 25

I hadn't stepped foot inside Althea's cottage since before the hurricane. I was relieved to see the storm hadn't damaged the charming home that had been in her family for two generations.

"It's private here," Althea explained as she slid out of the front seat of her bright yellow car.

Nestled within the lace of the Spanish moss draped branches of ancient oaks, the cottage was partially hidden from the road.

"We need to be careful," she said.

With Big Dog and Delilah unaccounted for, Althea was right.

"No one would suspect you'd come here with this kind of evidence," she said. "Not with the…um…troubles that have been brewing between us."

Another fair point.

But then I glanced over at the road.

There was a man standing at the edge of Althea's property.

He was staring right at us.

I jumped out of Althea's car, slammed her trunk closed, and hurried toward the road.

It took me a moment to recognize the man. He was the ghost hunter from the shop, the one who'd warned me to watch my back around the treasure hunters. What was his name?

He took one look at me and Stella charging toward him and set off running in the opposite direction.

"Call Gibbons!" I shouted to Althea as I picked up my pace. "Tell him…" *What?* "Everything."

Now, I might not be the fastest runner in the world. Those extra chocolates I'd been eating ever since the hurricane certainly hadn't done anything to help boost my speed. But, even so, I couldn't believe that by the time I'd reached the road, the man was nowhere in sight. Absolutely nowhere. I spent several minutes searching for him in neighboring yards and peeking in the windows of the few cars that were parked along the road.

Nothing.

He was gone.

"What in the devil is going on with you?" Althea asked somewhat testily when I returned with Stella panting by my side.

"There-there was a man watching us," I panted. "That ghost hunter, Brett Handleson. He was right there. Didn't you see him?"

Althea turned toward the road and shook her head. "There wasn't anyone there. I checked. Our find is too important to make sure there are no prying eyes around before pulling it out of my trunk."

"No, he was there," I insisted as I thrust my finger toward the road. "Right there."

"I didn't see anybody." The skin between her eyebrows wrinkled. "Did you see where he went?"

"No. It was like he"—I hated to say it—"vanished."

"Where in blazes is my love potion, Althea?" Trixie complained from her perch on Althea's sofa. Barbie, seated next to her, snorted.

"Tell me again who invited those two," Harley whispered in my ear.

"They overheard Bertie talking on the phone with me and insisted on coming. They said they had vital information," I whispered back.

"My guess is they were getting vitally bored spending all their time in your living room and were desperate for a change of scenery," he said with a chuckle.

"You're a naughty girl, Althea, letting me go this long without that potion. A girl has needs." Trixie waggled her hips provocatively, which was a feat since she did it while seated.

"That's one sight I didn't need to see," Bubba said and whirled to look out the window.

Althea patted Trixie on the shoulder. "I understand completely. But, honey, you don't need that potion. You've got the magic in you and more. All you need to do is get out there and wag those hips at the man you want, and he'll come crawling after you."

"You hear that?" Trixie shouted over at Barbie. "She said I'm a magic man magnet."

Barbie snorted. "You're a magnet for something, all right. Remember what happened with you and Oscar, that crusty old coot?"

"Poor man couldn't peel himself away from me." Trixie tsked. "Twasn't his fault he got all wound up in my net. Did him a kindness and tossed him back into the sea. Couldn't keep him. Not with his bad heart and all."

"And bad manners," Barbie added.

"Perhaps we can save the love talk for another time," Gibbons said as he swept into the room after Bubba opened the door for him.

The detective was the last of the group to arrive. Althea, who had wanted to smash open the box immediately, let out a loud sigh of relief. With a look of excitement, she picked up the crowbar.

Gibbons deftly slipped the tool from her hands. "We need to do this by the book."

"This is why I didn't want you to call him," she grumbled.

"*You* called him," I reminded her.

"Only because you told me to."

"I don't understand something," Bubba said as he approached the muddy box cautiously. "From everything we now know, presumably Joe brought this box of stolen money with him when he moved here from Virginia. So why in blazes would he spend all his time these past several years searching for it?"

"You were there when Bertie explained it to us," I said. "Just the other day Trixie and Barbie agreed with Bertie's assessment," I added with a smile in their direction. The two sisters puffed up. "Joe was showing signs of memory loss. Was he suffering from dementia or something else? We may never know. But we do know that a few years after moving to Camellia Beach he started his obsession with searching for pirate's treasure."

Bertie tut-tutted. "The poor man forgot where he'd buried his own treasure."

"Impossible," Bubba growled. "How could a man forget something so important?"

"Oh," Bertie said with a sage nod, "I can see that happening. Wasn't it just this morning you lost the keys to your shop? You spent two hours searching for them."

"That's not the same thing," he grumbled.

"No, perhaps not," I agreed. "But you do have to agree that Joe's obsession with treasure hunting did seem a bit outrageous. I mean, he had no way of really knowing if Blackbeard's treasure was on the island. But he would know for certain that he'd buried a treasure of his own somewhere on the island...and then lost it."

"That would explain why he'd only quote the Wikipedia page whenever he talked about Blackbeard," Bubba grudgingly agreed.

"And he did seem genuinely surprised to see the gold coin Stella had dug out of that crab hole," Althea added. "Didn't he say something like, 'I didn't really think it existed'?"

He had.

"Now can we see what's inside the treasure box?" Althea bounced on the balls of her feet like a little kid anxious to open a birthday present.

"You can tell everyone back at the station that we opened it before we called you, if you need to," I told Gibbons, feeling nearly as eager as Althea looked.

"I suppose we could take a peek inside it to make sure that this is stolen goods and not just a box of pirate research," Gibbons said after he'd snapped several pictures of the box's exterior.

I suspected he was as excited about peeking inside the box as the rest of us. After all, he'd been chasing after Big Dog around the Lowcountry thanks to the contents of this box. When Gibbons handed our find over to his captain, the box would likely be given to that cranky Detective Prioleau. Prioleau, who'd openly expressed his distrust of me, would hide the contents like a dragon hiding its treasure.

With a look of determination Gibbons picked up the crowbar and with a quick movement broke the rusty lock.

Chapter 26

"**Whoa, I wasn't** expecting that," Althea breathed.

"What? Move out of the way, you big lugs. I'm too short to see." Trixie used her cane to knock Harley and me out of her path.

"Good thing it wasn't paper money," Bubba said. "Looks like water got into the box."

"Well, you have to give the man credit. When Joe told us he was searching for gold, he wasn't lying," I said unable to take my eyes off the gleaming bars in the metal box. No wonder both Althea and I had struggled to pull it out of the hole and carry it.

"This is the work of someone who really thought through the crime. Marked bills would be too hard to spend. Gold, you can sell anywhere," Harley said, sounding impressed.

Either Joe or Sammy had stuffed crumpled paper in the gaps between the bars. Gibbons pulled out the soggy paper lumps while we all leaned closer to get a better look. The bars didn't fit neatly into the box. It looked as if they had once been neatly stacked but had all shifted into an untidy pile.

Gibbons pulled bar after bar out of the box, lining them in an orderly row on Althea's kitchen counter. "That's the last of them," he said at last. "Ten gold bars."

Harley whistled. "That has to be at least five million dollars' worth of gold."

"Really?" I wrinkled my nose. "That's not nearly enough to kill for."

Everyone in the room turned to look at me with a strange expression.

"Someone *has* killed over this, dear," Bertie gently pointed out.

"Twice," Althea added.

"Well, let's not get ahead of ourselves," Gibbons warned. "We don't know that Joe was murdered, and we don't know why someone

211

wanted Sammy Duncan dead. And now that we know what's in this box, I think it's time I turn it over to"—he sighed—"Detective Prioleau."

As he returned the bars to the box, he speared Harley with a sharp look. "I trust you haven't heard from Big Dog."

"I gave you my word," Harley snapped right back. "And, besides which, he didn't steal this gold or hurt anyone."

"That reminds me," I said quickly, uncomfortable with the tension between two of the dearest men in my life. "Were you able to find out anything about that ghost hunter Brett Handleson? I spotted him outside this cottage when Althea and I returned with the box. He was just standing at the road watching us. He took off when he saw that I'd spotted him. I gave chase but lost him almost immediately."

"Y-you gave chase?" Harley sputtered.

"Not very well," I said. "I didn't see where he ran off to."

Gibbons frowned. "I did look into his background. Whoever you were talking with gave you a false name. Brett Handleson died in a boat accident three years ago right off this coastline."

"Are you sure you weren't talking to a ghost?" Althea asked me. "Has anyone else talked with him? Seen him?"

Ghosts indeed.

Of course that was where Althea's mind would go. I rolled my eyes. "Yes, people have seen him. He was in the Chocolate Box on a crowded day for goodness sake. Besides, there must be more than one Brett Handleson in the world. Or perhaps the man I spoke to lied about his name. Perhaps he's scared, or maybe he's after Joe's treasure. There has to be a reason why he was watching us."

While I was making my case against conversing with a dead man—which I could hardly believe I'd ever do in my life—Althea ignored me. Instead, she tapped on her phone.

"Is this the man?" She turned her phone's screen toward me.

"That's him. Brett Handleson, right?" I asked.

The way her eyes glittered with excitement made me nervous. "I wonder why he's interested in you," she mused.

"It's not me he's interested in. It's the treasure. Clearly, he lied about being a ghost hunter," I said. "What?" I asked when I noticed how both Gibbons and Harley were frowning as they passed Althea's phone between them.

"That can't be the man you saw," Gibbons said.

"No, it is the man. I'm sure of it. That's the face I saw not much more than an hour ago. Will someone tell me what's going on already?"

"Now don't explode on us," Althea warned. "But the picture I showed you is the picture the newspaper ran for Brett Handleson's obituary three years ago."

I didn't explode. Or implode. Or do anything embarrassingly emotional. Before reacting, I took a long, slow breath. I then smiled. I shrugged. And finally I did something I hated—I lied.

"Clearly, the man I talked with looked like this man. A brother? A cousin? Whatever." But deep down in my heart, I knew—*knew* down to the marrow in my bones—that the man in the picture was the same Brett Handleson who'd warned me to be careful around the blood-thirsty treasure hunters. He was the same man standing at the road this morning watching.

I had no idea how Brett had managed to fake his death…or why. Obviously, he had his reasons, just as he had his reasons for coming "back from the grave" now.

One thing was obvious, though. What better way to get away with murder than to become a ghost? Perhaps this Brett Handleson—ghost hunter extraordinaire—had spent the past three years traveling around the Lowcountry committing all manner of crimes. Or perhaps he'd been biding his time, waiting for this moment.

Later that day, as I hunched over the counter in the Chocolate Box, I added Brett's name to my suspect list. Like Joe Davies, he had gone to a great deal of trouble to disappear from his old life. How, I wondered, was Brett connected with Joe's stolen gold?

All the names on my list had more questions beside their names than answers.

"You-you're g-g-going at it from the w-w-wrong angle," Fletcher stuttered. His voice like a rasping ghost right next to my ear, startled me nearly to death.

"I thought you agreed to take a few days off," I said once my heart had settled in my chest. "And how did you sneak up on me like that?"

He adjusted his deerstalker hat while giving me a smug look. "I'm here as a paying customer. Delilah, who-who sh-sh-shouldn't be on your l-l-list"—he tapped the paper—"has g-g-gone into hiding thanks to your b-b-bungling. I hope to clear some things up with Detective Prioleau so she'll feel safe enough to return."

"You invited that mean detective here? Now? You do know that if he arrests me—wrongly, mind you—you're going to be out of job?"

Instead of answering, he tapped his finger against Brett's name. "D-d-don't know him. But he's not our killer."

"Then who is?" I asked.

"I had my m-m-money on Big Dog, but now I'm wondering if he's s-s-still alive."

"Who do you think is going around our town killing people?" I asked again.

"Now, if I told you that, you'll just take credit for solving the mystery like you did last time," he sang.

"I did solve it," I reminded him. "And I saved your life."

He grunted.

"Just tell me what you think is going on," I said.

Fletcher shook his head. I probably would have argued with him further, but the bell on the door chimed and in walked Detective Prioleau looking as if he'd swallowed a lemon.

"D-d-detective!" Fletcher smiled broadly as he crossed the room to greet him. "I-I think w-w-we have l-l-lots of information to sh-sh-share."

"I'm not here to share information." Prioleau cut his sharp gaze in my direction for a moment before turning back to Fletcher. "I'm here because you said you had important information for me."

"Y-yes." Fletcher adjusted his deerstalker hat and smacked his lips. The detective's icy attitude clearly made the young man nervous. "I-I do. I-I'm also trying t-t-to help Delilah, um, M-Mrs. F-F-Fenton."

Fletcher glanced over at me before directing the detective to sit at a small table as far away from the front counter as possible. No matter how hard I tried I couldn't hear what either man was saying.

Eventually, I stopped attempting to eavesdrop and instead spent my time wondering about Fletcher's odd devotion to Delilah. Though Fletcher was young and prone to jumping to conclusions, he wasn't a fool. I circled Delilah's name on my suspect list. There had to be something about her story that had convinced him to become her champion. Perhaps it was simply a case of romantic attraction. He wouldn't have been the first person in the world to make bad decisions because he'd followed his heart.

I closed my eyes, picturing Delilah. She always scowled at me. Why? What threat did I pose to her?

I opened my eyes and circled her name on the suspect list again.

It has to be her.

Delilah saw me as a threat. Before even meeting me, her body language had communicated her dislike. To be fair, on that first meeting I'd reacted stiffly to her. She reminded me of Florence, my perfectly turned out and perfectly unfriendly mother.

Still, it has to be her.

After meeting Mary and hearing how Delilah was the quintessential wicked stepmother, how could she not be my number one suspect?

If her description didn't fit the profile of a greedy killer, I don't know what did.

Dear sweet Mary. She'd lost her father twice and didn't know why. I needed to call her and tell her about finding her father's *treasure.*

I dug around in my purse until I found her card. Without remembering that she'd written the number for her cell phone on the back of the card, I dialed the number for the car dealership. Instead of ringing, the line beeped and an automated voice announced that the number had been disconnected.

Wait. Disconnected?

Mary had said that she worked at her father's old car dealership.

Poor Mary. Her father's leaving town had not only severed their relationship, it had also wrecked her career.

I had dialed the number for her cell phone when it hit me. Her father had left Cedar's Hill eight years ago. If he was the glue that held together the dealership, and losing him was the reason it had closed, why was Mary carrying around that business card? I flipped over to my phone's search engine and typed in *Cedar's Hill Imports.*

Perhaps it had only recently closed.

After scrolling past several websites that had nothing to do with the dealership in question, I found what I was looking for—an article in the local newspaper announcing the surprise closing of Cedar's Hill Imports. The article was dated eight years ago.

Curious about what Mary had been up to in the ensuing years, I typed her name into the search engine. She might have taken a break from work to have had kids or started work at a retail shop that didn't provide their employees with business cards. The fact that she still held onto old, useless business cards only underscored the trauma she must have suffered at her father's abandonment.

216

The first item to pop up from my search was a photo from a high school reunion. It featured a picture of three women who were clearly friends, including Mary with blonde hair instead of red. She had her arm around another woman whose hair was as red as Mary's was now. Before I had a chance to click on the page to read the caption, someone knocked sharply on the counter immediately under my nose. I jerked my head up.

"Yes? What can I do for you?" I asked Detective Prioleau. "Are you interested in a pumpkin seed truffle? They're new."

"I suppose it's packed full of pumpkin spice," he said and made a gagging sound.

Customer service, I silently reminded myself.

"Perhaps something else?" I suggested. "Our wholesale supplies have been delayed because of the hurricane, but we do have—"

"What I want is for you to understand that I'm not going to play games with you." He raised his voice and added, "With any of you." He lowered his voice again. "The next time you find a vital piece of evidence, you don't tamper with it. And you don't call Gibbons, you call me. I'm the detective in charge of this investigation. I'm the only person you should be talking to. I'm the only person you should be worried about because I'm looking into your involvement in this and other crimes."

I took several deep breaths before trusting myself to react. "I see."

Should I say more? He was standing there looking at me as if he expected me to say more.

Finally, he relented. "My instincts tell me that you're at the center of the troubles here on Camellia and have been ever since you arrived."

"That's not your instincts, that's Chief Byrd talking. He and I have never rubbed together well."

Prioleau coughed. "Well, my instincts agree with him." He tapped the counter with his finger. "And my instincts have never been wrong. I'll be watching you."

I held my breath, not sure what I should say to that. Telling him he was wrong would be a waste of my time. We stared at each other for at least a minute.

"Okay, then." I took another deep breath before saying, quite calmly, "Let me fix you a small box of chocolates to take with you." It's what I would have done for Gibbons.

Prioleau's posture grew even straighter. His gaze hardened. "Ms. Penn, I don't take bribes."

Chapter 27

"If he's meeting with Fletcher and throwing threats in your direction, it's a pretty good indication that he has no leads. He's floundering," Harley assured me over the phone a few hours later. He was picking up his son from his ex-wife's house. "Don't worry about him."

"But he didn't accept my chocolate."

"Maybe he doesn't like chocolate," Harley suggested. He started to say something else, but abruptly cut himself off. "Oh," he groaned. "Jody's coming out with Gavin. And she looks angry about something. I need to go."

It was just as well, a group of three shaggy-haired men wearing black hats with white stitching spelling *Palmetto Ghost Hunters* came into the shop, talking loudly. I brought up the picture of Brett Handleson that had run with his obituary onto my phone's screen and, after taking their orders, asked them if they'd seen him around.

"That's Brett," one of them said while slowly shaking his head. "He'd love to be here. Always said he wanted to catch sight of the Gray Lady. He had a picture on his wall of the Gray Man that he took himself. But the Gray Lady? She's an elusive one."

"No one has ever snapped a picture of her," another said.

"She don't like the camera," the third man chimed in. "But if anyone were to get a picture, Brett would have been the one to have gotten it. He had luck and then some when it came to ghost huntin'."

"Didn't he show you?" I asked. "Just a few days ago he showed me a smudgy picture of what he claimed was the Gray Lady."

The men paled a bit as they exchanged glances.

"That's not who you saw," the tallest man snapped.

"Yes, it is. He was in here in this shop." I pointed to the picture of him on the screen. "I'm good with faces. And I know this is the man I saw."

The three of them took several steps away from me. "Don't know what you playing at, girly," the third man drawled. "Our hats say *ghost hunter* not *stupid*. You show us a picture from an obituary and expect us to jump around like we have rocks for brains believing you conversed with a ghost?"

"I—" I was taken aback by his anger. "I don't think he was a ghost."

"We're not going to do it," the tall man said.

"Do what?" I asked.

"Lie for you so you can get more free publicity for your shop. Brett didn't come back from the dead. Has no reason to."

"Didn't they say he died in a boat accident?" I asked.

"Yeah. So?" the tall man stepped forward again.

"Was his body recovered from the water?" I asked as gently as I knew how. These men were obviously Brett's friends. "Is it possible that he somehow faked his death?"

"Girly!" the third man shouted. "I saw his bloated body in the casket. We. All. Did." He clapped his hands as he spoke each word. "There was no mistaking who it was."

The second man, who hadn't said much up until now, quietly added, "I was with him on that boat. I was the one who dragged his lifeless body from the water."

"I'm sorry." I truly was. "Did he have a brother or a cousin who resembled him?"

The men glanced at each other before shaking their heads.

Not sure what to say, I bit my lower lip. There was no question in my mind. The man I'd met had looked identical to the man in the obituary.

"You say the person you spoke with claimed to be Brett Handleson?" the tall man asked as if he still couldn't believe it.

"Yes. He showed me a picture of the Gray Lady, not that it was a good picture. He then told me to watch out for the treasure hunters."

The tall man frowned. "What did he say exactly?"

I started to repeat what I'd just said about watching out for treasure hunters, but that wasn't what Brett had said to me, not exactly. I closed my eyes and tried to recall his exact words. With my eyes still closed, I said slowly, "He asked if I planned to search for the pirate gold. I told him I would if that was where my investigation took me. To that, he said that the Gray Lady might have something to say about that."

I opened my eyes to see that the three ghost hunters now appeared paler than the plastic Halloween ghost decorations that had been popping up in the island's shop window displays.

"What?" I asked. "What did I say wrong?"

The men exchanged glances as if they were having a conversation with their eyes. Finally the third man nodded and then said to me, "Girly, you'd best heed that warning because that wasn't Brett you were talking to, that was the Gray Lady."

"It's frustrating," I told Althea as I flipped open my notebook to my crumbling suspect list.

After closing the shop later that afternoon, I had headed straight to her crystal shop where I found her finishing up the installation of a door to her shop's newly rebuilt back office.

She used a rubber mallet to hammer in the pins for the door hinges before turning toward me.

"What's frustrating?" she asked.

"That all my suspects keep ending up dead."

"To be fair, that Brett fellow didn't end up dead. He started out that way," she said as she tested the swing of the office door.

"I didn't talk to a ghost." Why was I telling her this? What did I want her to say to me? "I was thinking that Brett had somehow faked his death, and that he was sneaking around, pretending to be his own ghost. But one of those ghost hunters was with him when he died."

She nodded.

"I didn't talk to a ghost." I reiterated. She was smart enough not to say anything. After several tense moments of me waiting for her to tell me that I had, indeed, had a conversation with a specter from beyond, I asked her, "Can I help you with something?"

"I could use a hand putting away the tools and cleaning up."

We worked side by side in silence. "Why are you doing the work? Where are the workers your mother had hired to fix everything?"

Althea groaned. "They didn't show up this morning. And I hate to see things sitting around not getting done. Have you heard from Gibbons about our box of gold?"

"No. But Detective Happy stopped by to talk with Fletcher and growl at me. He didn't like that we peeked inside the box and that we didn't call him."

"Do you think Fletcher knows where Delilah is hiding?" she asked.

"No, and he was grumpy as a bear about it." I picked up one of the thick iron pipes that were scattered on the floor. "What do you want me to do with these? They're heavy. What are they?"

"They're the old water pipes. When the wall came down, they did too. The workers replaced them with PVC piping. You can stack them up over there." She pointed to a back wall. "I need to find where I can take them to be recycled."

While we continued to work, Althea speculated about the man who'd called himself Brett and whether he was a ghost or not. She tried to convince me that there were cosmic forces at work on the island and that we all needed to be wary. She gave several examples from ghost lore of how ghosts had ruined lives in the Lowcountry.

"These aren't just stories to the people who lived them," she argued, even though I hadn't said anything. "Some of the people I mentioned have documented proof that their lives were turned upside down by something they couldn't control."

I was only half listening to her. My mind kept going back to something I saw in that picture of Mary and her friend. Something that nagged at me. I tried to remember what Mary had said about the relationship between her father and Sammy Duncan and her relationship with her stepmother. I gathered up some more pipes. There was something about what Mary had said to me that no longer rang true. Or perhaps it was something Delilah had said to me that reeked of lies—the deadly variety.

"I hate it when people lie to me," I snapped.

Apparently, Althea thought I was referring to the lie she'd told me and the rift it had created between us. She dropped her tools into the toolbox with a loud clatter and turned toward me. Something inside her had snapped.

"We're going to talk about that again, are we? You're not exactly the easiest person to be friends with, you know? You act like you're doing us some grand favor when you offer an occasional kind word. And let me tell you, those kind words are occasional. As in, hardly ever. But I laugh it off because I know that you're not really a bad person. I understand you sometimes can't help it. But heaven help me, all this drama is tiring me out. And I'm Southern. We eat drama for breakfast." She fisted her hands on her hips. Fire flashed in her brown eyes. "I guess what I'm saying is knock it off. If you want to walk away from one of the few friends you're ever going to have, do it now. If not, get over yourself. We all make mistakes. I'm not perfect. You're not perfect. It's high time you start practicing a little forgiveness."

I opened my mouth then shut it again.

It felt as if she'd punched me in the stomach. No, a punch to the stomach would not have hurt this much. Althea was right. Knowing it only sharpened the sting.

"Well?" she said. "Aren't you going to tell me how everyone is always out to get you? Aren't you going to tell me that anyone who professes to believe in"—she feigned a shocked gasp—"*ghosts* is a con looking for a sucker?"

I wanted to tell her that I wasn't thinking anything of the sort. The heavy lump in my throat caught the words that should have made everything better and held them hostage.

She drew a deep breath. "Aren't you going to tell me that I'm not good enough to be your friend?"

I swallowed hard. The lump refused to go anywhere. The best I could manage was a quick shake of my head. A denial. A silent one. An inadequate one.

Tears filled my eyes. I spun away from her. I hoped I'd moved fast enough that Althea hadn't seen them. I detested tears. They revealed weakness. They opened me up to getting hurt.

"Oh, no you don't. You don't get to run away without offering me...something." She grabbed my arm and spun me back around.

I cried out. Not from pain. Althea's slender fingers had a feather-light touch. It was her will that was steely. And like a dam breaking, tears burst from my eyes.

"Crap. You're crying." She tried to pull me into her arms.

I danced away from her.

"Y-you're right." I struggled for a smooth breath. "I am a terrible friend. I've always been a terrible friend."

She made a shushing noise and pulled me close for a hug.

"No," I said. Every muscle in my body stiffened. I tried to wiggle from her embrace. "No. Stop hugging me."

"I won't." Althea tightened her arms around me. "Not until you realize."

"You don't understand. I've suddenly realized everything."

"Everything?" Althea asked.

"We can finish this later," I said as I wiggled loose from her embrace. "But right now, I need to go find Byrd. Or Gibbons. But Chief Byrd would be faster."

"Hank? Why?" Althea frowned at me.

Bonbon with the Wind

"Because, thanks to you, I know who killed Joe Davies."

Chapter 28

Chief Byrd was out of the office. I left a message for him to call me. Gibbons answered his cell phone on the first ring. I explained how I'd figured everything out about Joe's and Sammy's deaths. He was silent for a long time before telling me two things. First, all the information I had was conjecture. And then, he reminded me that he wasn't working the murder investigation.

"Then do you think I should call Detective Prioleau?" I asked. *Please say no. Please say no.*

"No." He hadn't even had to think about it. "He won't want to listen to your hunches any more than I do."

"But—" I started to argue that my information was so much more than a hunch.

"Keep away from Prioleau," Gibbons snapped. "The man doesn't trust you. And he's under pressure to close this case quickly."

"Pressure? From whom?" I asked. "Not Big Dog's brother, I hope."

Gibbons groaned at the mention of Silas Piper. "You didn't hear it from me, but Piper is concerned his half-brother is responsible for Sammy Duncan's death. He wants both his brother found and the murder case wrapped up quickly and quietly. He's making the sheriff miserable with all his haranguing phone calls, which in turn is making the rest of us miserable."

"Tell Piper you know who killed Sammy Duncan. Tell him that this will soon be over," I said. "Tell Piper that."

Gibbons sucked in a sharp breath. "If you know where Piper's brother is hiding, you'd better tell me now."

"I wish I knew where he's holed up." I did feel bad I couldn't help Gibbons more. The strain he was feeling was evident in his voice. "If you'd just listen to what I'm telling you, I'm sure this case would be closed in no time."

"I can't follow hunches, especially when they're not even related to my investigation."

"It's not a hunch." Why couldn't he see that? My voice grew louder. "When you look at all of the pieces of the puzzle, this is what I see—what anyone with any sense would see."

The silence on his side of the line stretched for so long that I wondered if he'd hung up. Finally, a tired, much subdued voice said, "Promise me, Penn, you won't do anything rash."

"Of course, I won't," I promised. But that didn't mean I planned to sit on the sofa and watch classic TV with Trixie and Barbie. The steps I took to prove what Gibbons had dismissed as a *hunch* would be well thought out, not only by me but also by my friends.

As soon as I'd disconnected the call with Gibbons, I dialed Fletcher's number.

"We need to work together," I told him. When he scoffed, I added, "Believe it or not, a ghost is my main suspect right now. I need your help in figuring this all out."

"I w-w-won't help you fr-frame Delilah," he snapped.

"You care for her. You're trying to help her." Just like I was trying to help Mary. "I would never ask you to do anything to hurt her. All I'm asking is for you to help expose a murderer."

After going back and forth a bit like this, I finally agreed that he should take the investigative lead—whatever that meant—and that *I'd* be helping *him*. With that assurance, he told me to meet him at the Chocolate Box in ten minutes.

Fletcher arrived at the Chocolate Box on time and with his usual chip on his shoulder.

"I'm not going to help you hurt Delilah," he sang.

I took a bite of one of my chocolate chip brownies. "I already told you that I wouldn't ask you to that. I would like to speak with her, though. And I'd like to get a look at the map she took from Sammy's body." I wanted to assure myself that the dream map that had helped lead us to the treasure had been created only because my mind remembered the details of the map that Delilah had briefly shown me.

He snorted. "That-that's not going to h-h-happen."

"Fine. Let me tell you what I know." I sat down at one of the shop's small round tables and invited him to sit with me.

"I-I'm n-n-not going to l-l-let you lie to me about h-h-her," he announced before dropping into a chair across from me.

I offered him a brownie. He refused.

His leg bounced up and down with restless energy as I told him about the metal box with *Cedar's Hill Consolidated Bank* stamped on the side that Althea and I had found. I didn't tell him that we'd opened the box or that we'd turned the gold over to the police. I just made it sound like I was perplexed by this discovery and asked Fletcher if he, perhaps, could help me figure out why such a box would be on Camellia Beach. Perhaps Delilah had told him something?

To Detective Prioleau's credit, he'd kept the information about the recovered gold on a need-to-know basis. And our small group of friends who'd been on hand when we'd opened our treasure chest had all agreed that it might be dangerous to talk about what we'd found.

Fletcher had reacted with genuine surprise upon hearing about our "treasure chest." However, instead of sharing any useful information of his own, he told me that he had somewhere he needed to be and hurried away.

HE'S DRIVING AWAY NOW, I texted to Harley.

I hated to do it. I truly did. Despite his chronic bad attitude, Fletcher was one of the good guys and the best employee I'd ever known. Following him felt like a betrayal.

But there was a killer on the island. This wasn't a time to worry about hurt feelings.

Bonbon with the Wind

While waiting to hear from Harley, I ate the chocolate chip brownie Fletcher had refused. And I fidgeted worse than Fletcher had.

Finally, my phone pinged with an address. It was to a property located on nearby Bowman's Island. I thanked Harley and texted that I was on my way.

Harley didn't like my plans to root out Delilah. But since he knew there was no stopping me, he insisted on supporting me. I hated taking Harley away from his son on one of the few weeknights Harley got to spend with Gavin. And I certainly didn't like putting Harley in any kind of danger, but as Harley had pointed out, if we were going to be in a relationship, we needed to trust each other. We needed to let each other into our lives.

After checking in with Bertie, who was feeding Gavin a hearty meal and making sure he was doing his homework, I drove over the bridge and across the causeway to Bowman's Island, a long, narrow marsh island that visitors had to cross over in order to get to Camellia Beach.

I turned off the main road and onto Bowman's Island. The paved road on the island quickly ended, giving way to a deeply grooved and rutted one-lane dirt path. Homes sporting long boat docks sat tucked in around sprawling oaks heavy with Spanish moss.

Harley's motorcycle—which ironically wasn't a Harley—was parked off the road and partially hidden within a copse of trees. I spotted Harley leaning against the trunk of a tree. The corner of his mouth lifted when my car approached.

Gracious, did my heart truly need to beat so heavily every time I saw him?

I pulled off the road as best as I could manage and then turned off the car.

"After Fletcher headed down this way, I remembered he has a cousin that married a Templeton who has a family home out here on this island," Harley said after brushing a quick kiss against my cheek.

"Gotta love small towns, everyone knows everything about everyone," I said with a smile.

"I still don't know nearly enough about you," he said with a playful sparkle in his eye. "But let's go talk with Delilah, huh?"

I twined my fingers with his, and we walked down the driveway toward a large white-washed plantation-style house. I recognized Fletcher's car parked near the front door. A black and tan hound dog barked at us from the porch.

"So much for sneaking up on anyone," I said.

Harley gave my hand a squeeze as we climbed the steps. The hound, bored with barking, had flopped back down by the time we reached him. "Think we should just ring the bell?"

"Yeah, I think that would be best," I said. "We can't really kick down the front door. That's against the law."

"Glad to hear it," Harley said with a smirk. "I didn't wear my kicking boots."

I rang the bell and waited.

I hammered my fist against the door and waited.

I shouted, "I'm not here to accuse you of killing your husband," and waited.

Finally the front door lock clicked. Fletcher tossed the door open. "I knew you'd have someone follow me."

"If you knew it, you should have saved us all the trouble and invited me over," I said. "I just want to talk with Delilah."

"You know that police detective that you've been so friendly with over the last couple of days wants to talk with her too," Harley added.

"I k-k-know," Fletcher huffed and stepped aside. "Sh-sh-she didn't d-d-do anything wr-wr-wrong."

"She tampered with and took evidence from a crime scene, but…" Harley said and shrugged.

"I took what was mine," Delilah said as she came into the living room. She was impeccably dressed. Not a hair was out of place. I wouldn't have appeared so put-together if I'd been on the run from the police.

"That was your husband's map," I said.

She gave a sharp nod.

"You'd known all along that he'd come to Camellia Beach," I said.

"Admitting that would be admitting I was an accessory to a crime," she said while Fletcher opened and closed his mouth like a fish that had found itself tossed onto shore.

"You must have suspected she knew more than she was telling," I said to Fletcher, honestly surprised. "None of the revelations about her husband has surprised her."

"J-j-just because she's n-n-n-not an emotional mess, doesn't-doesn't mean she's involved," Fletcher stammered even more than usual.

"No. But remember how I saw the Gray Lady and remember how I thought she looked familiar?" I turned to Delilah. "She was you, wasn't she? You were warning Joe—I mean John—that Sammy was out of jail and coming to Camellia Beach. You were the reason that he was so upset the morning before the hurricane. And I suspect you also knew he'd started to have trouble with his memory and had misplaced the stolen gold."

Instead of answering, she gave a haughty sniff.

"Stolen gold?" Fletcher whirled toward her. "Delilah? You knew?"

"Of course she knew," I answered since she was determined not to incriminate herself. "And we're not the police."

"Actually, as a lawyer I'm compelled to—" Harley started to say.

"Could you go stand outside for a second?" I asked him. "Not that we'll be discussing anything illegal, mind you. I simply don't want Delilah to feel intimidated, seeing how she's not your client." I didn't understand all the rules governing lawyers, but I didn't want to accidentally cause Harley any ethical dilemmas.

He hesitated for a moment before giving a sharp nod. "I'll be right outside the door."

Once he was gone, I said, "You met with Joe at the beach because you knew Sammy was on his way. You wanted to warn him. Isn't that correct?"

"I did," she admitted.

I had to tamp down an urge to do a little victory dance.

"You were also skulking around Althea's shop, weren't you? Have you also been dropping gold coins for me to find?"

"What are you talking about?" She scowled at me.

"I'm talking about The First Wish, the crystal shop on Main Street. I saw you poking around the shop. Did you drop a gold coin inside her shop to confuse us?"

Her scowl tightened. "Why would I do that? You clearly don't need my help to get confused."

Fletcher snorted.

I wasn't sure why she was lying about the gold coins, but it really didn't matter. "We found the stolen gold."

"Pirate gold?" Fletcher demanded.

"No, not pirate gold. It was gold Sammy stole from the bank where he worked. Joe took it. He hid it. And lost it. Isn't that true?" I asked Delilah.

Her shoulders dropped. "Fletcher told me you found the box. And I'm sure you and your friends plan to keep it."

"No, we turned it over to the police."

"Ah." She plastered a brittle smile to her face. "Such heroes. Are you here to rub salt in the wound?"

"No. I'm here because I'd like to take a look at the map."

"Why?"

"Call it curiosity," I said. Plus, I was hoping it would help provide some evidence against the person who killed Joe and Sammy, evidence that would convince the police to listen to me.

She closed her eyes. "How did you manage to find the box? John had this map. Heck, he made the map, and he still couldn't find his way back to the gold. No one has been able to."

"Dumb luck, probably," I said, not willing to go into a long explanation about how my dreams and Althea's knowledge of the island brought us straight to the hidden box.

"Dumb luck." She opened her eyes and looked me up and down. "I can believe that." She left the room for a moment and then came back with the map.

It was a copy of a hand-drawn map on graph paper. It was mainly a series of lines with numbers of steps written next to them. There weren't many identifying markers. A bush here. A tree there. But no way to know if the trail was located on the ocean-side or marsh-side. No wonder Joe had had trouble following it once he forgot the rest. And even if he'd started in the right place, the trail Althea had followed was so well hidden, he might not have been able to find it again. I doubted I could find it again and there was nothing wrong with my memory.

I had no idea how my dream-mind had managed to make sense of such a sparse map. But somehow it had, right?

"How do you think Sammy got hold of this map?" I asked. "Joe's place had burned to the ground. Do you think Sammy confronted Joe before the storm?"

"No, Sammy came to me after the storm had passed," Delilah said quietly. "He threatened to tell the police about my role in helping them get away with the gold. I had no choice but to give him the map."

I blinked back my surprise. "How did you get it?"

"After John realized that he'd lost the treasure, he sent me a copy."

"You stayed in contact with him?" That seemed risky.

233

"We were careful," she admitted. "He kept promising me that he was close to remembering where he'd buried the gold. He had been afraid that someone would steal it out of his house, so the numbskull went and buried it."

Okay, that made sense. But there was something I didn't understand. "If he stayed in contact with you, why didn't he also stay in contact with his daughter? How could he abandon her? She was working with him at the car dealership. When he ran, it closed, leaving her without a father and a career."

"Mary?" Delilah wrinkled her nose.

"Yes, Mary." I felt a need to defend the poor girl. Even though she was an adult, her father had abandoned her.

"Well…" Delilah bit her lower lip. "You see…"

"You were lying about that rosy relationship between her and you," I said, trying to be helpful. I'd had stepmothers who lied about being friendly with my father's children when the reality was no relationship existed. I doubted any woman wanted to be cast as the evil stepmother.

"No. No. It's just…" She bit her lower lip again. After several tense moments, she blurted in one breath, "Mary isn't good with secrets. To protect her, I told her that her father lost the business and ran off in shame. I told her that I didn't know where he went and that I couldn't contact him. He didn't leave her in a lurch. He signed his savings account over to her and gifted her one of the car lot's best used cars. A real cute sporty two-seater.

"And I have lunch with her every week. We sometimes go antiquing together on weekends. She loves coming to me for makeup and fashion advice. I'm not a monster. I freely share my knowledge with her. She's easy to get along with. We're very much alike."

"Ah," I said. I didn't have time to argue that Mary had described their relationship differently. I hated it when people lied to me. My tone grew sharper. "You do know that you need to contact the police as soon as I leave here? You need to give them the map and tell them everything else you know."

"She-she-she c-c-can't!" Fletcher looked as if he wanted to murder me.

I held up my hands. "I have a good feeling the police will be making arrest tonight." In a few hours' time if everything worked out the way we'd planned. "Call Detective Prioleau, Fletcher. He likes you. It'll be best for everyone if Delilah turns herself in."

And with that small piece of advice, I left. My friends and I had a busy night in front of us, and a murderer waiting to be caught.

Chapter 29

COME TO THE RUINS NEAR THE LIGHTHOUSE AT 8PM, the text message had pinged my phone while I ate dinner. It had originated from a blocked number. COME ALONE.

That was the text we'd been waiting for. Still, when it came, my stomach lurched.

After our meeting with Delilah, Harley had sent a series of texts to Big Dog's phone, a phone we weren't even sure Big Dog still had on him, providing him with information similar to what we'd told Delilah about the gold we'd found—suggesting that we still had the bank box.

Harley and I had met up with Bertie, Althea, and Bubba for a light dinner. Before sitting down at the table, I'd sent a quick text to Mary to update her about what was going on. I told her about the treasure chest of gold and promised to let her know whenever we knew more. After a short back and forth, we'd planned to meet up and discuss things much later tonight at the Chocolate Box.

"Any idea who sent this cryptic text?" Bertie asked as she peered over my shoulder and read the part about needing to *come alone* out loud.

"I'm pretty sure it didn't come from a ghost," I said.

Althea snorted. I didn't know if she'd snorted because she agreed with me or because she thought ghosts could send text messages. I was wise enough not to ask.

I drew a long breath. These were my friends. And as hard as it was for me, I had promised to share everything with them. I needed to tell them my theories because before the night was over, we were going to meet up with a killer and we needed to get through this with no one ending up hurt or worse. I needed to tell them everything.

While finishing off the rest of my chocolate chip brownies, we sat around the table and quietly discussed the who, what, and whys of what was going to happen tonight. And I was fairly certainly none of it would involve a ghost.

It was easy to imagine why the island was fertile ground for ghost stories. There was heartache and death crowding every chapter of the local history book I'd started reading last night. I huffed as I drove toward the narrower northern end of the island where the abandoned old red-and-white striped lighthouse now stood stranded in the water.

Even though the sun was still visible over the marsh, a full moon sat on the horizon over the ocean as if waiting for its turn to take over the sky.

I drove alone in my Fiat, just as the text message had asked of me. But I'd faced enough dangerous situations in the past year to know that doing as the mysterious message had directed would be beyond stupid. And I had no patience for stupid.

Harley and Althea had left ahead of me.

WE'RE HUNKERED DOWN IN THE BUSHES TO THE RIGHT OF THE RUINS, Harley texted. NO ONE IS HERE YET.

Gibbons also knew what we were doing, although he'd told me that he thought it foolhardy to do anything other than ignore the text. He had fussed so much that I regretted calling to tell him about it. But after he'd settled down, he insisted on having a team nearby.

Bertie, Bubba, Trixie, and Barbie were also in on the plans. Fletcher was not. I wished he was, but ever since Delilah had arrived in town, we seemed to be working against each other. I couldn't risk him doing something impulsive that might put the rest of our lives in danger.

This was it. I parked where the road ended. I swept my gaze over the empty street. Harley had hidden his old BMW well. The far end of the island felt vacant, deserted. With a shiver, I stepped out of the car and headed down the sandy path that led toward the ruins near the lighthouse and whoever waited for me.

A Coast Guard base used to watch over the nearby Charleston harbor from its vantage point at the far northern edge of the island. It had been abandoned decades ago. The ruins of its crumbling concrete block buildings, only partially removed, were slowly being eroded away from the top by the relentless wind and swallowed by the sandy beach at the ground level.

This is where the person who'd sent the text had wanted to meet.

"You have no proof a killer even sent that text," Chief Byrd had complained when I'd gone to him to show him the message on my phone. "People don't like outsiders like you poking in their delicate business, Penn." He rubbed his nose. "People with secrets get mighty anxious when you start asking questions. Any one of them could have sent that text in your hand."

Like Gibbons, Byrd had advised me to ignore the text. Like Gibbons, he'd insisted on being on hand where the action was going to happen.

As I approached the ruins of the old Coast Guard base, my heart began to pound. Was Byrd right? Was I walking into trouble of my own making?

I hated surprises.

Hopefully, everything would go according to plan.

I headed straight for the remains of what looked like a storage building. It was the only building that still had four walls and an opening where a door used to be. This had to be the place.

ANYTHING? I texted Harley.

YOU'RE THE FIRST PERSON WE'VE SEEN SINCE GETTING HERE, he texted back.

I focused on a thick clump of underbrush where I suspected Harley and Althea were hiding. I couldn't see anything.

I glanced around some more. No sign of Gibbons.

That was good. Right?

For some reason, I wanted to see them. But if I could see them, others could too.

I'M HEADING INTO THE BUILDING TO WAIT, I texted before pushing my phone into my back pocket.

As soon as I stepped foot into what remained of the small building, I knew I wasn't alone.

I nearly tripped over my own feet when I saw the man who was waiting for me in the shadows of the building, a building we had all thought was empty. "You-you're early."

His hair was in disarray. His eyes wide with panic. He marched toward me like a man who wanted revenge.

"You don't need that gun." I struggled to sound calm while my heart hammered painfully against my chest. How had our carefully thought-out plan failed so dramatically? He wasn't supposed to have a gun. And how had he hidden himself so well that no one knew he was here? Certainly Gibbons and Harley would have taken a look around before getting into position.

I threw my hands in the air. "You-you don't want to shoot me."

He barked a laugh. "Missy, you don't know what I want."

"I think I do know. And I think we can help each other," I said because I sure as heck didn't want to get shot.

I swallowed around a lump in my throat. This wasn't the first time I'd found myself on the wrong end of a handgun. In the past, I'd been lucky to escape with my life. Had that fantastic luck of mine finally run out? "Big Dog, you don't want to shoot me."

"Weren't you listening?" With a look of pure rage, he shook his gun at me. "You don't know what's going on in my head!"

I closed my eyes, fully expecting him to pull the trigger and end things right then and there. When nothing happened, I said very quietly, "I know you didn't kill Joe Davies."

He didn't answer. Had I spoken too quietly? Had he not heard me? I began to repeat myself, talking a bit louder this time when he cut me off. "You're lying."

I shook my head. "No, I'm not lying. For one thing I know what it's like to be the black sheep of the family. Your brother believes the worst of you. Always has and always will. Well, both my mother and father treat me the same way. It stinks. I'm not going to do that to you."

He frowned at that. But his gun remained locked in place.

"I know you came to Camellia Beach in search of the gold. I know—"

"There's no pirate treasure!" he shouted. "That was a lie!"

"Yes, but Sammy stole gold from the bank. From under your nose. Why was the bank stockpiling the gold in the first place? Was that your idea? Is that why the feds suspected you of the crime?"

Big Dog shrugged. "I didn't make any changes to how things were run at the bank. It was the trustees who had lost faith in the federal government. They feared the dollar might collapse, so they started to buy gold bars as a safeguard. Other banks around the country having been doing it too. Or so they told me. I honestly didn't care."

"I see. And after Sammy was released from jail you followed him to Camellia Beach in order to find those stolen gold bars and hand it back to the bank. You wanted to prove to your brother that you aren't the screw up he thinks you are, isn't that right?"

"Not that he'd believe it," Big Dog grumbled.

"No, he won't. Put the gun down. I know you didn't kill Joe. But if the police come running in here, they might not see things the same way."

The hand he was using to hold the gun was trembling. "Maybe I found Joe before the storm. Maybe I no longer care about the gold. Maybe I'm here because I'm looking for revenge. Sammy and Joe are gone. Maybe my task is done."

"Come on now," I said. "If that were true, you wouldn't be here. You wouldn't be skulking around in an abandoned storage building. You'd be in another country by now. My arms are getting tired. Can I put them down now?"

He nodded, but he didn't lower the handgun. I still had quite a clear view down its shiny barrel.

"I don't have the gold," I told him.

He rolled his eyes heavenward. "Harley lied, didn't he? He lied to lure me here."

"Don't be too hard on him. He's worried about—"

With an angry growl, Harley charged into the shadowy ruins like an enraged bull. His head lowered, his right shoulder leading the way. He tackled Big Dog with a loud smack. The impact knocked the wind from Harley's friend. He landed hard with a groan.

"He didn't do it!" I shouted as Gibbons and an armed police officer ran into the building behind Harley with their guns drawn.

No one seemed to hear me. Harley pinned Big Dog to the ground and pried the handgun from his grip. With efficient movements of a man who knew his way around a firearm, which I found in equal parts sexy and frightening, he checked the chamber to see if it was loaded.

"It's empty," Harley looked up at me and said.

"That's because he's not a killer."

"He sure has a funny way of showing it," Harley said, his voice deep with rage.

"Brandishing a weapon and threatening people with it is a crime," Gibbons said. He then turned to the officer and said, "Cuff him."

"Wait!" I waved my hands in the air, trying to get everyone's attention. "He had a gun, but he wasn't threatening me." As much as I hated to lie, I felt this was one that needed to be told. I looked at Big Dog. "Isn't that right?"

"I—" He glanced at me and then at Harley. "Um…"

"He wasn't threatening me," I insisted. "He's trying to find the bank's gold, but he's not breaking any laws."

"He's been hiding from me," Gibbons grumbled.

"Not illegally," I pointed out. "A man has a right to avoid his brother."

Gibbons grunted.

Harley rolled off Big Dog and then offered a hand to help his friend up.

"Did you have to tackle me so hard? I think you cracked a few ribs, man," Big Dog complained as he rubbed his chest.

"He didn't kill those two men?" the officer asked, scratching his head. "Then what are we doing here?"

"You're helping mend a relationship between two brothers," I said.

"We're doing our jobs," Gibbons said. "We're following orders that come from the top."

Big Dog held up his hands. "I'm not going to let you drag me in front of Silas like a truant teen. I came to Camellia Beach to clear my name—and catch some gnarly waves—but mostly to clear my name. But with Sammy dead and the gold still missing, I don't see how that can ever happen."

"Harley didn't lie to you," I said. "We found the stolen gold. The police have it."

"You-you found—?" Big Dog's voice cracked. He quickly turned away.

"Will you come down to the station with us, Mr. Graham?" Gibbons asked. "We'd like to take your statement regarding the theft and the murders. And your brother would like to see you."

"Your brother is not going to apologize or change overnight. You know that," I warned. "But you owe it to yourself to stop running from him."

Big Dog kept his back toward us as he nodded. "You're right. I'll go." The tone of his voice was rusty. "Not that I think it'll make any difference. I wasn't the one who recovered the stolen gold, so I'm still the failure, the screw up."

Harley laid his hand on his friend's shoulder. "Not to us, man."

Gibbons and the uniformed officer led Big Dog out of the ruins. Harley looked at me and frowned.

"He'll be okay," I said. "We're ending this tonight, remember?"

"I know, but I still feel like a jerk for what I did to him. He is my friend."

"You helped him."

His shoulders sagged. "He threatened you with a gun. I don't know if I'll ever be able to forgive him for that. We should have handled things differently. We shouldn't have pushed him over the edge like that."

"We didn't push him to the edge. He walked right over that particular cliff on his own when he left your apartment and disappeared." Which reminded me of something. I chased after Gibbons.

"Who told you that they saw Big Dog going up the steps toward Harley's apartment the morning after Sammy's murder?" I asked Gibbons.

He hesitated before saying, "I suppose it doesn't matter now that I've found Mr. Graham. It was your new friend. Mary. She was Joe's daughter, right?"

"That's what I thought." I bit my lower lip.

"That's a lie. She didn't see me. After I left that night, I didn't come back," Big Dog said like a man who'd been roundly defeated. "Not that anyone is going to believe me."

"I do," I said.

Big Dog looked at Harley, who'd come to stand next to me and shook his head. "You're probably the only one who believes that. And here I am. I failed to prove I wasn't involved with the theft. I failed to recover the gold. And now these guys are going to charge me for Sammy's murder."

243

"No, Gibbons wouldn't do that," I said.

"That's for Prioleau to decide," Gibbons warned.

No, it wasn't. The night wasn't over, and the plan we'd put into place hadn't worked its way to the end.

"Althea took my car and is headed to the Chocolate Box," Harley said as we watched the police lead his friend away.

I nodded. "Good."

At the same time my gut clenched. While the pieces for catching a killer tonight were falling into place as I'd expected them to, that didn't mean I had to feel happy about it.

Chapter 30

Harley drove while I called Chief Byrd to make sure he was still willing to help out with our *unwise caper* as he'd grumpily called it.

"I'm already in place. But only because Gibbons sweet-talked me into it. This *plan* of yours is going to turn out to be a big, fat waste of everyone's time," he grumbled and then hung up.

I hoped to prove him wrong, didn't I?

My gut clenched again.

Harley glanced over at me before turning onto the road that led to the Chocolate Box. He didn't say anything. He didn't need to.

I had promised Mary that I'd help her find the villain who had killed her father. And I prided myself on keeping my promises.

A light wind rustled the leaves in the ancient oak tree that guarded the entrance of my shop. The Spanish moss hanging from its sweeping branches waltzed in the moonlight like debutants at an otherworldly cotillion.

Harley parked my car in one of the parking spots reserved for our upstairs apartments. He then turned off the ignition. We sat there in silence for several minutes.

"I don't like the idea of you going in there alone," he said finally.

"You have a son, Harley. You have to think of him," I said.

He reached across the console to cover my hand with his. "I get what you're saying, and I don't disagree. But I also think you need to send Hank into your shop and stay out here with me."

"Byrd will be in there, but if we're going to get a confession, I need to talk with the killer. Alone."

Harley squeezed my hand. His eyes darkened with concern. "I hate this."

His concern touched me more than I'd expected. I understood how he felt. If our roles were reversed and he was the one going into

245

the shop, I'd hate it too. I'd turn into a warrior woman set on protecting my man. He cared about me. And I cared about him. I cared probably too much.

"I love you," I said.

What. Just. Came. Out. Of. My. Mouth?

My heart stopped.

Harley's heart must have stopped dead in its tracks too. His entire body stilled. The pressure of his hand on mine remained unchanged as we sat in my car staring at each other like a pair of feral cats who'd crossed into each other's territory and didn't know whether they wanted to strike or run.

My head suddenly felt cold. I knew I needed to breathe, but my lungs had seized.

The words were out there. I couldn't take them back. Heck, I couldn't open my mouth to laugh or say something flip that would chase those other *stupid, stupid* words away.

They floated between us like living things.

What would Harley do with those words? Would he use them against me? Would he laugh? If he laughed, I'd die of mortification.

After hundreds of long, long moments, the corners of his eyes crinkled. Just a bit. The hard edges of his mouth loosened. Just a bit. The grip of his hand on mine tightened. Just a bit.

"Penn"—my name was a soft prayer on his lips—"don't panic."

Three words.

Not the three words most women wanted to hear after such an impulsive declaration, but they were the three words I *needed* in that edge-of-death-by-mortification moment.

"You go do what you need to do. I'll make sure everyone is where they need to be." His mouth lifted into a cautious smile. "And while you risk your neck, I'll risk mine and go raid Bertie's hidden stash of Amar chocolates so you'll have as much comfort food as you might need when this is all over."

246

At a loss for words—*he'd promised me chocolate for heaven's sake*—I pressed my mouth to his before hurrying out into the night and toward the shop.

I'd barely made it to the Chocolate Box's front door when my phone chimed. I read the text. It was from Althea.

THERE'S TROUBLE AT MY SHOP, she wrote. I NEED HELP.

What was Althea doing at her shop? She was supposed to be at the Chocolate Box coordinating with Byrd. Everyone, even Trixie and Barbie had been given vital roles to play in our plan to catch the villain. Going against my instincts, I'd not kept any part of the plan a secret from my friends. But by doing that, it meant I needed everyone focused on the plan and not running after trouble elsewhere.

WHAT'S WRONG? I texted back, and then added, I NEED YOU HERE.

She replied with only one word: HURRY.

I frowned at the screen.

Well, it was going to be at least another half-hour before our plan got underway. The crystal shop meant the world to Althea. I could understand why she would rush over there if something seemed amiss. Whether I trusted her completely or not, it didn't matter. Althea was my friend. And she deserved all the help I could give her.

After sending a group *"be right back"* text, I jogged over toward the car. Harley was already heading around the building to the steps. When he saw me hurrying his way, he quickly changed course.

"What's going on?" he asked.

"Althea texted that there's trouble at her shop."

"At her shop? What is she doing there?"

"I don't know, but she says she needs help. Will you come with me?"

"Of course." He slid into the passenger seat.

While the shop was only around the corner, with our plan already in motion driving seemed safer than walking. I parked in front of her shop. The place was dark.

"It shouldn't be this dark," Harley said. "She's been keeping construction lights on inside the building all night for security."

A light danced around inside. It looked like a cell phone light.

"Althea?" I called and pushed on the door.

It opened. The bell above the door chimed.

"She shouldn't have left this unlocked," Harley said, his voice a low grumble. But this was Althea we were talking about. We all knew she wasn't all that vigilant when it came to security.

Harley stayed by my side as we entered the store, using our phones as flashlights.

"Althea?" I called again.

Still, no answer.

We stepped further into her shop. Nothing looked out of place.

"I don't like this," Harley said.

I tried calling Althea's cell phone. We could hear it ringing in the rear of the shop. And that's where we found her, in the back office that she'd just finished framing out. She was lying on the sawdust covered wooden floor. A dark puddle of blood pooled around her head.

"No!" I shouted and ran to her side.

Why would someone attack Althea? No one was supposed to get hurt. I'd shared my information with my friends. We'd spent hours creating a plan designed to keep everyone safe. It was supposed to be foolproof.

I found a pulse, but she remained as still as death.

"Call EMS!" I shouted.

"Already on—" Harley started to say.

And then there was a sickening thud.

I jumped up in time to see Harley crumple to the ground.

"No!" I shined my cell phone flashlight in his direction.

The petite Mary stood like an innocent lamb—if lambs held heavy iron pipes. The pipe was one of the pipes I'd stacked for Althea earlier that day. Mary stared with those large eyes of hers as if she couldn't believe what she'd just done.

"What are you doing?" I demanded as I dialed my phone like mad.

"If you don't want me to hit your boyfriend again, you'd better drop that phone." While her voice sounded soft, gentle, she lifted her arm, prepared to take another swing.

I opened my hand, and the phone clattered to the floor, but it fell in such a way its light still shined in her direction.

"He's my beau," I corrected. I never thought my first opportunity to use it would be in response to a crazed killer. "And I'll kill you with my bare hands if you touch him again."

She sniffled. "You were supposed to help me."

I took a step toward her with the goal of leading her and that heavy pipe of hers away from Harley. I prayed he was still alive.

"I *was* trying to help you," I said, holding my hands wide to show her that I was no threat.

"My father…" She looked up at the ceiling and blinked. When she continued, her voice cracked, "You know who killed him?"

"Yes. I know who killed both Joe and Sammy," I said. She still was too close to Harley. I choose my next words with care. "I also know Joe helped Sammy Dalton steal five million dollars' worth of gold. That's why he left Cedar's Hill. He took the gold, changed his name, and moved here."

Mary took a step toward me. "But, the gold? It's gone, isn't it?"

"Everyone I talked with commented on how Joe was obsessed with finding Blackbeard's lost treasure." I moved closer to Harley. Close enough that I could block Mary if she tried to swing that iron pipe again. "But Joe was never searching for Blackbeard's gold. It was my friend Bubba who pointed out that Joe never provided any detail beyond what someone could read on a Wiki page on the Internet. Others have mentioned how he had moments where he forgot…things. The aging residents of the island have seen the signs before. They believe he had dementia."

"Oh great, I gave up my life for a man who was losing his mind?"

"Gave up your life?" I asked. I glanced down at Harley, and nearly cried with relief when I saw that he was still breathing. "I thought you didn't know where Joe had gone."

"I didn't." Her voice turned sharper. "He up and ran away, didn't he? He didn't care about how his leaving affected those he left behind."

"You're talking about the car dealership closing," I offered.

She nodded. "I worked there since high school. I put everything into that place. Everything. And then he ran off and left the dealership buried under crushing debt. It didn't last even a month after he abandoned it."

"I don't understand," I said. "It's not like you expected to inherit the shop."

"I-I-I—" She sputtered. "Why would you say that?"

"Because it's true."

"You mean because of my stepmother?" Her pretty cheeks turned pink.

I didn't let her distress deter me. "No, that's not what I mean. Let's stop pretending. Your name isn't Mary, and you're not Joe's daughter."

She opened her mouth to protest. But she must have recognized the futility of denying what I clearly knew was true, because she quickly shut it again.

"I admit that you had me fooled until I accidentally called the number for the car dealership on Mary's business card. When I discovered the number had been disconnected, I did a quick Google search. I was feeling so sorry for poor Mary. And that's when I saw it, a picture of her with two of her friends—Sammy's daughter and you. You seemed genuinely upset that day we met, but you're not Joe's daughter. You may have dyed your hair red to look like hers, and your face is similar to hers, but you aren't her. No, you're Joanna Waller, Mary's friend, aren't you?" I tilted my head to one side. "Why do you think you should have gotten anything from Mary's dad?"

"I worked for her dad at the used car lot."

When she didn't offer anything else, I asked, "You were what? His private secretary?" The pieces seemed to settle into place. "Delilah was Joe's secretary before he married her, wasn't she? I imagine they'd been having an affair long before his wife died." I drew a slow breath. "Were you his mistress as well as his secretary?"

I hated it, but I'd worked in the business world long enough to know that some men expected their secretaries to be a co-worker *with benefits.*

"He promised he'd leave Delilah and make me his partner both in marriage and in the dealership." Her eyelids snapped angrily. "But that was a lie. He disappeared only a few days after making that promise. Neither Mary nor Delilah seemed at all put out by his abandonment, not even after the car dealership collapsed in bankruptcy. He'd hidden what he'd done from everyone. He'd been taking out loans left and right on the dealership, putting the money in his personal accounts.

"He left Mary and Delilah sitting high in hog heaven. And me? What did I get as a reward for letting that old goat near me? Not a crumb. That's what." As she gave her impassioned speech, she lifted the lead pipe as if preparing to play a game of baseball. "It took me a while to figure out what he and Sammy had done. And then I had to wait and wait for Sammy to get released from prison before I could follow him, here, to this little rat-hole by the sea."

"And when Joe couldn't tell you where to find the gold, you lost control?" I asked.

"It was an accident. He kept saying he couldn't take me to the gold and that he needed to get away. I hit him because he kept saying over and over that he didn't know where the gold was. The lying bugger. He fell down his house's front steps and died on me. He died before he could give me the gold. He gave those other women everything and left without even thinking what his leaving would do to me. I deserved that gold."

"Is that why you burned down his house after you killed him?" I stepped over Harley. I needed to move Joanna further away from him. "Because you were still angry?"

She sniffled. "The gold wasn't there, and I knew I needed to get rid of the evidence that I had been there."

"And then, after the storm, you dyed your hair red and returned, pretending to be the grieving daughter. But why do that?"

"Are you an idiot? I came back because the gold is here. And I needed help finding it."

"You set out to use me?" I'd blindly trusted her. I'd felt sorry for her. And she'd been pulling my strings all along.

"Everyone on the island says how you're the one that can figure things out. Heck, everyone was talking about how you found John's body and how you were already asking questions about his death."

"So you followed me to his burnt house? You contrived our first meeting?"

She was right. I was an idiot. And in my attempt to be honest with my friends, I'd pulled both Althea and Harley into her trap. They were hurt because of my stupidity. They could *die* because of me.

She shrugged without showing a lick of remorse.

"But I wasn't getting the results you wanted, so you went after Sammy, isn't that right?" I asked. I had to keep her talking. And I had to hope that the call I'd placed had gone through.

"He had a treasure map to help him locate the gold. I'd watched him steal it away from Delilah. I'd been watching him ever since his release from prison, which wasn't easy. That surfer who used to work at the bank was following him on and off too. Never knew when that one would show up."

"Wait. I'm confused. Why didn't you let Sammy find the gold for you, then? Why did you attack him?"

She pushed out a sharp breath. "The fool man kept leading me around in circles. He'd pull out that map, swear, and then wander around in circles all over again. He clearly didn't know what he was doing. I needed to get my hands on that map and do it myself."

I shook my head. That didn't ring true. Delilah had taken the map from Sammy, not Joanna. "But you didn't take the map," I pointed out.

"Didn't I?" She smiled. "Couldn't make things look too obvious. I took a picture of the map with my phone."

"Ah," I said. That's all I needed to say. I could tell by the way pride danced in her eyes that she was bursting with a need to share how she'd outsmarted everyone, including the police. Of course, I also realized that her openness to share all this with me meant that she had no plans of letting me leave Althea's shop alive.

"The map is flawed. No wonder John lost track of where he'd buried it. No one could find the back of their hand following it." She shook her head with dismay. "But I've been watching you. And I know you're just about as clever as I am. And you know this island."

"I don't know the island as well as some," I admitted.

"Come on." She stepped toward me, while still gripping the iron pipe. "You found the buried gold."

I swallowed down a lump of worry and nodded. "Yes. Just today, I found the gold."

"Where is it?" She charged toward me. "It belongs to me, you know."

I backed away from her and nearly tripped over Harley. "You came to me pretending to be someone else. You pretended to be grieving, and I promised to help you." I wasn't sure why I said that.

Surprisingly, despite having lived my life expecting the worst of others, the sting of betrayal still hurt.

"Oh, you're going to help me all right. You're going to hand over that gold you have no right to. And in return for that favor, I'll help you end this miserable life of yours. Your best friend has turned her back on you. Your mother won't talk to you. Anyone with a brain would understand why you'd snap and attack your boyfriend and ex-best friend. They'd fight back, and everyone ends up dead."

I shook my head. "No, you're wrong. No one would believe that. And I made up with Althea."

She shrugged. "Doesn't matter, does it? You being dead and all. That's the important part."

She swung the pipe like it was a baseball bat.

I ducked.

"You thought you were so clever setting that trap for me." She swung again. I jumped out of her way. "But I knew what you were doing. I stood outside your apartment and listened as you and your silly friends made plans."

With a downward motion, she tried to knock me down with the pipe again. And again, I managed to avoid her. "If you kill me, how are you going to find the gold?"

"You'll be begging me to let you tell me where you hid the gold before I'm done with you." She swung the pipe.

I needed help. Where were the police? Where were my friends? I'd hoped my aborted call had at least caught their attention.

Where was Chief Byrd? He should be here.

Mary came at me again. Swinging wildly.

The pipe caught me on the back. I went down hard and landed on Harley. He groaned.

"Help!" I cried.

With a banshee yell that had my hair standing straight up, Bertie—*not Chief Byrd*—came crashing in from the back door. And she had a gun. A big one.

"Give me the gold!" Joanna growled as she hit me in the back again. The force of the blow knocked the breath from my lungs.

"The police have it," Bertie shouted. "Leave her alone."

"Where's Byrd?" I wheezed.

"Prioleau called him off," Bertie growled. "Said he already had the killer in custody."

"The detective must mean Big Dog." I coughed. "He didn't do it."

"That's kind of obvious," Bertie lifted the gun. "Don't even think of swinging that thing again, honey."

"Where's Bubba?" We needed help in cornering this swinging she-devil. She was too dangerous to let get away.

"He's coming."

But it wasn't Bubba who burst in like Bertie had, but Trixie and Barbie with Stella on a leash barking like a hellhound. The ruckus distracted me more than it had Joanna. Before I knew what was happening, the madwoman grabbed me up from the floor and used me as a shield between her and Bertie's ginormous gun.

At the same time, Bertie shouted, "Honey, I warned you to leave my girl alone!" She then squeezed off a shot.

I closed my eyes tightly closed, fully expecting the bullet to slam into me.

It didn't.

But Joanna, obviously realizing she was dealing with a group of armed lunatics, released me and dove to the ground.

I took the opening and jumped on top of her. My back screamed in pain as I did it. Those glancing whacks I'd taken from her iron pipe hurt like the devil. I could tell they were going to leave a rainbow array of bruises.

Bertie fired again. Plaster and splintered wood rained down on my head.

"Bertie, put that gun away," Byrd hollered.

I looked up in time to see the police chief, moving faster than I'd ever seen him move, run into Althea's shop. Bubba followed him through the back door along with several Camellia Beach police officers.

Things moved quickly from there as Byrd and his men took over. Sirens blared as EMS was called. Althea still hadn't moved. Bertie had rushed over to her. She cradled her daughter's head in her lap. I did the same for Harley. His eyes fluttered before they opened. He reached up and put his hand on my cheek.

"You okay?" he asked.

I had to shake my head. "I'm not the one who got conked over the head, you numbskull."

He smiled. "Glad to hear it."

By that time Marion had arrived with her crew. "Again, we meet under the worst conditions," she said in place of a greeting.

I pressed a kiss to Harley's lips before turning his care over to her capable hands.

I was relieved to see Althea had woken up. She was talking quite animatedly to Bertie. She then grabbed hold of her mother's arm. "Mary tricked me," I heard Althea say, her voice scratchy but urgent. "When I was driving to the Chocolate Box, I saw my shop's front door was wide open. I stopped and check it out. I barely saw her before she knocked me out."

"She knocked you out after you sent those texts to me?" I asked, even though I was pretty sure I knew the answer.

"Texts?" She shook her head. "I didn't send you any texts. Once I got to the shop, I only expected to be there long enough to check things out and then lock the front door."

Marion nudged me out of the way. "You can catch up later. Right now, we need to take care of your friend."

"They're both going to be okay," Byrd assured me, sounding surprisingly kind, as my two closest friends were wheeled out on stretchers. Before she left, Marion laid a heavy blanket over my shoulders. I didn't realize until then how badly I was shaking. Both Althea and Harley could have been killed.

"It's over," Bertie said as she wrapped her powerful arms around me. "It's over."

True, it was over. I looked at the stains of blood on the floor and started shaking again when I thought about what could have happened. Joanna had been one step in front of us the entire time.

"She didn't win," Bertie said as if she knew what I was thinking. "Harley and Althea will be okay. As soon as Hank lets you go, you're going to come with me to the hospital and we'll both see to them ourselves.

She was right. Joanna was going to spend a very, very long time in jail. And my friends would recover. "It's over," I agreed and silently vowed to give up sleuthing forever.

Chapter 31

Three weeks later...

It was nearly morning and I still hadn't gone to bed. Trixie and Barbie had moved into the newly renovated Pink Pelican Inn the previous day, so I finally had a bed instead of a sofa to sleep on. Still, ever since that night we'd confronted Joanna, I'd felt unsettled, restless. It was as if an invisible hand was tugging at me, willing me to do something. But I had no idea what that "something" could be.

Well, there was the fact that I'd never actually talked with Harley about that moment in the car and how I'd blurted out that I loved him. Instead of facing it, I'd avoided him. Not that it had been too difficult. We were both busy. Me, with helping residents make repairs on their homes. And him, with helping residents file claims with insurance agencies and making sure no one got taken advantage of. There simply hadn't been time for us to explore what it meant to be *us*.

He'd asked me out on a date a couple of times, and I'd turned him down, claiming I had too much work to do in the shop. It wasn't a lie. The wholesalers were catching up with their backlog of deliveries. Supplies were rolling in, and I spent most days and nearly every night in the kitchen downstairs with Bertie by my side as we worked to rebuild our stock. And whenever I had a free moment, I worked with Althea to get her shop back up and running. I'd catch a few hours of sleep only whenever exhaustion demanded it.

I had no time for sleep, I kept telling myself.

But this morning, as the grayness of morning lightened the inky night sky, I forced myself to face the truth. I'd worked myself ragged so I wouldn't have times like this, time to stop and contemplate what had happened three weeks ago.

I stood outside my apartment door and leaned against the railing that looked out over the marsh and the river beyond. Stella

258

stood next to me, her tiny body a warm comfort pressed against my leg. After a long, hot summer and equally steamy fall, the air was finally starting to feel cooler. A delicious, crisp breeze brushed my cheeks.

The door to the apartment next to mine opened then closed again. I kept my face turned to the marsh, but my heart beat faster as I listened to footsteps approaching behind me.

Harley stopped right next to me, his shoulder nearly touching mine.

It was too early in the morning for Stella, who liked her sleep, to do anything other than offer a low growl of protest at his nearness.

"Hello, stranger." Harley's voice sounded raspy, as if he'd just rolled out of bed.

"Good morning," I said, still without turning my head to look at him. If I saw kindness in his eyes or the gentle crease of his smile I might blurt out that I loved him again and again and again. And what a mess that would be.

"I hear the Chocolate Box has been having record sales lately."

"The ghost hunters are still prowling the island." I chuckled. "I should have a sign made that says, 'Come for the Gray Lady. Stay for the chocolates.' As much as I hate to admit it, the group has been a boon for everyone in the business district. But they won't stay forever."

"Speaking about people not staying forever, Big Dog has told me that he's leaving this morning. After grumbling and growling about it for weeks now, he says he's accepted his brother's invitation to stay at the family home for a while. He complains that it's your fault."

I smiled at that. "I did talk with him a bit about family."

"You found time to talk with him and not me?" There was no mistaking the hurt in his voice.

"I understand how Big Dog feels. It's hard always being on the outside looking in, never belonging. But I also think it'd be wrong for him to completely cut his family from his life. I mean, if his brother is truly trying to reach out to him in a gesture of goodwill, he owes it to himself to at least hear what Silas Piper has to say."

"That's sound advice. Does that mean you've finally answered the texts you've been getting from Peach and Florence?"

My smile faded. "It's Peach that's sending the texts. Not Florence. And no. I've been too busy to answer her."

"That's not quite true." He put his hand over mine. "You've been keeping yourself busy."

Instead of admitting he was right, I dived in with a description of the new chocolate flavors I'd been developing for the upcoming Christmas season. I'd been experimenting with a dark chocolate bonbon with a delightfully tart orange center, a white and dark chocolate mint swirl, and a chocolate gingerbread cookie guaranteed to melt even the hardest of hearts.

"That all sounds amazing, and now I'm hungry. But, Penn, you don't have to run from me. Please, just tell me what's bothering you." When I didn't answer right away, he added, "I hope you're not worried about my expectations after what you said three weeks ago because if you are, you don't—"

"I know," I stopped him. My smile returned. "You're patient and exactly what I need. And things would be so very simple if I didn't feel this awful need to run all the time."

"It's okay," he said being so perfectly patient again. "There's no need to rush."

Still too much of a coward to look at him, I nodded.

There. It was done. We'd talk through my blurted admission of love. Why, then, did my nerves still feel so prickly?

"There is something else bothering me," I admitted both to him and myself.

"I suspected there might be."

I did look at him then.

He must have read the surprise in my expression. He chuckled, low and sexy. "I'm not so conceited to think your feelings for me are the cause of all your misery. Tell me, Penn. Maybe talking about it will help you feel better."

"I keep thinking about Joe's death and our investigations into what happened." My fingers shook as I touched my hand to my temple. "Brett Handleson spoke to me. Or-or someone who looked like him and claimed to be him spoke to me. Then there is the gold coin I found in Althea's shop. Where did that come from?" My voice grew louder. "And-and…" I uttered an oath in frustration. "There are no such things as ghosts, so why can't I come up with a rational explanation—even to myself—for those happenings?"

The wind screamed with a sudden gale as if trying to provide an answer to my questions. It whipped the palm fronds and branches of nearby oaks, causing them to chatter like old bones. Stella jumped up, barking frantically.

And then, as suddenly as it had started, the wind stopped.

"Shush, Stella," I said and showed her a treat to help calm her down.

"That's the cold front coming in," Harley said seemingly unfazed by the weird weather.

"I suppose it—" Before I could finish that thought I spotted it.

A gold coin lay at my feet on the porch deck. I crouched down and picked it up, turning it over in my hand. Like the coin Joe had found and the coin that had somehow gotten into Althea's damaged shop, this was a Spanish gold coin that looked as ancient as the others.

"Did you drop this?" I demanded.

Harley shook his head. "I-I don't know how that could have gotten there. Honest."

"It wasn't here when I came out," I said.

Harley and I stared at each other. Neither of us were willing to say it, but I'm sure we were both thinking it.

Maybe ghosts are real.

After several minutes Harley cleared his throat. Twice. "Um… Tell me some more about the orange chocolate bonbons you've been making. Are they holding together?"

I jammed the gold coin into my pocket. "Amazingly, they are."

As the morning broke over the island, the two of us talked about chocolate and spices and fruits. For the first time in weeks, I could draw a breath without having to battle the tension coiled in my chest. Finally, my life on Camellia Beach felt right again.

Recipes Snipped from the *Camellia Current*, Camellia Beach's Local Newspaper

Penn's Pumpkin Spice Bonbons

Penn has done it again. She's been proving herself quite the genius when it comes to mixing flavors. This time she's captured the flavor of fall with her pumpkin bonbons with their sweet and salty pumpkin seed butter, and dipped in a slightly bitter dark chocolate. And for decoration, she's sprinkled pumpkin seeds on the top. This food editor is in pumpkin seed heaven!

Ingredients

For the Pumpkin Seed Butter:
1 Cup Pumpkin Seeds (Shelled, Roasted, and Salted)
2 T Honey (Local is best)
Pumpkin pie spice, to taste
Add water as needed

For the Chocolate Dip:
6 oz of Fair Trade 85% Dark Chocolate
Pumpkin Seeds (Shelled, Roaster, and Salted)

Grind the pumpkin seeds in a food processer. Add honey. Continue to grind until it makes a smooth paste. If mixture is grainy, a teaspoon of water at a time to loosen.

Roll pumpkin seed butter into small balls. Freeze.

Melt the dark chocolate chips using either a double boiler or following the microwave directions on the bag. Dip the frozen pumpkin butter balls in the melted chocolate and place on a tray covered with parchment paper. Sprinkle pumpkin seeds on top. Place bonbons in refrigerator for 30 minutes to 1 hour to cool.

Store in the refrigerator. Makes approximately 2 dozen.

Althea's Cacao Nib Encrusted Salmon with White Chocolate Sauce

Now reader, stick with me. You're thinking this will taste sickly sweet. And it won't. Althea Bays fixed this dish for me last Thursday to prove that it's a wonderful way (chocolate lover or not) to cook salmon. The cacao nibs exactly like one would use any kind of spice, such as black pepper. In fact, the recipe calls for the nibs to be ground in a pepper grinder. It's a light and flavorful dish that any home chef would be proud to serve. We're extremely lucky Althea has finally agreed to share her special recipe with us.

Ingredients

For the Sauce
3 T Butter
3 t All-Purpose Flour
1 Cup Fish Broth
6 t Fresh Lemon Juice (unsweetened)
1 oz White Chocolate (not too sweet)

For the Salmon
6 T Cocoa Butter (cooking grade)
5 T Cacao Nibs (ground in pepper grinder or in food processor)
2 lbs Filet of Salmon cut into 4-5oz portions
Salt

Melt 3 tablespoons of butter in a small saucepan over medium heat. When the butter has melted, whisk in the flour. Mix until smooth. Add fish broth, stirring constantly to cook the flour. Let the sauce cook on low heat for 15 minutes, stirring regularly. Add lemon juice, white chocolate, and salt to taste.

Spread 3 tablespoons of melted cocoa butter on salmon skin. Press ground cacao nibs into salmon. Sprinkle with salt. Flip over and repeat. Heat remaining cocoa butter in a pan over medium heat. Fry fish for about 5 minutes per side until it has browned.

Serve with rice, sauce, and cooked leeks, asparagus, or broccoli.

Penn's Surprisingly Simple Chocolate Chip Brownies

The secret to this recipe is not to over mix the batter. Penn has shared with this editor all the other ways that she's messed up this ridiculously simple recipe, but dear reader, we know that you have more sense than to repeat any of her appalling mistakes. This is a recipe that was given to her, so she doesn't know the original origin. But, let me tell you, I've tested this one myself. And although there are only three ingredients, if you use a good quality chocolate, you're going to find it difficult not to eat all of these brownies for yourself.

Ingredients

> 1 can Sweetened Condensed Milk
> 2 cups Graham Cracker Crumbs
> 6 oz of Fair Trade Chocolate (I prefer dark or semi-sweet)

Mix together all the ingredients. Spread in 9X9 square inch pan (ungreased). Bake 350 degrees F for 30 minutes. Let cool for at least 15 minutes before cutting. Depending on how you cut the brownies, the recipe makes about 2 dozen.

Thank you for reading

BONBON WITH THE WIND

If you enjoyed this book, I would appreciate it if you'd help other readers enjoy it too. After all, most books are sold by word of mouth. What can you do?

Recommend it. Please help other readers find this book by recommending it to friends, readers' groups, and discussion boards.

Review it. Please tell other readers why you liked this book by reviewing it.

To learn about new releases, sign up for my newsletter at www.dorothystjames.com.

Thank you!

Also by Dorothy St. James
Read all of Dorothy's delicious mysteries.

Southern Chocolate Shop Mystery Series
Book 1: Asking for Truffle
Death in a chocolate shop.
Book 2: Playing with Bonbon Fire
Beach music, spicy chocolates, and murder.
Book 3: In Cold Chocolate
Sea turtles, chocolate turtles, and a shot in the dark.

The White House Gardener Mysteries
Flowerbed of State
The Scarlet Pepper
Oak and Dagger

Birds of Paradise
(An Aloha Pete Short Story)

About the Author

Mystery author Dorothy St. James was born in New York but raised in South Carolina. She makes her home in South Carolina. Though writing has always been a passion for her, she pursued an undergraduate degree in Wildlife Biology and a graduate degree in Public Administration and Urban Planning. She put her educational experience to use, having worked in all branches and all levels of government including local, regional, state, and federal. She even spent time during college working for a non-profit environmental watchdog organization.

Switching from government service and community planning to fiction writing wasn't as big of a change as some might think. Her government work was all about the stories of the people and the places where they live. As an urban planner, Dorothy loved telling the stories of the people she met. And from that, her desire to tell the tales that were so alive in her heart grew until she could not ignore it any longer. In 2001, she took a leap of faith and pursued her dream of writing fiction full-time.

Visit Dorothy St. James at:
http://www.dorothystjames.com
http://www.facebook.com/dorothy.stjames

CPSIA information can be obtained
at www.ICGtesting.com
Printed in the USA
BVHW072026010120
568264BV00004B/9/P